Praise for
Reading for Children

Judith Gustafson's translation of Zacharius Topelius' work for children brings out the gentle but strong, moral and ethical messages of right and wrong the author shared in his day. Topelius shares a beautiful panorama of his native Finland in an impressive and inspiring way. The unique style of the book commends it be read to or by young children. Zacharius Topelius has written to children in their everyday world, thus making the stories very attractive and interesting. Gustafson has caught this spirit and brings it out warmly in these delightful literary selections.

—William Sandstrom, covenant pastor

Reading for
Children

Judith Gustafson

Reading for
Children

*May your life be enriched as
you read H. Topelius' sagas.
Judith Gustafson*

TATE PUBLISHING & *Enterprises*

Published by Tate Publishing & Enterprises, LLC
127 E. Trade Center Terrace | Mustang, Oklahoma 73064 USA
1.888.361.9473 | www.tatepublishing.com

Tate Publishing is committed to excellence in the publishing industry. The company reflects the philosophy established by the founders, based on Psalm 68:11,
"The Lord gave the word and great was the company of those who published it."

Book design copyright © 2010 by Tate Publishing, LLC. All rights reserved.
Cover design by Lance Waldrop
Interior design by Stephanie Woloszyn

Published in the United States of America

ISBN: 978-1-61566-468-9
1. Fiction / Christian / General   2. Fiction / Cultural Heritage
10.04.26

Dedication

Reading for Children, or *Läsning för barn,* is dedicated to my dear husband, Rev. Charles Gustafson; our children: Dr. Deborah Gustafson and Dr. Paul Gustafson; and our grandson, Maximilian Gustafson Wassmer. May the Lord bless you along life's journey as you read the pages from this insightful Finnish author, Zacharius Topelius.

Table of Contents

Foreword

Traveling excites a passion in us because of the unexpected adventures at each turn in the road and the opportunity to observe the tapestry of people we meet along the way, each with their unique culture and dialect. The memories we have from our travels sustain us in our quiet reflective moments for the rest of our lives. Perhaps we benefit most from travel by the appreciation and comfort we have of our own home when we return. In every culture there are fairy tales or stories that have been passed down through generations, stories that have excited the imagination of children and provided ideas that have fed the souls of man. Among the oldest recorded stories are from the Old Testament of the Bible and the New Testament teachings of Jesus, which have laid the foundation of moral living and led us to discover man's purpose: the development of a personal relationship with God. Subsequent authors from every generation have tied their literature to this moral message.

Translator, educator, and author Judith Gustafson has traveled extensively all over the world and has come to appreciate and embrace her Scandinavian roots as well as her godly heritage. In her travels, she discovered the fairy tales and timeless sagas written in Swedish by Finnish author Zacharius Topelius. Fluent in Swedish, Judith was able to translate these stories into English while preserving the lyrical and poetic style of the writer. One of these stories is The Boy From Pernå. In the story, the boy yearns to translate the Bible from the Greek and Latin so that all the Finnish people could read the Bible for themselves in order to discover a personal God. Likewise, Judith has translated these fanciful tales so that English speaking readers, especially children, can appreciate her Scandinavian heritage of tales by a Finnish author and learn of biblical moral themes.

Since humankind first rudimentarily communicated with each other and subsequently taught each other, the challenges for educators have remained the same. Teachers ask themselves, "What are the most salient topics to teach my students in the endless body of knowledge? How can I motivate my students to learn? Once I have decided what to teach, how I can break down the tasks so the students will understand the concepts? How do I evaluate that they have grasped the concept? How can I ensure retention? How can I incorporate the concepts of honesty and morality in my teaching?" Judith Gustafson is like all dedicated teachers seeking to find the best approach to enhance learning. As a woman of integrity and a strong woman of God, she emphasized moral themes in her teaching while motivating her students with special needs. Judith interpreted *Reading for Children* to leave a legacy for her students and her own children. She demonstrates how Dr. Arnold Goldstein's role-playing theories can be adapted in her instruction with children and even adults. They can learn morality through reading stories with moral themes and role playing the stories. Enter the Topelius tales. Judith has combined her appreciation of Topelius' moral tales into her teaching. As a special needs educator, Judith is particularly fond of Topelius' Finnish tale, *The Boy Who Heard the Silent Speech,* as it incorporates several moral themes which can be adapted for kinesthetic learning through role playing.

In interpreting *Läsning för barn,* Judith has collected some of Topelius' best stories that are endearing to children, as well as adults, that touch the heart and conscience of all readers. Enjoy the journey.

—*Barbara I. Schulz, D.Ed*

Syne in Summer Village
Syne i Sommarby

In the village of Sommarby, the shoemaker and the tailor had differences of opinion on various issues. For example, the shoemaker had feelings of jealousy toward the tailor who named his son *Ahasuerus*. In those days, many people had long names adopted from well-known persons, places, or events. Consequently, the shoemaker named his son, *Zephyrinus*, or Rinu, and his daughter was named *Mormässa*, or Morsa. The tailor's son was named *Ahasverus*, or Sveru, and the daughter was named *Euphrosyne*, or Syne.

Sometime later, the shoemaker and the tailor's wife died. The tailor thought he should marry the shoemaker's wife because they were neighbors. After becoming a blended family, the parents realized all four children, Rinu, Morsa, Sveru, and Syne had their differences. This resulted in a tense relationship between the parents because they had conflicting opinions when they raised the children.

The tailor's first wife had been good-natured. Now he was hen-pecked and in a tangled mess with his new wife, Priska, who became the boss in the house. Each of the four children had distinct personalities. For example, the shoemaker's children included well-mannered Rinu, and argumentative Morsa, while the tailor's children were ill-tempered Sveru and gentle Syne.

The two argumentative children, Morsa and Sveru, were

mother's favorites because they never disobeyed her. Morsa was somewhat like her biological mother who was lazy and lied.

Soon winter passed, and it was early in the spring. The fresh, green hay lay on a sparse meadow. The hungry cows ate two weeks worth of hay in a few days. Mother Priska, Syne's stepmother, commanded Syne, saying, "Go outside and care for the farmer's cows."

"Yes, Mother," Syne said obediently.

"Get a piece of bread to take with you for the day," Mother continued.

"Yes, Mother," Syne answered

"Yes, yeesss!" Mother mimicked Syne grumpily. "One never hears anything else but "yes!" Besides, don't freeze, you good-for-nothing!"

"I will run to keep myself warm," answered Syne.

"Do not leave the cows! Watch them from the same place all day!" Mother shouted.

"I will try and be near them all day, Mother," Syne answered quietly.

Eight-year-old Syne went into the pasture. She did not have any shoes or socks to wear in the wooded hillside. Of what good were socks without shoes? She had one short wool skirt and a linen undergarment that Priska thought was enough.

Syne brought a short mountain ash branch to the innkeeper's farm to help her walk and call the cows. The cows gazed at the sun and sniffed the fresh spring air for the first time after six months being imprisoned in the dark cow barn. The cow's spring wonder was quite humorous.

They stared at the daylight and ran wildly with their tails in the April air, not knowing where to go. One ox, seven cows, and two lanky-legged calves were seen in the pasture. Syne watched the cattle in case they became confused and wandered into the forested area. The oxen were the only ones that maintained their composure because they took pleasure in honoring God's open nature. Syne finally heard the long, monotonous *moo*, which showed the cow's happiness.

The calf danced naturally and noisily with its bells. Syne drove the cows to the meadow at the foot of the wooded hillside that was completely red with wild strawberries. There were patches of snow between the withered yellow grass from the autumn season, and spider webs were seen in the midst of the high snowdrifts.

"I am eating a poor diet because of little grain, and I want something better," Syne thought to herself. There were dry, blackened birch leaves and sprigs of bilberry. If necessary, Syne also ate yellow and red berries. The cows tried the bilberries, but they had difficulty trying to chew them. It reminded one of poor people who ate potato peelings.

Brrr! It was such a cold, blustery wind that blew Syne's thin, short skirt. As she gathered her cows walking through the field, she noticed a good place on the hillside behind a large stone where she could count them. There she had protection from the wind, and a small piece of bread for breakfast. She could not scratch the cows with birch bark branches and milk them simultaneously.

She sat behind the stone for a long time with nothing to do—not even a book to read. From a distance she looked for something like a stick of wood, pieces of bark, or pinecones. She built herself a little stuga with the stones, a fence with a gate, and a barn. She gathered twigs for the oxen's horns and the seven fat cows. She took bark and cones from the spruce trees to help with her creativity.

I will create a good-natured woman who will tend to the animals, Syne thought. She dressed the bark piece in a skirt with red leaves and made the head from a half spruce cone. The eyes, nose, and mouth were used from last year's lingonberries. The arms and other bones were made from twigs. Syne's creative skills were so amazing! She decided to walk farther into the forest to see what she could find, and at the same time, she must keep her eyes on the cows.

As she walked, she looked between the trees. There lay something in the heather under the high Scotch pine. What could it be? A little gray bird had frozen to death! She took the bird in her hand, placed it under her linen dress, and warmed it. Its heart felt like a piece of ice as it was cold inside and outside. Syne began to tremble from the cold. When the bird lay some minutes next to Syne's warm heart, it began to move its wings. "He lives! He lives!" Syne shouted.

She was extremely happy, took the bird in her hand, and kissed his beak. "You little, innocent friend, thank you for living! Tell me who you are and how you froze to death!" The bird shook its numbed wings a couple of times, stretched them out, and flew away.

"The bird is as merry as a lark," she exclaimed, happy and annoyed at the same time. "Has anyone ever seen such a helpless little thing? The next time it will freeze to death."

Now Syne had built her own farm. Her father, the tailor, would be the master. However, where would she get a good tailor in the midst of the forest?

She looked between the tall trees, and under a snowdrift lay something special. It was a small, old, broken stump baring its roots and branches. It had arms and bones. Exactly where the head should be, it had a large knot with a gray beard, eyes, nose, and mouth. Syne dragged the cumbersome stump to her farm, wiped it clean with moss, and placed it at the gate.

Syne did not have a lot of space in her cottage; however, she had many sewing tools from father in addition to her iron and scissors. In the midst of her creativity, Syne thought about Priska and wished she would be kinder to Syne's father, the tailor.

To take her mind off Priska, Syne began to count the ten calves. "One … two … where is the red calf? Oh no! It is gone!" Syne shouted.

She ran down to the pasture and asked the bell-cow if the cattle would look out for each other. The bell-cow turned around and looked at Syne reproachfully, as if she wanted to say, "You are a calf-aunt, so give me my reddest child again!"

Syne was afraid as she looked around the pasture, the fence, and the wooded hillside. There was no red calf! She looked under logs and stones and up in the trees to see if the calf wanted to annoy her. There was not so much as a red piece of straw that she could find. Suddenly a brown tail was seen moving quickly between the branches. A squirrel! What would she do with a squirrel? She could not carry it home and then say, "It is a calf!"

Syne sat on a stone crying as she ate her dinner. "Where is the half piece of bread I saved for supper? It is gone like the calf!" Syne asked herself. Then she noticed the bread had fallen in the moss. The slender squirrel went down the tree, sat on its spine, took the morsel between its front paws, and ate it quickly. Did Syne laugh at the squirrel in all her distress?

"Such a miser! The squirrel ate my dinner! I need to be optimistic! Even though I am certainly hungry, you are perhaps more hungry than me." Meanwhile, Sveru was on the road looking for Syne and saw her nearby.

"Hi, Syne! How is it going with the cows? Where are they? Let's look in the pasture. There should be ten. I see one, two, three … eight calves. Where are the rest of them?" Sveru asked Syne.

"The calves?" asked Syne startled.

"Yes, both calves. Has the wolf taken them?" Sveru questioned.

"Dear Sveru, help me find them!" Syne asked.

"Look yourself," replied Sveru.

"Please ask Rinu to come here immediately to help me look!" Syne stated excitedly to Sveru.

Sveru laughed. "Rinu is sitting in the cellar because he spilled the milk bowl when he was looking for his jackknife in the cupboard. Mother reads to him in the evening, and she will read to you when you come home with the calves. What is that mess you built by the stone? Well, good-bye for now," Sveru said to Syne.

As he left, Sveru kicked the beautiful newly built farm with the fence, gate, and all the cows in the barn Syne had created.

She looked at her farm and saw the gray stump that stood

alone to the left. Syne thought to herself, "If you were now my living father, you would have helped me. But you are only a poor, old, fallen piece of trash, gray stump."

"Do not cry. I will help you!" said a hoarse voice that was heard from someone standing next to Syne.

Syne looked longingly over the pasture, the road, and the forest hillside. There was no one except for the grain and a swarm of mosquitoes that danced the quadrille in the sunshine by the fence. Whose voice was it? It was now spring; however, it was fall in Syne's sorrowful heart.

"Here I am," said the voice. Syne noticed to her unbelievable fright that it was the stump that spoke, sounding just like her father the tailor!

"Why should you be afraid of me?" continued the stump. "I am only the poor, old, crown-fallen tree. Do you understand what I am saying?"

"Yes," said Syne. She thought she noticed the voice was clearer the longer the stump talked. It reminded her of when the dead skylark first moved its wings and finally began to chirp.

"That is good," said the stump. "Now listen to what I say! Remember when you warmed my frozen skylark with your childlike heart and warmed it back to life? You have not given the calves their milk and soon you will be thirsty too. The squirrels will eat your bread, and you will soon be hungry. Do you not believe that all animals and growth despise stumps? Do you not believe there is a living spirit in all plant life and animals? Tied animals are not unconstrained like your free spirit. They are the same Creator's work and live their lives as you live yours. They speak, but people do not understand them. It is because people have separated themselves from nature. Good, unspoiled children understand nature's language; however, others believe it is only their imagination. It is like a saga or a long involved story. More exists in the saga than people believe."

Syne was not afraid anymore. She knew the stories that spoke of everything in God's creation; however, not everyone could understand it. She pondered each word and wondered what the stump had been.

The stump continued as if he read her thoughts: "Do you wonder what I am? I am a poor old stump and nothing else. I have been a large tree; I have been as old as the others and broken from the storm. Throw me into the fire, and I will burn; cut me to pieces, and I will not be anything else but shavings. I am so wretched and corruptible! I want the power God has provided in nature to be given also to me. You are a good child by dragging me out from the snowdrift, drying me clean, and placing me as a guard of honor on your farm. I will reward you. How many fingers do you have?"

Syne was not sure. She counted to ten using her fingers and answered, "Ten."

"Precisely! The saga's good fairy usually fulfills three wishes, but I will be more generous and fulfill as many wishes as you have fingers on both hands, as my power is able. I can finally give you what nature provides, but I cannot alter God's will and people's hearts. Every wish of yours is one missing finger. Consider yourself correct and sensible! Now we will begin. Raise your thumb!"

"I want to have my healthy calves back!" Syne said without hesitation.

The stump broke a dry branch from its rough front, put it to its mouth and blew like a pipe. Immediately Syne was very happy. First the red and then the white calf plodded along in front on their lanky bones between the stones.

"Why have you caused the girl so much worry?" asked the stump.

"The wolves took us," answered the honest calves.

"The wolves?" questioned the stump.

"Syne counted ten of us on the hillside, and then we became frightened and ran."

"Return to your mother in the pasture and do not run away in the future!" exhorted the stump.

The calves were confused, and the stump continued, "Raise your hands with your index finger pointing upward!"

"I am freezing and so hungry!" said Syne. Immediately there was a dish with steaming warm palt bread and a wooden spoon with warm milk in a separate bowl. The stump looked at the hungry child eating with satisfaction.

"Raise your index finger!" continued the stump again as Syne ate.

"The oxen, cows, and calves eat and are satisfied!" said Syne.

Soon the pasture was covered with luxuriant, green foliage where the hungry creatures waded in the tall grass and gulped down more than they could eat. Syne clapped her hands with delight. The wild anemone was like the bilberry!

"Raise your hand's ring finger!" the stump commanded Syne.

"All the animals, people, and living things get to eat to their satisfaction!" shouted Syne in her happiness.

"My child," said the stump, "the Lord provides for all His creation. In your childlike faith, you were given warm palt bread. Now raise your little finger."

A little discouraged, Syne answered after some thought. Raising her little finger, she said, "I wish Mother would be good-natured toward Father!"

"Pray to God that he will speak to your mother to love as he himself is full of love toward all his created work. I cannot answer your prayer. You have wished for everything from your raised hand. Think about your well-being! Now raise the thumb on your left hand," the stump commanded.

Syne raised the thumb on her left hand, answered the stump with a lump in her throat and said, "I wish Mother, Sveru, and Morsa would be kind and happy. I want to attend school."

The stump answered, "Yes, of course. Early tomorrow you will begin. You will receive your own ABC book with a rooster on it.

Little Syne, you will have the book with my help. Do not waste your personal wants and desires on that which does not last, like Sveru and Morsa do.

"No stump, you know I do not wish for more things…Wait, yes! Papa was quite stiff and sore from constantly sitting at the table with his legs crossed. He needs a ride on a beautiful horse!" Syne suggested.

"Yes, yes, that is both dangerous and a pleasure for a tailor's spindly bones. Has your father ever sat on a horse?" questioned the stump.

"No, I do not think so. It is so beautiful when the sheriff, Kalle, rides to church with a feather in his hat. I want my father to be proud," observed Syne.

The stump said to Syne, "I will teach your father early tomorrow when his horse is saddled in the yard! You now have two fingers left. Show me the ring finger on your left hand!"

"Two fingers? Everyone's most beloved stump asked me what I wanted. Do I want Papa to have money?" questioned Syne.

"Find something better!" The stump suggested.

"I wish Morsa would have rice sausage, Rinu should have a picture book, Sveru…I am not sure; and Mother…what shall I wish for her?" Syne asked.

"Well, Sveru has broken up your farm and Mother has sent you outside without a sweater in the cold wind," the stump reminded Syne.

Syne replied, "No, no, Sveru will get a new hat, and Mother will get a new cotton dress. Then they will both look nice."

"You have wished for four gifts instead of one, and you will get them. But now you have only one finger left. You must wish something sensible for yourself! Show the little finger on your left hand!" urged the stump.

"Yes, you are asking what I want for myself! Is it proper if I ask for all the money in the world, to be an empress, to learn the ABC book by heart, or to receive a pair of new socks because my old socks have a hole in the heel? How will I get oxen, cows, and calves home when there are wolves in the forest? I would rather have ten wolves safe and sound in the barn! I would also like to get two pieces of sugar on Sunday mornings for my morning coffee," noted Syne. "Stump, how will I get the oxen, cows, and calves home when there are wolves in the forest?" Syne mused.

"You will see your livestock coming home safe and sound on the main road, and you must see to it your cattle are well cared for," the stump reminded Syne.

"Maybe I want something else," Syne continued.

"Children wish for small things when they could wish for something bigger; however, you have thought more of others' fortune than your own. I, the old and gray stump, do not blame you. Go home and always be God and nature's good child. Good-bye, little Syne!" the stump concluded.

When Syne came with the cattle, Mother Priska stood with the cellar key in her hand at the gate. She said to the gatekeeper's mother, "The wolves attacked two calves, and we need to pay for two more. It is a loss to us. Syne needs to be in the cellar for seven days and seven nights."

The gatekeeper's mother said to Priska as she counted and examined the cattle, "They are all here. See how fat, shiny, and well behaved they are early in the spring? We have never had such excellent female calves."

"You had Sveru lie to me!" shouted Mother Priska to Syne. Sveru saw his sister coming and wished her much luck in the cellar. Sveru put the broomstick (used for discipline) securely on his shoulders. Syne began to pray for him.

"Don't hit him, Mother! The calves were away when Sveru came to me on the hill, but they came back!" Syne shouted.

The whole village wondered how Syne's cows had gotten so fat. However, even something greater occurred on the following morning when a beautifully saddled horse stood at the tailor's farm. "Whose delightful colt is this? Could it belong to one of the carriage patrons of the estate?" Papa asked.

"It is my horse, Papa," said Syne, who could not hide her happiness.

Father replied, "Now you will be able to ride every day. May I ride it also?" He laughed.

"Oh, you can try," answered Syne. Her father was persuaded, and he climbed up onto the horse's back landing like a heavy blanket.

"Oh, ouch!" The tailor shouted.

"What gifts did each of you receive?" Syne asked.

"I was given a picture book!" Rinu yelled.

"I have a new hat!" cried Sveru.

"I have rice sausage!" Morsa said happily.

"Oh my goodness!" rejoiced Mother Priska. "I have a beautiful cotton dress!"

Syne smiled quietly to herself, but the others did not notice it.

"You know something, Syne," Morsa said. "You know something about Father's new horse. Tell us! Tell us about it!"

Poor Syne, she could not tell a lie; she told everything that happened to her that strange day when she went to the pasture with the gatekeeper's cows. She had forgotten how good she had been to the animals.

"Syne," said Mother Priska, "you are a smart and thoughtful girl because you have given me a beautiful cotton dress. You will begin school today. Morsa wants to quit school because it is too difficult for her."

Syne thanked her mother. She had already received an ABC book with the rooster's picture on the cover.

"Mother, may I get the gatekeeper's cows in the morning?" asked Morsa.

Mother had nothing to say on the contrary.

Morsa said to Sveru, "It was really something of Syne to get what we needed!"

"Yes," responded Sveru, "I will come with you to get the cows."

The next morning Morsa and Sveru went to the pasture where the gatekeeper's cattle were grazing. They had brought good food to eat along the way and warm clothes. With a nudge now and then, the cows trudged ahead to the pasture. When they walked through the yard, there sat Sveru and Morsa eating breakfast on Syne's destroyed farm. The old gray stump stood quietly to the left while the children looked at it inquisitively. Was it possible that such a miserable tree stump with a wooden leg gave everything? What more could one want of him? They wanted to know.

"Poor stump," commented Morsa. "Please get me a string of pearls!"

"I want a rifle!" ordered Sveru.

"I will be the most courteous person in the church," responded Morsa.

"I will shoot all the larks and squirrels here in the forest," declared Sveru.

The stump stood quietly as before; however, if Syne had been there, perhaps she would have noticed his beard moved a little as if he had pulled his mouth. He could not speak to them as they would not be able to understand him.

Now Sveru was annoyed. "Don't you know how to obey? I will teach you to do as you are told, old, withered, parched, and frightened stump!" Sveru gave it such a clever blow with his cane that it fell down in a heap.

"What have you done? He was sorry he did not give us any gifts," lamented Morsa. Sveru was careful to place the stump upright and put butter on its mouth to calm his anger.

"Stump, get me a gun or I will light a fire on you. I have matches in my pocket, and a candlestick in my hand," threatened Sveru.

"Is that what you want?" Morsa shouted.

"Of course!" laughed Sveru, and he went to get the matches. "Should I or should I not get a gun?" he continued.

The stump was silent. Morsa wanted to pull the match away, but he was pushed and fell backwards.

"Is it right that I do not get a gun?" shouted Sveru. "I will teach you to obey, old man stump!"

Then Sveru held the burning candlestick under the stump's long beard. It was dry and flammable as gunpowder, and soon it stood in flames. Soon thereafter, the wind died down, the forest was dry, and Sveru was able to clean the meadow. Now he was able to expand his lungs and blow on the fire. No sooner had Sveru done this when the flames were engulfed under the stump's long beard. From the stump to the moss, from the moss to the heather, from the heather to the juniper twigs, and from the juniper twigs to the Norway spruce, pines, and birch trees. Oh, it was a terrible fire engulfing the whole area!

The wind danced the polka as it blazed, throwing the fire over the field in the dry, leafy pasture. The airborne swans were seen; however, the wolves did not look at anything else other than the fearful stump in the forest hillside. I do not have the heart to speak about how it went with the wretched cows and calves! Soon the wind died down, and in a few weeks Sveru had cleaned the meadow, and the forest was dry. Now he had to work by expanding his lungs and blowing on the fire.

Morsa dashed home and told of the misfortune. The ox came mooing after her—the only four-footed beast that was fortunate to be saved. The whole village came running, and the people hurried out to the woods to quench the fire. What could they do? What could they accomplish? The whole forest was aglow with the pasture in ashes. The stump had fallen over, and its clothing was on fire.

In the midst of catastrophe often there comes some good. The gatekeeper was pleased with his new horse. Priska now had a positive attitude. Priska remembered the day when she sent the children to get her a long woven piece of cotton. Her changed, positive, interpersonal relationships taught Morsa, Rinu, and Syne to be good friends.

The following spring, the woods remained bare with some burned stumps resembling a dirty chimney. The dark pasture had green straw sprouts coming out of the ashes. The soft and gentle spring with beautiful new life out of nature's grave had already begun to extinguish the devastation's mark on this ravaged, desolate waste.

The children looked in vain to trace the peculiar stump that at one time had been the master in Syne's farmyard.

Morsa reminded Syne, "The stump was the forest king who dresses itself for children and hunters."

"So says the fairy tale," Syne answered. "Morsa, we should be good toward all the living. "Even as the living spirit was in the stump, so it exists in all living plants and animals. We need to be good toward all growth and animals. We should never grieve the living spirit which lives in them."

The Old Man
Gamla Herrn

r. Sedmigradsky was an older man whose name sounded so formal that children could barely pronounce it correctly. He was of Polish descent and came to Helsingfors as an art teacher. The young girls thought his hair looked unkempt, and they were afraid of him. When he spoke kindly to the children on the avenue, they wanted to run away. He kept a small tin box in his waistcoat pocket that held the photo of a young woman whose name was Maria, some caramels, and sugar cubes. Taking out his canister, he offered the children some candy. They would occasionally run away, or if the youngsters took some sweets, they often would not say, "Thank you."

Mr. Sedmigradsky often sat alone, and no one cared about him. He had two or three former students who greeted him, but he was not much older than they, and they usually kept their distance. He thought, "I must find something better for the children than caramels and sugar pieces. What shall I do so the children will like me?"

He wondered about this as long as he lived because he was so alone in the world. He did not have a wife or children, although he would like to. It annoyed him that he was a stranger in Helsingfors, and some distance from those who were dear to him in his younger days in Poland. He was not an old and ill-humored person; on the contrary, he was cheerful and talkative. Life had been good to him, and he enjoyed associating with others.

When he went out for walks in Helsingfors, he always wore his old, gray hat, his well-worn coat, and his torn, blue dress suit with shiny buttons. He never engaged in activities that cost money. His small income and a few expenses left him with nothing left over. People thought Mr. Sedmigradsky was stingy. Even though Mr. Sedmigradsky appeared destitute, he had a treasured collection box. Oh! Who will inherit his goods? Maybe his cat will finally take his gold, or someone else might say, "I want your worldly goods."

Mr. Sedmigradsky wondered what others said and thought of him, including the children. His housekeeper was unhappy because there were those who told her stories of him being wealthy yet stingy. In spite of what people said, he was relatively content and cheerful. As time went on, people kept talking about the old man's money and how he hoarded his goods.

One day he was sick and lay in his bed. The people wondered if he should do his last will and testament and who would receive the treasured box. The neighbors wondered if the stingy man's housekeeper would inherit his wealth, and the housekeeper wondered the same. She knew a lot about him; however, she was certainly unaware about some will and testament.

One day the doctor said to the housekeeper, "Mr. Sedmigradsky does not have much longer to live."

The minister continued, "Has he set aside any money for the poor?"

"Not even his old blue dress suit," answered the housekeeper.

The minister thought it was selfish for the old miser to not leave some money for the poor and needy.

The old man lay there cheerful and satisfied as he always had been. However, now he found something better than caramels and sugar cubes that would encourage the children to stay with him and talk. Perhaps he should leave a legacy for his students. After all, he wanted the children to have pleasant memories of him after he died.

He passed away and was buried. Surprisingly, the old man left his treasure box and an unexpected will and testament. Nothing was willed for the relatives, including his property. The schoolmaster opened the sealed document. The neighbors were so curious as they pushed into the hall in order to hear the great news. They whispered to each other, "The housekeeper will get all his gold! Oh, such a stingy wolf!"

However, it was not the housekeeper, but it was the small children who received the unexpected remembrance of him. The old man had finally written his last will and testament. All of his property was willed for a large school carrying his name. No one could dispute the last will and testament was drafted in legal form. Because the old man had worn his old blue suit and saved on personal pleasures, he could now build a legacy.

Following his death, a female teacher was hired for about one hundred students, who learned, played, and sang. When the students were older, they went to a secondary school, and younger children enrolled in the older students' place. So it went year in and year out, generation after generation. It was a fine school for each group of new children. There they learned well and were happy. An old portrait was hung in the middle of the wall in front of the entrance of Sedmigradsky's School.

The school has been open for forty years. I have been there many times and seen the old man in his blue suit looking down from the picture on these obedient and fortunate children in the high, big, and light classrooms. Every visit to the school I have thought of the old man and how alone he was while he lived. The children can no longer forget him. Every day he is among them at play and hears their happy singing. They cannot look up without seeing him in front of them. The treasure box is forgotten. No one remembers it anymore, and no one is greatly desirous of *things*.

Here exists something better than caramels and sugar pieces. Those who all look up at his portrait think so much of him. He is the same old man who people called stingy and miserly, and now they see what he contributed! Before, many people thought he should have new clothes, eat and drink well, amuse himself, and live well with his savings. However, what would it have been like if he had not contributed his money for generations to come? The cat, the housekeeper, nor the children took his treasure. Miserly, Mr. Sedmigradsky, saved for others' fortune. One must thank God because excessive desire should not exist in the world.

Last winter just before Christmas, I was at the children's Lucia celebration on December 13, the longest night of the year. There stood a big julgran, or Christmas tree, with bright lights and many beautiful decorations. More than one hundred children stood there in a circle around the tree and had an indescribably pleasant time. Encircling the old man's portrait was a wreath with greenery and flowers. As the children viewed his picture, they sang and praised him even though so many years had passed. It is the memory one cherishes. One needs to forget disgraceful words and thoughts from people! It occurred to me as a young child that as the old man looked at the children, he was saying, "Do not run from me anymore!" Once more it was as if he should say, "Not me, Lord, not me, but to your name be the glory! It is your work, my God, and I have been your poor instrument. Your name is blessed.

Little Lasse
Lasse Liten

nce upon a time, there was a boy named Lars who later was called Little Lasse. He was a courageous and adventurous person because he thought of traveling around the whole world in a pea pod.

It was soon summer when the pea pods grew green and long in the garden. Little Lasse crept into the pea pod territory in between the banks where the closed peas grew high over his hat. He broke seventeen large, straight sheaths or coverings, hoping no one saw him. However, God sees everything, and he saw Lasse break the sheaths.

One day the gardener came walking with his rifle on his shoulder, and Lasse heard something rustling in the pea patch.

"I believe it is sparrows! Money! Money!" Little Lasse shouted. However, no sparrows flew because what he saw had no wings; only two small sticks.

"Wait. Now I will load my rifle and shoot the sparrows," the gardener stated.

Then Little Lasse was scared and crept out of the pea patch, saying, "Excuse me, dear gardener, I would like to look at some beautiful boats."

"Only this time. The next time you must ask permission to look for a ship in the pea patch area," replied the gardener.

"Okay," answered Lasse. It was so bare on his way to the bank. There he found a pea pod, ripped it along its edge with a pin, split it carefully and cut small slits for the rowing seats. He took the peas that were in the shell and laid them in the boats. When all the sheaths were ready, Little Lasse had twelve boats or one big warship. He had three ship lines, three large warships, three brigs, and three schooners. The largest ship line was named Hercules, and the smallest schooner was called Loppan. Little Lasse laid all twelve ships in the water, and they floated so splendidly that no large ship danced as proudly over the seas' waves.

The ships would travel around the world. A large islet away was Asia; however, the largest stone he chose was Africa. The little islet was America, the small stones were Polynesia, and the beach from where the ship sailed was Europe. The whole fleet traveled a long way to different parts of the world. The ship lines sailed straight away to Asia, the frigates traveled to Africa, the brigs went to America, and the schooners journeyed to Polynesia. However, Little Lasse remained in Europe and threw small stones out in the world's harbor. Yes, he was in the mood to travel out to the parts of the world even though Papa and Mama had forbidden it.

At a beach on a European coastline, Little Lasse stepped into Father's beautiful white painted boat. The pea pod boats were so small on the vast oceans resembling small blades of grass.

"*I will row a little way out,*" he thought. "*I will soon take the solid Hercules boat near Asia's coast and then row home to Europe again.*" Like a man, Little Lasse managed to free the tight chain. He rowed and rowed as best he could. He had rowed so often on the step at home when he pretended the step to be a boat and Papa's large cane was the paddle. Sometimes when Little Lasse wanted to row at home, there were no oars in the boat. What should Little Lasse do now? They were tied onto the beach shed, and Little Lasse had not noticed the boat was empty. "It is not easy rowing to Asia without oars," Lasse thought to himself.

What should Little Lasse do now? The boat was already quite far out on the lake, and the wind blowing from the land drove him steadily out farther. He was frightened, and he began to scream;

however, no one was on the beach to hear him. On the beach Lasse eyed a large hook attached to a large birch, and below it the gardener's cat lay in wait. Neither the birch nor the cat cared the least for Little Lasse, who drifted out further.

He felt badly that he did not listen to his parents. Perhaps he could disappear on this large lake, and Mother and Father would never know. What should he do? When he cried and was tired no one heard him. He clasped his small hands and said, "Dear God, I hope you are not upset with me!" He soon fell asleep.

After some hours it was daylight, and old Nukku Matti sat on the beach of Fjäder Harbor. He took his fishing pole, and he held it out into the shoreline so the children could grasp it and be drawn into shore. Nukku Matti dragged the boat toward shore and laid Little Lasse on the rose petals at the bottom of the boat he had collected on the water's surface.

Soon afterwards, Nukku Matti fell asleep and dreamed about Little Dream Boy. Nukku said to him, "Pretend you are traveling with Little Lasse so he will not be scared." Little Dream Boy had blue eyes, light hair, a red cap with a silver band, and a white sweater with pearls on the collar.

He came to Little Lasse and asked, "Do you want to travel around the whole world?"

"Yes, I would like that," said Lasse in his sleep.

"Come and let us sail in your pea pod vessel. You sail on Hercules, and I will travel on Loppen," suggested Dream Boy.

They sailed from Fjäder Harbor, and after some time Hercules and Loppen were a long way at the end of the world on Asia's shores. Far away at the end of the world the Arctic Ocean flows through the Bering Strait together with the Pacific Ocean. Long away in the winter mist, Nordenskjöld was seen with the steamship Vega to search for an open channel through the ice. Here it was so cold, so cold. Here a large whale lived under the roof of a tall glittering iceberg. The huge iceberg gleamed strangely, and the large whales lived under the iceberg roof. They were not able to thrust a blow into the ice with their clumsy heads. Around the empty, desolate beaches was snow as far as the eye could see. People were seen dressed in light, hairy, leather skins. They were traveling in small sleighs through drifts led by a team of dogs.

"Should we land here?" asked Dream Boy.

"No," said Little Lasse, "I am afraid the whale will overpower us, and the large dogs will bite us. Let us travel instead to another part of the world."

"Okay, let's travel to America," said the dreamer with the red cap and silver band.

In America the sun shone, and it was very pleasant. The high palms stood in long rows on the beach with coconuts on top. People were red like copper and were prepared at full speed as they threw their spears toward the buffalo that turned toward them with their sharp horns. Suddenly, an enormous king snake crept up on the highest palm stem and then slithered down onto a little llama that grazed in the grass at the foot of the palm tree. In a short time, the llama died from the snake's venomous tongue.

"Should we go into the countryside?" asked Dream Boy.

"No, I am so afraid the buffalo will butt us with their large horns and eat us up. Let us travel to another part of the world," said Little Lasse.

"That is what we should do because it is not long to Africa," said the dreaming boy with the blue eyes. It was no sooner said than they were on the vast African continent.

They anchored at the mouth of a large river, and the beaches were as green as the greenest velvet. Part of the river spread into the desert sand where the air was golden, and the sun was so hot, as if the earth was burning to ashes. They prepared to go through the desert on camels as they saw the thirsty lions and the large crocodiles opening their mouths out of the river with their lizard-like heads and sharp white teeth.

"Should we enter the country here?" asked Dream Boy.

"No, the sun will burn us, and the lions and crocodiles may

hurt or attack us," replied Little Lasse. Let us travel on to another part of the world," suggested Little Lasse.

"We could sail back to Europe," suggested the dreaming boy with the light hair. With that suggestion, Little Lasse and Dream Boy returned to Europe.

Upon arriving, everything was so cool, familiar, and friendly. There stood the tall birch with its hanging leaves, the old crow, and the gardener's black cat creeping slowly on a branch. Not long from there was a yard where little Lasse sat before. In the yard was a pea patch garden with long pea pods. Little Lasse and Dream Boy reminisced about the old gardener who always wondered if the peas were ripe.

Old Stina was being milked in the cowshed. A familiar woman was seen in her checkered wool shawl that the weavers had bleached on the green grass. There was also a very well-known man in a yellow summer coat with a long pipe in his mouth, who observed how the harvest team measured the field. A boy and a girl ran on the shore and shouted, "Little Lasse! Little Lasse! Come home and eat a sandwich!"

"Should we go into the country here?" asked the dreaming, blue-eyed boy who appeared so mischievous.

"Come, and I will ask Mother to give you a knäckebröd sandwich and a glass of milk," said Little Lasse.

"Just a minute," said Dream Boy. Now Little Lasse saw how the kitchen door stood open, and from there he heard a slow rustling as when one hits the yolk of an egg with a spoon in a hot frying pan.

"Do you think we should travel back to Polynesia?" the happy boy whispered dreamily.

"No, they are frying pancakes in Europe," Little Lasse noted. He wanted to run out into the country, but he could not because he had tied himself with a string of flowers so that he could not move. A thousand small dreamers surrounded him and sang the following little ballad:

The world is so big, so big,
Little Lasse, Lasse!

Larger than you ever believe,
Little Lasse, Lasse!

There it is hot, and there it is cold,
Little Lasse, Lasse!

But God follows everywhere,
Little Lasse, Lasse!

Many people live there,
Little Lasse, Lasse!

Fortunate then, who God holds dear,
Little Lasse, Lasse!

When God's angel goes with you,
Little Lasse, Lasse!

No serpent will get to bite you,
Little Lasse, Lasse!

See how you flourish most?
Little Lasse, Lasse!

Away is good, but home is best,
Little Lasse, Lasse!

At the conclusion of the ballad, Lasse went once again in the boat. As he lay in it, he fell asleep. While he slept, the wind had shifted, and the boat drifted out from the shore and slowly drifted back. He thought about the pancake griddle sizzling at home. It was a daring, slow, ripple when they hit the stones on the beach.

Rubbing the sleep out of his eyes, he looked around. Everything was as before—the tall birch tree, the cat in the grass, and luxurious pea pods on the shore. Some of the ships had been lost, and some drifted back to shore. Hercules came back from Asia, and Loppan came from Polynesia. All parts of the world were exactly there as before.

Little Lasse did not know what he should believe. He had so often been in the Fjäder Harbor cavern, and yet he did not know how dreams sometimes played tricks. Little Lasse was not bothered with such things. He pulled himself together on his ship and rowed toward shore and back to the farmyard.

Then his brothers and sisters ran toward him and shouted, "Where have you been so long Lasse? Come home for a smörgås!" The kitchen door was open, and he heard the strange sizzling.

The gardener stood nearby crying and watering dill, parsley, and parsnips until night. He asked, "Where has Little Lasse been so long?"

Little Lasse gently pinched the gardener's neck, looked self-assured, and answered, "I have sailed around the world in a pea pod boat!"

"I see!" said the gardener.

The Sea King's Gift
Havskonungens gåva

A t one time, there was a fisherman named Laxmatte who lived on a large sea. Where else would he live? He had a wife whose name was Laxmaja. What else would she be named? In the winter, they lived in a little cottage on the seashore. In the spring, they moved out to a red, rocky cliff in the sea and lived there the whole summer until fall. There they had a smaller cottage with a gray stone fireplace, a flagpole, and a windmill on the roof.

The rocky cliff was named Ahtola and was not larger than the market place in the city. Between the cracks in the ground grew a little mountain ash, four alder shrubs, tufts of fine velvet grass, some straw reeds, two herb plants with yellow pericarp that was called tansy, four tall plants of rosy epilobium, and a beautiful, white blooming plant called trientalis europåa. All of these plants grew there because of the falling and rising tides. But the most pleasant were the three tufts of chive Laxmaja had planted in a cleft where they had a stone wall on the north side and the sun on the south side. It was not a large area, but it was spacious enough for Laxmaja's spice garden.

All good things come in threes. For example, in the spring Laxmatte and his wife fished for salmon, in the summer they fished for Baltic herring, and in the fall they caught whitefish. On the weekend when the weather was beautiful with a pleasant wind, they sailed on Saturdays into the city and sold the fresh fish. On Sundays they went to church.

For many weeks, they were often alone on the Ahtola cliffs, and they did not see anything else other than their little, golden-brown dog named Prince, some bushes, flowers, the harbors' gulls, fish, the stormy clouds, and the whitish-blue waves. The Ahtola cliffs sat at the outskirts of the archipelago, and there was no islet or people for ten kilometers around them. As Laxmaja and Laxmatte sailed, they saw only a clipper here and there, red varieties of stone, and the Ahtola that constantly waved foam. They brought butter, bread, fish, and soured milk for their trip. What more would they need?

Laxmatte and Laxmaja were peaceful and hardworking people who lived contentedly with Prince, who thought he was rich when his masters salted so many fish. Life was difficult during the winter. They burned corn and chicory to provide flavor for their food and drank coffee.

Everything was good now; however, Laxmaja had a secret desire of becoming rich. She asked her husband, Laxmatte, about buying a cow.

"What will you do with a cow? How will we get the cow to the rocky cliff? Besides, if we are able to get the cow to the cabin, we won't have anything to feed it," Laxmatte continued.

"Here are four alder shrubs, sixteen pieces of sod, three chunks of chive sod, and salt Baltic herring. I have an idea. Let's bring Prince who will catch the gulls with the fish in its mouth, and then we will clean them," Laxmaja suggested.

"Oh, get that idea out of your mind, wife; everything is fine as it is!" countered Laxmatte.

Laxmaja sighed. She understood Laxmatte was right, but she could not forget. The old, sour milk no longer tasted like coffee cream. Laxmaja thought the fresh cream and fresh soured whole milk was the greatest thing in the whole world.

One day while the husband and wife cleaned herring on the beach, they heard Prince bark, and immediately they saw a beautifully painted barge with three young men wearing white hats steering the clipper. The men were students, who had been sailing a long way for relaxation, and they were now looking for land to embark and get fresh food.

"Give us some soured milk!" they shouted.

"Yes, whoever has it!" sighed Laxmaja.

"Get a can of sour unskimmed milk," continued the students.

"Yes, whoever has it!" sighed Laxmaja.

"Don't you have a cow?" asked the students.

Laxmaja was silent. It gripped her so deeply to answer such a question.

"We do not have any cows, but we will give you a couple of warm, smoked Baltic herring," Laxmatte answered.

"Okay, we will have smoked Baltic herring," responded the students as they tapped their cigars and pipes against the jug as it lay down in the ground. At the same time, fifty silvery-white Baltic herring were brought to the smoke oven.

"What is that small stone called in the lake?" asked one of them.

"Ahtola," answered the old man.

"Now, what do you need when you live in the sea god's region?" one student asked.

Laxmatte did not understand everything because he had never read *Kalevala*. He did not know anything about the ancestor's troll, *Ahti*. The students explained who Ahti was in the following way:

"Ahti is a powerful king who lives in his court, Ahtola, on a rock in the deep harbor with an abundance of precious treasures. He manages all fish and other sea animals. He has the most beautiful cows and the quickest horses that graze on seaweed in the sea bottom. Ahti certainly was a rich man. He is also easily provoked, especially when someone throws a stone into the water. Ahti does many things such as retrieving items thrown into the sea. He walks up the harbor in a storm, pulls the sails down, sees beautiful sea swallows, and combs and shapes Vellamo's long hair, Finland's goddess of war."

"Has she seen everything that exists here? According to the almanac, the weather should have been clear; however, the wind blew and there was a downpour as if the heavens opened," Laxmatte asked.

"Yes, it comes from the almanac that has the privilege to fib, and that privilege is kind of depressing. Therefore, the licence to fib must be true," the students said.

Laxmatte shook his head. Now the Baltic Salt herring was ready and the students ate for six persons; while Prince relaxed and ate cold beef bones. The students gave Laxmatte a shiny, silver coin, thanked him for the good food and drink, and went on their way.

Laxmatte and the students felt sorry for Prince who sat with a sad countenance, relaxing on the beach, viewing the barge's white sail on the blue harbor.

As Laxmaja arrived to the troll's antelope, she sat on the beach and thought about what to tell her husband about Ahti. She got to the point and refreshed her memory about Ahti. It was quite something to come to one of the troll's cows. It was something to milk on such a splendid morning and evening.

"What are you thinking about?" asked Laxmatte.

"Nothing," replied the old woman. In quietness she wondered about the old troll runes; stories she heard in her childhood of a limping old man who would have good luck fishing.

It was now Saturday, and on Saturday nights Laxmatte usually did not put out his Baltic herring bait because he wanted to be sure people would not dishonor the Lord's Day. Toward evening, the old woman suggested, "Let's lay out the herring drift net."

Laxmatte responded, "No, there is no benefit or reward to fish on Sunday night."

"But last night it was so stormy, and we caught so few fish," countered his wife. "Tonight the harbor is as clear as a mirror, and with the wind the Baltic herring will swim inwards."

"The northwest sky looks foreboding, and Prince has to eat grass in the evening," reminded the old man.

"Will he never eat my chives?" asked Laxmaja.

"No. It will be bad weather tomorrow even with the sun shining," observed Laxmatte.

She replied, "Listen, we will prepare the well-cared for pasture, which is encased in shallow ice, and fill it one-fourth full with fish."

Laxmatte was persuaded, and they rowed out to sea. When they were in the deepest part of the ocean, Laxmaja hummed the old troll Ahti's tune from memory:

> *"Ahti with the long beard,*
> *Ahti in the deep sea,*
> *You have many fine treasures,*
> *The sea's fish are your glory,*
> *As the sea's pearls*
> *Collecting in your kingdom,*
> *The sea's beautiful fat cows,*
> *Grass on your meadows..."*

"What are you humming?" asked Laxmatte.

"It is only an old ballad which I know in my mind," answered Laxmaja. So she raised her voice and continued to sing:

> *"The king in the wide body of water,*
> *I do not desire the golden treasure,*
> *I do not want to be adorned with pearls,*
> *Nor silver do I consider;*
> *Two are even and one is odd;*
> *The sea's king gives me a pillow,*
> *I will grant you a reward.*
> *The golden sun and the moon's circle..."*

"It is a dumb ballad," said Laxmatte. "What else will one desire other than fish from the king's harbor? It is not appropriate to sing such a song on a Saturday night."

The old woman pretended not to hear him and sang everything in the same monotonous key while they were in the sea depth. Laxmatte did not hear anymore; rather, he sat and rowed the heavy boat because he thought of his pipe and the tobacco. Then they came back to the rock and relaxed.

Laxmatte and Laxmaja lay in their bed, and neither of them said anything at first. Then one of them thought about the unholy Sabbath because they fished on the Lord's day while the other thought about Ahti's cows. When it was past midnight, the old woman sat up in bed and said to her husband, "Do you hear something?"

"No," he replied.

"The person said it is storming, and we need to go out and harvest," she noted.

Both husband and wife went outside as they contemplated fishing in the morning. The summer night was dark like October, and the storm was ferocious. As they stood outdoors, there was a huge sea as white as snow around them in the night, and foam spread high up over the roof of the fish hut. On such a night Laxmaja reminded Laxmatte never to go out and experience something dreadful on the high seas. "It is not worth the effort pushing the boat out to the ocean to salvage the refuse from the storm," she said.

Laxmatte and Laxmaja stood on the steps amazed. They stood near the door entry as the water was splashing on their faces. He said, "Remember when I said there is some blessing to fish on Sunday night? Laxmaja stood there so flabbergasted she did not think about Ahti's cows. When there was nothing more to see, they went into the house again. Their eyes were very heavy due to the late night hours. They slept so soundly and would not have awakened even if a stormy sea had roared about their solitary rocky island.

When Laxmatte and his wife awoke, the sun stood high in the heavens. The stormy weather stopped. Only the sea's ground swell was high, as if it was playing and shimmering in the sunshine toward the red boulders.

"No, what is this?" the old woman shouted when she looked out through the door.

It looks like a sea dog, Laxmatte thought.

"It certainly is not a cow!" exclaimed Laxmaja.

The splendid, fat, and exuberant cow was of the best kind. One would think she had eaten spinach her whole life. The cow walked as quietly as possible along the beach and was not enamored with the poor, small tufts of grass.

Laxmatte could not believe his eyes when the cow birthed a calf. The husband began to milk her, and he filled the pail with the most delightful morning milk. The wife shook her head and went out to look for her lost herring drift net. It was not long before they found the waves had washed many shimmering Baltic herring up on the beach, and they could not see the mesh net.

"It is a good thing we have a cow," said Laxmatte, as he cleaned the herring. "What should we feed her?"

"It should be something rough or coarse," replied the old woman.

The cow walked into the water toward the ocean grass that grew along the banks near the edge of the ocean. Now Prince found a rival as he barked at it.

From that day, cream and sour whole milk was in abundance on the red rock. Everyone managed to be constantly filled with herring. Laxmatte and Laxmaja were fat from good living, and every day they were richer because the old man churned many pounds of butter. In fact, he hired two farm workers, and he was able to fish more. To him the sea was a large fish chest from which he collected as many fish as he wanted.

It was fall, and as Laxmaja observed their cottage, she said,

"We need to build a better stuga next year because this old one is too small for us and the farm hands." They moved to the mainland and the following spring they returned to Ahtola where they stood on the rock.

Laxmatte agreed with his wife about building a new cottage. He built an excellent stuga with heavy, secure locks and a fish house. He hired two men, who fished for long periods of time so that he was able to send a lot of salmon, Baltic herring, and whitefish to Russia and Sweden.

"I will talk with the neighbors and see if I can get a maid to help me because we do not have enough milk for our hired help. I think we need three cows," noted Laxmaja.

"Why don't you sing a ballad for the troll?" Laxmatte said, provoking and joking.

So on Sunday night she went out and sang:

> *"Ahti with the long beard,*
> *Ahti in the deep sea feared*
> *A thousand cows you have in the sea:*
> *Be so kind and give me three."*

The following morning the three cows stood on the red rock and ate the sea grass.

"Are you satisfied?" Laxmatte asked his wife.

"Certainly I am content because I have two maids for housekeeping, and I have better clothing. Have you noticed I am called 'Madam' or 'Missus'?"

"Yes, I have noticed," he replied.

"Now everything is better than in the summer. You should build us a two-story house with a tree garden. I would like to sit and look out onto the sea. We also need a fiddler to play in the evening, and a little steamer to take us to church when it is windy," Laxmaja suggested.

He made everything his wife wanted. "Is there anything else you want me to build for you? Are you satisfied?" he continued. Ahtola was now so pleasant and Laxmaja was so dignified-looking that even the sea's bullheads and Baltic herring were in awe. Prince was fed roast veal and waffles with cream until he was as round as a sprat.

"Certainly I am content; however, we need thirty cows," replied the wife.

"Ask the sea king," suggested her husband.

Laxmatte went out on his new steamer and sang for Ahti, the sea troll. The next morning stood thirty cows on the beach.

"You know husband, it is too cramped here on this little wretched Ahtola rock. We do not have room for so many cows," said Laxmaja.

"I do not have any advice other than to pump out the sea. You can try it with your pump on the steamboat," he continued.

Laxmaja thought the idea was ridiculous, and she did not like that suggestion. She replied to her husband, "I cannot pump out the water from the ocean, but perhaps I can fill it if I build a huge dam out in the depths. I will put down stones and sand so we can cut twice as much grass in the spring."

The old woman loaded her new vessel with stones and went out into the depths of the sea. The violinists and cellists were aboard and played their instruments beautifully. Ahti, the king, and Vellamo, the Finnish goddess of war, and all the sea swallows in the Arctic Circle flew to the surface of the water to listen to the stringed instruments being played.

"What is it that glitters so beautifully on the waves?" Laxmaja asked the musicians.

"It is the harbor's foam that glistens in the sunshine," answered the violinist.

"Throw the stones out!" Laxmaja shouted to the people on the ship.

Passengers on the steamer began to throw stones out onto the foamy sea. One stone hit the nose of Vellamos' close, friendly, sea swallow while another scraped the sea queen and scratched her cheek. A third stone splashed near Ahti's head and tore away half of the king's beard. There was a noise in the sea, and the waves tumbled around each other like a pan of boiling water.

"From where did the violent weather come? It seemed as if the sea opened its mouth like a gaping-mouthed pike, and suddenly the vessel sank," Laxmaja observed.

Laxmaja sank with the vessel like a stone to the bottom of the sea, struggling with both hands and feet. She surfaced, grasped the cello, and floated on it. At the same time, she saw Ahti's disheveled hair with only half of his beard. "Why did you throw stones at me?" the decayed harbor king asked.

"Oh, merciful sir, it was a mistake. Your beard will grow back again," Laxmaja suggested. "Just shake the bear smell out of your beard."

"Wife, have I not given you all you desired and more?" Laxmatte reminded Laxmaja.

"Yes, of course, dear husband. Thank you so much for the cows! They milk just like camels."

"Where is the sun's gold and a piece of the moon as you promised me?" The Sea King asked.

"Oh, Sea King, every day and night when it was not cloudy you had it quiet on the sea," answered Laxmaja deceitfully.

"I will teach you!" shouted Sea King, and he tilted the bass viol so that the old woman could get up on it and return to Ahtola.

Upon returning to Ahtola, there stood Prince, just as starved as before. He gnawed on the crow bone while Laxmatte sat alone on the steps in his gray jacket outside the old, poor cabin with a rope around the net. "Look at Mother! Why are you in such a hurry? Why are you so wet?" Laxmatte noted.

Laxmaja looked around amazed and asked, "Where is our two-story house?"

"What house?" answered her husband.

"Our large house, farm, horses, pigs, the three cows, our steamer, and everything else?" the wife continued.

"Now you talk as if you were talking in your sleep. The students have caused you to not think clearly so that you sang silly ballads yesterday evening on the lake. You could not fall asleep before the early morning. It was inclement weather during the night, but the storm is over. I did not have the heart to awaken you," Laxmatte said.

"I have seen Athi," said Laxmaja.

"You have lain in your bed and dreamed only of madness, Mother. You went to sleep out on the water!" Laxmatte reminded Laxmaja.

"But there is the bass viol," said Laxmaja.

"Beautiful bass viol! It is just an old log, little woman," Laxmatte observed.

"It never blesses anyone to fish on Sunday nights," Laxmaja reminded Laxmatte.

The Boy from Pernå

Gossen från Pernå

 lof Simonsson was called a poor fisherman who served in Särkilak's mansion in Pernå parish located between Borgå and Lovisa. Finland's blue bays were between the promotory islands and the thickly foliaged forest heights down to the mirrored islands. Olof had a boy who was given the name Mikael, taken from the archangel, Mikael. Olof was a strong warrior, who in his youth fought against enemies in his country. He used a sword and a bow as oars to catch sea salmon.

During this historical period, Finland was distraught because Kristian Tyranns' Danish preditory coastal navy devastated the coastal villages. Olof desired that his son would one day liberate Finland and tread Tyranns' naval dragon under foot. It is for this reason Olof had his son christened, Mikael.

As Mikael grew stronger, he could lift his father's sword. One day Olof said to his son, "We should wait awhile before you attempt to use my bow. Perhaps you should try my hatchet first that is hanging in the cottage over my bed. See if you can strike the alder tree with one blow!"

Mikael took the hatchet, aimed toward the thick alder tree, and cut it with a single blow. "I knew you could do it," Mikael's father observed. "You are a capable person, and when you grow a head taller, you will be able to draw the bow toward Kristian Tyrann. In the meantime, you can row my large fishing boat, and your arms will be as strong as iron." Mikael agreed with his father. Nothing could surpass a pair of strong arms, a good steel bow, and a sturdy ax.

One Sunday Mikael followed his father to church, and as he entered, Mikael saw many decorations, pictures of saints, incense, and Latin prayers, as this was the Catholic era. "I do not understand anything. What are they singing?" the boy asked.

"It is Latin. What else would it be? One does not speak to God in any other language than Latin," said his father.

"Why can't we speak to God in Finnish?" He and most of the people spoke Finnish, and he thought it was strange that one could not speak to God in their own language and understand God's answer.

"God does not understand Finnish. God only understands Latin," responded his father. Mikael thought it was strange that God was so misinformed, and the boy did not ask further.

When the mass concluded, father went to the sacristy to discuss a matter with the minister, and Mikael followed. As they walked past the altar, there lay something big with peculiar, dark marks, and variegated colored pictures lying on the table. "What is it?" asked Mikael.

"It is a book," Father answered.

"A book? What is a book?" the boy asked. He had never seen a book. He looked at the strange object, contemplating it with so many pages and dark marks in it. It was what one usually called a Folio, a very thick book with elegant, strange letters. Some were blue, gold, green, red, but mostly black. On the edges were painted holy pictures with a gold halo around the head.

In Finland at that time, there existed a mass book printed in Latin and German. All the others were handwritten and very expensive, so that it cost as much as a farmer's homestead.

Mikku (his nickname) questioned his father, "What is meant by the crooked marks and lines?"

"They are called letters. To print them is called writing, and to decipher them is called reading," replied Father.

"Will I learn to read and write?"

"No, no one understands but the minister," answered Father.

"I want to be a minister," replied Mikael.

"You must first learn to speak Latin," replied his father.

"Is it very difficult, Father?"

"Yes, it certainly must be difficult because it is God's language and one must learn it in school."

"I want to attend school, Father, and learn Latin. When I become a minister, I will pray to God in Finnish, and if God does not understand me, I will say to him in Latin, 'Dear God, I will teach you to speak Finnish, so that we will all understand what you say! We want to speak with you.'" Mikael stated.

The minister heard the boy's comments, tapped him on the shoulder, and said, "Mikku, you speak as you have understood. The Bible is written in Greek and Latin. How shall God speak another language than that which is spoken in the Bible? It is not impossible for you to attend school and become a minister. I will speak with your father about this."

After the conversation between the minister and Olof, the father answered in an ill-humored manner, "The boy was given the same name as the archangel, Mikael, and he should become the people's soldier," so Olof thought.

The minister continued, "Your son, Mikku, would like to read, write, and speak Latin. He can be God's and the people's warrior, even with another weapon than a sword and bow," the minister stated.

Sometime later after a stormy day, the minister wandered on the shore in conversation with the praised headmaster in Viborg's school, Johannes Erasmi, who was visiting the minister. They confided with each other regarding the concerns of the evil times, about Kristian Tyrann, and Stockholm's incessant berating of the frightening heretic, Martin Luther. He wanted the papacy to grant permission for everyone to read the Bible.

As they strolled along the shore, they saw a fishing boat struggle against the waves and headwinds. A man was seen at the rudder, and the boy was rowing. The headmaster questioned the minister, "Why does the man leave the boy alone to row the big boat in such harsh weather?"

"I know the man. He is the fisherman, Olof Simonsson. He wants to educate his son to be a member of the armed forces and train him to do the heaviest work in order to strengthen his arms."

"It is nevertheless quite a heavy boat for such young arms," mentioned the schoolmaster. "See how he works! He must be a hardy lad!"

"Yes, he is as hardy as a worker bee. I believe whatever he undertakes in the world he will have the drive. He wants to attend school, but his poor father wants his son to be a member of the armed forces. I am willing to have him enroll in our school tuition free. I have never seen such a hardy boy," the schoolmaster stated.

The boat worked itself slowly over the roaring bay, and Mikael and father Olof landed safely at the harbor. It was obvious that the boy's cheeks were red like mature raspberries, and his hands were red and raw from the strong, biting wind. The schoolmaster and the minister went to meet them.

As they approached Olof and Mikael, the schoolmaster encouraged the father that Mikael attend school, and it would be tuition-free. The harsh fisherman was not immediately convinced, but he finally admitted that his son could travel with the schoolmaster to Viborg and attend school. Prior to this time, Mikael had never seen a book. He was the only one from his home district to be educated.

He was one of Finland's most learned and distinguished men. He traveled to many foreign countries, including studying in Wittenberg, Germany, under Dr. Martin Luther and Filip Melanchthon. Luther's reformation was on the eve in Sweden and

Finland under Gustav Vasa. Luther wrote to the king praising and recommending young Mikael from Pernå. Mikael was the first rector in Åbo school in nine years, and subsequently he became the bishop in Åbo. It was a high honor for a poor fisherman's son.

This young lad from Pernå questioned why God could not understand another language other than Latin. He thought it was a sin that so many people would not benefit from speaking to God in prayers or read what God said to them in his manifested word.

Martin Luther said to Mikael that God understands all languages spoken to him because God has given everyone gifts in various ways to understand him and his revealed word. God did not want prayers with unintelligible learned words, but rather with heartfelt, childlike faith.

The lad from Pernå taught the Finnish people to read and speak to God in their own language. He was allowed to print the first ABC book, the first Finnish prayer book, David's Psalms, and finally the New Testament in Finnish. At first it was not easy to understand the printed language. There was no printing company in Finland; consequently, the printing was done in Stockholm, Sweden. King Gustav Vasa supported Mikael's printing endeavors, and as a result, every boy and girl in Finland read God's word and said prayers to God.

Through Mikael's minister and the school headmaster, Mikael Olofsson became known as a learned man. He was known as Mikael Agricola; the latter name meaning farmer or agriculturalist. Mikael was God's and the people's warrior who could win victoriously without fighting with a sword.

One time I sat on the shore of Pernå harbor and saw the fishing boats struggling against the storm and high sea. I thought about Mikael Agricola who rowed in the storm in his father's boat. In my mind's eye, I heard the Finnish-speaking people singing about God in church, or I imagined seeing them read their Bible at home after Sunday dinner. I have once more thought of the one who taught the people how they can speak to and with God. Mikael Agricola wrote the following in his prayer book:

> *"He who sees in all hearts below,*
> *understands what is contained in the prayers."*

Virgin Mary's Ladybug

Jungfru Marias nyckelpiga

he Virgin Mary was nine years old when her mother, Anna, said, "Visit your aunt Elizabeth in Bethany and ask for my gold key that I forgot when I was with her yesterday." Anna did not think she had dropped the unusual gold key.

The Virgin Mary knew she was fortunate that her mother, Anna, trusted her. As the hot sun burned over Jerusalem, the little girl was tired, but she ran quickly to the bridge over the Kidron Brook with its rippling waves.

The waves asked the Virgin Mary, "Why are you walking over the bridge? Instead, wade through our clear water; you who have childlike stars in your eyes."

"I do not have the time," answered the Virgin Mary as she continued on her way.

The brooks' waves were filled with butterflies, and all the air's winged creeping things buzzed over the water in the shadows of the fig tree.

"What truth will the waves say?" asked the little dark red, speckled beetle sitting on an osier bush.

"It means that one always pretends to be better than one is," answered the spider while it spun its web extremely fine so that the flies would not see it.

"What does it mean to be good?" The beetle continued as it was not really content with its first answer from the spider.

"It means to be good toward yourself but poke holes in everyone else," the wasp said.

"What does it mean to be obedient?" the beetle continued to ask.

"It means to do all what one wills," answered the horsefly and buzzed so brainless that it fell on its back and was almost drowned.

"Ow! Ow!" shrieked the beetle. "What does it mean to be humble?"

"Of course it means none other than to be clothed in fine-looking clothes in order to be admired by the whole world," the yellow fly answered while she boasted with her shiny wings in the sunlight.

"I am sorry my questions are so dumb," moaned the beetle in distress. "I do not understand why people would ask questions about being good, obedient, and humble," the dung beetle buzzed as it lay on its back in the dirt looking up and crawling in vain.

Toward evening the Virgin Mary returned more tired than before, and she sat resting at the bridge.

"Come, wade through the brook, and we will cool your burning feet," the waves said as they rippled again.

"Oh yes, it is so beautiful," noted the Virgin Mary as she tucked up her clothing and waded through the brook. It was a delightfully refreshing venture as the brook happily splashed and kissed the Virgin Mary's bare feet.

"Thank you," she said, refreshed as she continued to walk toward her home in the city.

Upon returning, she became anxious as the sun was already setting. "Dear small waves, have you seen my gold key? I had it in my dress pocket and must have dropped it here when I tucked up my dress," the Virgin Mary asked the brook.

"I have asked the sun, and it answered, 'Do I have time with your key now when the fig leaf ripened?'"

"I have asked the mountain, and it responded, 'I have other things to do because I stand as a watch tower in order to see the Romans coming!'"

"I asked the moon, but it said, 'Ridiculous girl, do not bother me for I have not yet set!'"

The Virgin Mary continued, "Brook, you must know about the key because it was here when I lifted my dress to keep it from getting wet."

The Kidron Brook defended itself like the sun, mountain, and moon because it asked, "Do I have time to look for your key now when I must water all the water lilies after the hot day?"

The crow flew down and observed people walking along the shore, as butterflies dipped their wings in the water and spiders looked in their webs. The golden flies and the dor beetle, or dung beetle, which now finally came on foot again, trotted along leisurely on the way to the shore. Many living things looked at each other. The eagle asked the dove, the dove asked the lion, the lion asked the hare, the hare asked the fig tree, and the fig tree asked the water lily if they had seen the Virgin Mary's gold key.

None of them had seen the key except the little beetle with the six dark spots on its red-crusted wings. The beetle had seen the key shine between the small stones at the beach along the brook, and it buzzed zzzzzz.

> "*Sun winking on the waves*
> *no one saw it,*
> *only the foolish*
> *from the least and the silent*
> *the gold streaks*
> *in the gleaming water.*"

The Virgin Mary heard the beetle buzzing. She ran down to the beach, and sure enough, the little key was between two small white and red stones. Happily she said to the beetle, "Come here and sit down by my dress and look at my key! You shall be my ladybug!"

"But I am so little, poor, and dumb," said the ladybug.

"Before you consider yourself so poor, little, and dumb, you will become my faithful servant and follow me wherever I go," the Virgin Mary commanded.

The little beetle hummed cheerfully in her place and then followed her mistress everywhere as her ladybug. The little girl at the Kidron was the Virgin Mary who received the gold key from her mother.

The spider, wasp, horsefly, and the dor beetle were not surprised with the honor given to the beetle.

One day the Virgin Mary's ladybug was seen in the osier bush, and today she considers itself to be the least intelligent in the whole world. Have you seen her? The entire ladybug family has the given Latin name, *Coccinella Septempunctata*. Some have white dots on the gold-shelled wings while others have only two or three dark dots. The ladybug with six dots on its red-shelled wings is good and well-known among many children who play in the green grass. No one knows for sure if she exists in the Kidron Brook outside of Jerusalem. It is a long time since the Virgin Mary was nine years old and waded over the brook on her way home from Bethany.

About the Summer That Never Came

Om den sommar som aldrig kom

Do I know of a small child who wished for a summer that never came? I will tell you about this true short story.

At one time there was a little boy named Rafael. He was healthy, strong, and growing like a little European mountain ash.

One day, God said, "When this little boy matures, he will face many temptations and live a wayward life." Then God sent his big shining angel, Rafael, (from which the little boy received his name) who stated, "The boy is mine."

One winter day, the healthy and strong boy became ill. His parents and siblings agreed to wait a little while for summer when Rafael would be healthy.

The long light spring came when the birds began to sing in the trees and boughs. The children had a linnet in a cage. They released it in the mornings and let it fly freely in the park with the other small birds. Happily, with gratitude, he chirped only one tune, and the children thought they had never heard a happier song.

When Rafael's sisters arrived home, little Rafael lay sick in his bed. The small sisters patted his pale cheeks and his beautiful brown hair and said to him, "Rafael, when summer arrives, you will come with us, hear the linnet sing, and be well again."

God's big shining angel stood invisible at the boy's bed and stroked his shiny white wings over Rafael, as if to protect him against all evil in the world. The long angel's wings stretched over his pale cheeks as his breathing weakened. His clear brown eyes looked toward the angel, whom he alone saw. As the angel and Rafael were together, he died. On his small, pale lips lingered the peaceful, happy smile that one sees with small children when they notice that an angel is standing at their bed.

The parents said to the small sisters, "Now Rafael is happy because he is with God. As the linnet flew out of its cage to freedom, so Rafael's innocent spirit flew to heaven. We did not hear his happiness as we heard the bird's twitter, but we noticed in his gentle smile that he praised God when he received salvation's crown."

Then one of the sisters reminded the family, "The summer will never come when Rafael could have been free."

"Yes," agreed the other sister. "Rafael's summer will never come."

The parents wiped their tears and replied, "Certainly spring has come. If we could see far away in the heavens, we would see Rafael playing with the small angels in God's everlasting paradise. With the Lord it is always spring and summer, and fall and winter never come anymore."

Little Rafael's body was brought to the cemetery and laid in the little grave. The minister read beautiful prayers and promised him eternal life with the Lord. The boy's mother, who stood at the grave, said, "Now we will sing a hymn at Rafael's grave."

At the same time, a little bird sang loudly under the blue heavens in the spring sunshine. Rafael's father listened and said, "Hear the linnet, for it knows well for whom it sings! It sings hymns at Rafael's grave."

A large, shining angel flew with little Rafael's soul a long way over the earth's grave to the eternal summer in God's heaven.

How One Finds Fairy Tales

Huru man hittar sagor

his is a dragonfly's conversation about autumn with little Marie.

"Good morning, Marie!"

"Good morning, Dragonfly!"

"Yes, it is autumn now, Dragonfly," reminded Marie.

"The leaves are yellow and the nights are so dark," the dragonfly answered.

"You fly whether it is fall or spring," Marie replied. "I am one of those who is in nature's heart. When I was a child, I was so warm and never froze. Now we have Saint Birgitta's day on October 7 from the Swedish saint, Birgitta, who was devout and good.

When fall comes people know winter is near, and everything becomes so chilly and withered in the woods. However, some pleasant days come around Saint Birgitta's day. The fall is dressed in its gorgeous, gold, parade-like uniform and is sad when the migratory birds disappear.

Then summer looked one more time in fall's door, dressed in a green, bare, hunting outfit, and said to fall, "Does one need permission to step in?"

"Yes, of course. Here is a moss bench, cousin. Take your place, even though I am not always organized in the early morning," replied fall.

"No thank you," answered summer. "It is only a French visit.

I do not have much time because the North Polar train leaves for Egypt at seven o'clock tonight."

"Don't hurry," said autumn. "Saint Birgitta will greet the pope in Rome, and she peels apples for her hungry children."

"Well, I suppose. I will stay a little while and see how you look after my head of cabbage and if my flowers are still blooming. That is the manner of summer on the green tuft of grass, and the fall neighborhood with the pears, lingonberries, mushrooms, and such," answered summer.

Fall continued, "In a flash like a storm signal, the North Polar train went to Africa with all its passengers and chaffinch, as it whistled in the air. The crow flew to Estonia, the magpie leased a room during the winter in a permanent outhouse, and laughed at the crow in the closest birch."

"One must take advantage of the fall for garden cleaning, as the broom goes over land and sea, sweeping everything away. We must rake leaves, remove anchors from the dam, and have the children pick the gooseberry bushes for the final fall ingathering. It is time for work at home, Marie," fall said.

"It is fairy tale time, Dragonfly, because it is fall," Marie reminded Dragonfly. Dragonfly replied, "What? Haven't you had enough? Have you forgotten '*Sleeping Beauty, Adalminas' Pearl,*' and a hundred other fairy tales?"

Marie answered, "No, but ..."

Dragonfly continued, "Tell me any tale."

She continued, "I do not remember anything."

Dragonfly shouted, "Look!"

Marie answered, "I have not found anything."

Dragonfly asked, "Will you teach me to find fairy tales?"

She responded, "Oh, yes, Dragonfly! Once some small children played a pontoon game. They discovered they could not loosen it, so they would sit and look while the other children ate wild strawberries and milk. There was a boy who tried to untie the pontoon by telling a fairy tale, but he could not recall any stories, so he went to the school headmaster.

"'Dear headmaster, be so kind and give me a fairy tale; otherwise, I will not get to eat strawberries and milk.'

"Okay," said the headmaster, "What is nine times seven?"

"That is not a fairy tale," the boy answered.

"'Yes it is,' replied the schoolmaster."

"Well... I suppose," the boy replied.

He continued to look for fairy tales and asked his uncle, who was a general, "Tell me a fairy tale."

"You know what I will say. Blame the rifles," the uncle answered.

"But it is not a fairy tale," responded the boy.

"Well... it is an excellent fairy tale requiring military service. I have nothing else to say," the general stated.

The boy left and came to an older gentleman. "Dear sir, give me a fairy tale or else I will not eat strawberries and milk."

"With great pleasure," he responded. "It's about Stanislai with crown and sword."

"That is not a fairy tale," sobbed the boy.

"It is an honor you should ask. I have nothing else to say. Be content with that!" responded the older gentleman.

The boy went to his aunt who was at the home of a graceful duchess. "Dear Aunt, give me a fairy tale so that I can eat strawberries and drink milk."

Immediately the aunt replied, "Here is a chignon. It is the only thing I have."

Sighing, the boy responded, "It is not a fairy tale."

Once again the boy left and went to the butcher who sold meat at the market. The same question was asked and the butcher answered, "My heart is willing if I can earn a living with so little. See, here is ham with some jam. I have nothing else."

"It is not a fairy tale," the boy said.

"Why isn't it?" answered the butcher. "Won't that do? It is pork!"

The boy went out and came to Aunt Ulla, who wrote books, and he was sure to find a good fairy tale. Aunt Ulla was prepared to give him a thick book with moral tales portraying young people. "They are not fairy tales!" exclaimed the boy.

"Why not?" answered Aunt Ulla. "It is good literature with upright standards!"

Now the poor boy was confused as he walked to the little summer cottage made from hewn wood in the forest. "Dear crofter, give me a fairy tale or else I will not receive strawberries and milk. Is this some kind of prank?"

"No," said the crofter. "It is not a trick at all. Go in the woods, and there you will become familiar with fairy tales in all the twigs."

Wondering what the crofter meant, the boy went farther into the forest, and when he looked around, fairy tales grew on all the treetops and branches. The sagas even looked out between the birch leaves and hung like cones in the spruce. The juniper bushes were so overgrown with beautiful tales that one hardly saw the berries. The boy began to pick the berries, and soon his pockets, his cap, and arms were full. He was strong to carry all of these berries!

"It was odd he thought to himself to have an uncle, godparents, aunts, the butcher, and the schoolmaster, who did not have the slightest idea about fairy tales.

"Yes, now you see," said the juniper bush that always was inclined to scoff a little.

"The schoolmaster is certainly never satisfied," observed the boy.

"He is satisfied with his extensive learning," responded the juniper bush noisily and slyly with its sharp needles.

The boy went home with his large load, his strawberries and milk, and sufficient fairy tales for the long winter until spring.

"Now I will tell you how one finds fairy tales in many other places other than the juniper bushes," the dragonfly stated.

"Tell me, Dragonfly!" urged the boy.

Dragonfly continued, "When it is summer, you shall go out early in the morning while the dew is still lying in the grass and look closely at the fields. There lie fairy tales as pearls by the many thousands. Walk to the shore of the lake where small brisk waves go over the water with bright furrows in between. They are tales written with bluish letters that will teach you to read."

"In autumn you will hear the high pines whistling, telling fantastic fairy tales from antiquity. Or look in the heather and the yellow leaves that contain lonely, melancholy fairy tales with yellow and red spellings."

"In the winter, you read about frost in fine verses on the window panes and on forest boughs which portray beautiful pictures with painted hoarfrost, reading the star's silvery fairy tales. All the best and purer fairy tales have been created because God himself has written of them in the highest blue evening heaven."

"When it returns to spring, you will surely see a display of colors in the evening sky with all the vivid array of colors. In fall, winter, and spring, you will read of the stars silver sagas. They are the highest, best, and purest fairy tales that have been created because God himself has written of them in the highest blue evening heaven," Dragonfly continued.

"Oh you, Little Marie, if you knew how incredibly big, rich, and beautiful nature can speak to you; much, much, more than I now can mention!" Dragonfly continued, "Nature can speak to us in such big, rich, and beautiful ways! All the mountains, stones, trees, bushes, plants, animals in the woods, in the air, in the sea—all have their own histories. Everything lives, breathes, feels, thinks, and speaks. Nothing is dead! How could your heart be completely oblivious? You only need to take the time to listen to it!"

Marie, when nature was speechless, it noticed you were old and gray in your soul. Why should you have gray hair in the soul?

When you were young, little Marie, you were always God's good child in your heart. When you are old like grandmother in the rocking chair, you will always hear nature speak. Listen to the angels sing of God's love in the clear heights, and then you will never freeze in the world's sorrow," Dragonfly reminded her. So it was.

Nora, Who Did Not Want to Be a Child

Nora, som inte ville vara barn

will never play with dolls anymore," stated Nora. With that, she threw Lillepytt and Rosa Wäderflykt in anger and sat sulkily at the table with both hands under her chin.

Rosa Wäderflykt and Lillepytt were two dolls, a boy and a girl. Both china head dolls were kind, and they never made any trouble. The dolls had been Nora's small children when she was little. Now she tossed them in a corner because she was too big for Lillepytt and Rosa Wäderflykt.

"Why are you not playing with your dolls anymore?" asked six-year-old little Selma. She thought it was fun to play with Nora, who was eleven years old.

"I am no longer a child. The boys on the street tease me by taking my hat off, and my aunt's maid calls me Miss Eleanore. I associate with older girls in school, and besides, I have already read four novels. I can dance the polka, and I am old enough to know if my clothing looks nice or not. Three days after Christmas at the children's dance if you remember, I waltzed with a cadet, who said I was beautiful. What do you think, Selma?"

Selma ignored Nora's question, and taking the dolls from the corner as if they were her own, she answered with a sad tone of voice. "I don't think Lillepytt has a nose now."

"You are not very smart!" said Nora annoyed, as she went to the piano and played a polka-mazurka.

Selma looked at the dolls. Yes, that is correct; Lillepytt had fallen and chipped a piece from her nose. It was smaller now than before, and Rosa Wäderflykt had a large scratch on her forehead. Besides, they were ragged and shaggy like begging children. "Poor, small children, you will be able to relax, lay on the bed, and pretend to be sick. I will sew new clothes for you," Selma said as she dressed Lillepytt and Rosa Wäderflykt. She laid them in their bed in the doll's house and placed the doll blanket over them so they would not freeze.

It was now Christmas, and in the garden there was a long toboggan the boys had leaned against the stall wall. They had poured water on the hill the night before so that during the night, the water had frozen. Selma put on the little gray bonnet with the red tie, and the nice blue wool jacket she received as a Christmas gift. On the step stood the little, painted, fast toboggan that was nicer than all the other toboggans.

Severin, one of the boys, went to the top of the hill. Up and down the toboggan went in somersaults. There were many boys and girls with red noses and happy hearts. The girls who were afraid to go down alone always had a boy in back of them to steer the toboggan. The whirling snow blew about the person's face in front. Severin steered well and only two tumbles happened the entire morning.

Meanwhile, Nora was in the house and became quite tired playing the polka-mazurka over and over. Gazing out the window, she exclaimed aloud, "Oh, such silly children!" Inwardly she thought, "*I remember having so much fun when I was little.*" She turned, picked up her new clothing, and held it up to her as she stood in front of the mirror. She thought to herself, "*To think they are totally and beautifully mine.*" Then her thoughts turned to reading.

As she looked for a book, she remembered her mother had

hidden all the novels. When Nora could not find a book she liked, she was angry and sent the cat to its bed.

In the evening, the children played in the large dining room as much as they wanted. First they pulled the chairs together and acted out a marketplace, buying and selling. They played games such as "Hide-and-Seek," "Cat and Rat," "Crow Hop," "Secretive Shoe," and "May Curtsy." Finally they imitated "Homespun Weaving," and it was indescribably fun! The hardest part was when Selma and her friend took each other by the hand over each other's heads, and when they were all in a line, they fell down, including Selma, whose arms were too short to reach over her friend's head! Then the children decided to climb up on the roof.

What did Nora do when all the others happily stood on the roof? She thought to herself, "*Crazy children!*" Sitting down in a corner, she looked sullen as if a cloud were over her like a heavy fall mist.

Selma said to Nora, "Come with me, and we will do something fun together."

Nora replied, "What should we do because I am bigger than you?"

At night when Nora slept in her bed, she had an unusual dream. She saw herself standing in a summer garden in the midst of a green forest. Round about were tall flowers with small, growing trees that were charming and beautiful to see swaying in the summer winds. When the breeze blew over the branches and leaves, murmuring and singing was heard conveying a message through ballads. Gently and clearly they sang, "We honor small children in God's kingdom. Oh God, our praise, we honor his children!"

A large group of small boys and girls ran between flowers, kissed and loved them, and called them their small playmates. When the flowers and trees began to sing, the boys and girls sang, "We honor small, small children in God's kingdom. Oh God, our praise!"

Then the sun stood still with a glorious sunset in the evening cloud, as if God's eye slept in the night. However, his eye never sleeps; it is awake both day and night. Nora looked at the heavens gradually getting dark, and the stars began to shine one after the other in the blue half of the sky. Many thousands and millions of stars sank down in the horizon with their clear brilliance.

From where the stars descended, an angel went among the children, trees, and flowers. All the angels were small, innocent children because in times past they had left the earth as human beings, and God had taken them to their earlier form. The angels sang, "We are small children in God's kingdom. Oh God, our promised one, we get to be his children!"

Out of the large multitude, an angel appeared and said to Nora, "Why are you so sad?"

She turned away and responded in an angry tone of voice as she usually did, "Such children!" Immediately everything was changed around her in the dream, and she thought she was so completely alone in a large desert in the midst of a cold winter. There she did not have any friends to love, only herself. Those who love themselves have a heart like a desert waste in the cold winter. Nora thought back to the summer, the flowers, and the growing trees, and she began to cry bitterly.

Then the winter around her was warmer, and Lillepytt and Rosa Wäderflykt came wandering through the drifts and asked Nora, "Why are you crying?"

She answered, "It's freezing here in the snow; I am alone, and there are no other friends in heaven or on earth for me."

The dolls replied, "You could be a child! Don't you see that everyone in nature is blessed and fortunate to be small children? God said heaven's kingdom hears them. If you will be a friend to God and people, you shall be a child in your heart. When you are an older adult some day, you will still be a child in your soul. You will constantly be humble and respectful toward Him. Come, and we will go back to our summer again!"

Nora took the dolls in her hands and cried because she did not understand. When they returned to the green forest, the flowers, trees, angels, boys, girls, dolls, and Nora were present. They all sang, "Praise to Him because we are small children in God's kingdom."

Hjälteborg Fortress
Fästningen Hjälteborg

ow it is war!" shouted Mathias when he trudged indoors, completely red-faced with a sooty mustache, a rooster feather in his hat, and a wooden sword with the biggest blade.

"God save us! What is Mathias saying about war?" shouted frightened Maja who swept the hall floor early in the morning.

"Yes, it is war!" replied Mathias as he proudly placed the sword in the loop of his belt.

"What is that noise? War is terrible! It is awful when people kill each other, burn cities and villages, and trample crops along the way. Are the Turks here?" questioned Maja.

"I think so," said Mathias. Looking in the cupboard, he found a basket with half of a crisp bread cake. He spread butter on it and began to chew with great force. "The whole yard is filled with Turks," he said with a mouth full of food. "We should threaten them, or they will take Hjälteborg fortress."

Maja put the garbage in a dustpan and quickly carried it out to the garden. She was curious to see what the strange noise was, so she opened the door with her heart in her throat. She saw nothing but a whole garden full of schoolboys. In the corner toward the fence was a large snow castle with brick walls on which one of the boys placed a red handkerchief portraying a swinging devil atop a large pole.

Maja mumbled, "The painting on the brick wall is ugly." (She did not realize it was a handkerchief.) Annoyed, she returned to the house with the dustpan.

Maja did not notice the seven block long Turkish soldiers who fastened half-moons of paper on the back of the fence. Then the schoolboys placed snowballs in orderly fashion like a stack of wood against the fence. (The children are creating a war scene between the Turks and the Christians.) The Christians were inside the garden, and a spruce branch was used as an entrance through the button-holed sweater of the make-believe human figure.

"Where is the general?" asked one of the Christians with an uneasy expression, looking in the direction where the enemy waited.

"He is eating a sandwich in the cupboard, Mr. Captain!" answered another as he pretended to place his hand on the cap.

"It is not fit for a general to eat a sandwich when the enemy is attacking us," remarked the captain resentfully. "An armed person does not stand and mumble. Without commands, our leader quickly marched out of the cupboard," he noted in a firm tone of voice.

"It happens," answered the armed man.

Upon inspection, Mathias, the general, was seen on the steps. The first thing he saw was the red flag on the fortress wall. "Why are they hoisting the bloody flag in Hjälteborg?" shouted the general sternly. There was no answer.

The embarrassed captain responded, "Sir, I borrowed the red flag from Britasköks (Brita's kitchen) and paid the loan out of the war chest. I have no idea why her scarf was red."

The commander answered, "Captain, you do not understand colors and the devil any more than a cat in the kitchen. We honor pirate ships and piracy, so why should we not carry the red flag? White and blue are our colors. White stands for our winter's snow, and the blue represents our blue lakes."

The general took out pieces of a worn out flag handkerchief from the breast pocket of his sweater that his sister Sofi had sewn inside the day before. The red pirate devil celebrated, and the blue and white devil swung quickly at the top of the pole shouting, "The Turks are coming! Everyone to his post!"

There was a big commotion within the three troops of the Christian army. Two divisions were placed at the harbor because both sides met enemies with the fearful hail of bullets. The third division hurried into the fortress to arrange the drums as well as mend bricks with plaster after the snow had loosened parts of the structure. The general's eye was everywhere, and he showed mercy like a puff on one's back.

With a drum beat, little Fritz was so scared that he lost the drumsticks and retreated to his kennel.

The courageous Turks were almost double in number compared with the Christians who hurried through the door with a hailed, "Hurrah!" The Turks retaliated, and the smallest among them began to cry. Their commander, Genghis Khan, was a tall, six foot brave leader.

A dreadful cannon of snowballs descended while the Christians retreated as they pulled up their sweater collars in submission because the attack was too violent. In this crucial moment everyone depended on the drums. However, the drums that should have revived everyone's heroism were not heard. If the Christians had heard the drums, they probably would have won.

With a drum beat, the commander shouted, "Traitor!" But they stood there and did nothing. The enemy stormed in, and soon the Christians, with great bravery, defended every bit of the area. Finally the Turks submitted to the Christians and withdrew behind the brick fortress.

The general and his men escaped harm. While conquering the Turks, they were heard cheering loudly, crouching around the yard with their trophies from the battlefield including one high boot, two tree swords, seven hats, and fourteen or fifteen odd wool shrouds.

Now there was a short truce or cease-fire, and the Turkish pasha celebrated the victory with a magnificent feast of taffy at the war's expense. After that, a negotiator was sent, who in a commanding tone requested the fortress be surrendered unconditionally. Everyone should run over the sword, meaning everyone must lie down and pretend to be beaten to death.

The armed person who stood in front up on the wall reasoned this was a brazen request. Why should he get a snowball from the drummer, aim, and hit the overbearing Turk in the middle of the forehead? In the process, his hat would fly off and the Turk would try and grab the armed person's feet as best he could.

"It is contrary to international law!" shouted Genghis Khan standing in the yard.

"I agree!" shouted the army captain. At the same time, a snowball whizzed from his firm hand, and Genghis came close to being hit on the ear.

"Good job, snowball!" the general's voice was heard. Those who dare to speak about surrender are wimps! The army weapon was given to the second lieutenant, but the general raised his voice so that the following was heard over the whole area:

"The drum beat is weak! Courageous Muslims! Listen to what the great boasters say! I say this not just to speak to you, but in back of the fence there is a whole basket of toffee, and the first one who comes over the brick fortress will ... !" shouted Genghis.

"Hurrah! Long live Genghis Khan!" shouted the Turks rushing toward the fortress.

However, Hjälteborg fortress was not so easy to overtake as the unfortified courtyard. It hailed bullets like peas around the ears. The bullets could no more be used because men wrestled with each other, and broke bricks which fell.

They all fought until the last person was left, but unfortunately the Turks were so considerably superior they could not help but overtake the Christians. The general was captured, the flag was pulled down while the enemy rushed over the fortress brick wall, and then a drum beat was heard.

At this unexpected signal, the Turks lost their courage. They could not do anything otherwise, even though a new Christian army was approaching from behind. Headlong, they jumped down from the brick wall and ran out of the gate at some distance.

The general and his group crept from under the fortress ruins, and barely believing their eyes, there was little Fritz drumming in the courtyard.

When Fritz approached the general, he took his hat off, fell on his knees, and said, "Now the general can shoot me. I do not deserve better because I ran away from death when the enemy advanced forward. It is better to have been shot than be degraded to that of a lad porter, or mooring a ship by rope or cable. I heard enough of what the general said when I sat in the dog kennel with him kicking me. It is true, I was afraid of the Turks, but I was still more afraid to be called a big coward. Clenching my teeth, I proceeded forward beating the drumsticks, and thought to myself, *"They will kill me because I drummed! Instead I ran away."*

The general kissed Fritz, the drumbeater, on the ear lobe and said, "Comrades, the drummer, Fritz, has rescued Hjälteborg and all of us. In the presence of the whole army, I declare he is an honest and straightforward man. Let him grow a head taller so he does not take up space in the dog kennel. It is a disgrace for boys who sometimes creep into the dog kennel when it concerns the raiding of Hjälteborg! Be respectful of each other. We would rather fight to our death than throw away the drumsticks when it means preserving one's native country!"

The Ant Who Traveled to the Doctor
Myran, som for till doktorn

f I could just look up," said Child Ant.

"Wait, first I will see how it is in the world," replied Mother Ant. She looked out through an opening in the anthill, but she could not see anything because the sun shone in her face.

"Now I will look up," said Child Ant. So she crept out through the hole in the anthill.

The anthill was built under a large Norway spruce, and the warm sun melted the ice under the green branches. The ice fell and plopped down in the anthill, and hit the leg of Child Ant who crept out through the opening.

"What happened?" asked Mother Ant.

"I think I lost a leg," replied Child Ant.

Frightened, Mother Ant dragged Child Ant through the hole and began to treat the leg with resin. It seemed to set well, but when Child Ant began to creep, the leg fell off.

"It does not go well in the world sometimes. We must travel to the doctor," Mother Ant commanded.

Mother Ant made a little bag of withered lily of the valley from last year, placed the leg in the sack, put Child Ant on her back, and they proceeded on their way. The anthill was on a mound almost near the railway. Mother Ant knew where the marching path was. The train came... *burr, urr, urr!* Mother Aunt jumped from the rail to the wheel, spun around some turns, climbed safely with her child up onto the train car, and traveled without a ticket to Helsinki, Finland's capital.

When they arrived in Helsinki, Mother Ant crept cautiously. She was scared to death as she walked with Child Ant on her back, with the leg in the bag, and hurried to the hired carriage and taxi driver. "Now we will go to the doctor. I wonder what the horse will think about carrying such a heavy load?" Mother Ant thought.

"What is this white hill?" asked Child Ant when they drove by the large stone house.

"People live in those heaps!" exclaimed Mother Aunt.

When Mother Ant and Child Ant arrived at the hospital, they were in such a hurry that Mother Ant forgot to pay the hired carriage taxi driver. She climbed up the steps with Child Ant on her back. As they entered the office, the doctor sat at his table and read a book about the skill in constructing new noses. Mother Ant climbed up on the table and then to the top of the book. The large doctor looked at her and flicked her with his finger. However, Mother Ant climbed up on the page again and began to tell the doctor about the ice lump and Child Ant's leg.

"Oh, is that all?" asked the big doctor. He wanted to set the little leg, but his pliers were too thick, and he tore off one of the healthy legs.

"Oh no!" Child Ant said loudly to Mother Ant.

"What is it?" questioned Mother Ant to Child Ant.

"It was nothing; it was only me who lost my other leg," answered Child Ant.

The large doctor blamed the mistake on his glass eye and went to look for finer pliers; however, Mother Ant did not have time to wait. She packed both loose legs in the sack, placed Child Ant on her back and crept away.

"We must travel to the marine doctor," said Mother Ant to Child Ant. She succeeded quickly to get another hired driver to visit Dr. Ewerth. Another male passenger with a large stomach was in the carriage taxi also.

As they entered Doctor Ewerth's office, he was standing beside the large sitz bathtub. He wanted to submerge the fat man in it just as Mother Ant climbed up on his hand. Quickly the doctor saw Mother Ant before he submerged his hand in the water!

Mother Ant rescued herself as she sat on the edge of the portable bathtub. When she regained her composure, she did not see her child because the fat man ferociously splashed in the portable tub water. However, Child Ant was safe and sound.

"How are you?" shouted Mother Ant.

"At first I was a little damp, but now I feel drowned!" responded Child Ant, who was drenched.

Mother Ant heard a feeble voice in the splashing bedpan. She flung herself in the middle of the torrent and dragged Child Ant up to dry, but the poor thing appeared lifeless. "*I wonder what doctor I should see now?*" she thought.

"I must travel to the people's doctor, Dr. Bäck," Mother Ant decided. Dr. Bäck arranged a time to be in Helsinki; otherwise, Mother Ant was forced to wait in the steamship waiting room because she could not walk to Vasa through the snowdrifts. She proceeded with the dead Child Ant and both detached legs to the doctor who did not wear a doctor's hat. Upon arriving to Dr. Bäck's office, he and Mother Ant untied the leg.

Doctor Bäck took a large glass, looked at the apparently lifeless Child Ant, and said, "One must massage it, but I cannot do it because I have large fingers."

Mother Ant thought about this and would willingly have asked the swallows to help her, but they had migrated. "I want to see behind the large kitchen stove," Mother Ant said as she crept in back of it and found a half-dead cricket, which had lain there since last fall. Struggling, she dragged it in front of the sunlight, where it revived, and the cricket began to cheerfully massage Child Ant's leg.

Three minutes later, after the cricket rubbed Child Ant's leg, Child Ant and Mother Ant were delighted that Child Ant was restored to health.

"What shall I pay you, Dr. Bäck, for your trouble?" Mother Ant asked.

"You should give food to the Virgin Mary's ladybug in your cottage, when she comes the next time to your anthill," answered doctor Bäck.

"I will do that," answered Mother Ant, gratefully. "I will make so much honeycomb and spruce resin, that she can hardly eat it."

"That's good. Good-bye to you, Mother Ant. I have six arms and four legs that are waiting for me to repair," stated the doctor. "Your Child Ant will soon be as good as new."

"Good-bye," responded Mother Ant, and she began her way home with her little healthy Child Ant.

When Mother Ant arrived home to her anthill, it was already spring, and all the neighbors had crept out of their homes. The ant's main road was seen over the forest hillside, for the snowdrifts had left a lot of rubbish. It was delightful among all the different groups of inhabitants, and they all would see and know about Child Ant.

At the same time, along came the Virgin Mary's small, hungry, tired, and frozen ladybug climbing over the grass in the forest hill. The ants took their sharp spears of spruce needles and wanted to drive away the wanderer. Mother Ant put herself on the ladybug's back feet with the green blade of grass to protect it.

As a token of thanks, Ladybug was invited by Mother Ant to her home on the anthill for a party and conversation. The cricket sang table music, and the ant children danced with their healthy legs. The sun shone, and the spring's little insects flew with swishing wings over the green forest hills.

Even as an ant carries one of their own on their back, so we need to shoulder responsibility by caring for those in need.

—translator's addition

Honor Your Father and Your Mother

Hedra din fader och din moder

What I am about to tell you is very short, but so remarkable that both adult and child clearly see how God wants father and mother to protect their children, and children need to respect their parents. What I am about to tell you is an old history which many people have told before me, and it can be told many times over.

There was a man and wife who had, in addition to their children, one of their fathers living with them. Grandfather was gray and so weak from old age that his hands trembled.

One day as he sat at the table with the other family members, he could not put the spoon to his mouth without spilling soup on himself. The family members thought this was ill-mannered, so they tied a napkin on him as when one ties a bib on a toddler when it ate. With trembling hands, he put the soupspoon to his mouth, and again he spilled; however, this time he spilled on the clean napkin.

The husband and wife were harsh and ungrateful toward their father and father-in-law. They did not realize how much work and patience their parents had with them when they were small. With angry words they said to the man, "If you do not stop dropping the napkin, you will eat with the pigs in the corner."

Grandfather could not help spilling his food because he was so old and frail. Then they sat him alone in the corner and put the trough of wood in front of him as one usually does for pigs. There Grandfather ate all alone in the corner, while the husband and wife ate at the table, lightly smacking their lips.

This made Grandfather very, very, unhappy. It is difficult to see oneself despised because of one's age. Yet, it was the only reason Grandfather was held in contempt by his only child. The ungrateful heart is the heaviest burden the earth bears.

Grandfather sat in the corner and cried so quietly that no one saw the tears which ran down his withered cheeks and down into his snow-white beard. It was only God who saw everything. He sees the sorrow, people's hard hearts, and he knows the instruments that humiliate.

One day Grandfather ate as usual in the corner, and the husband and wife sat at the table. On the floor, their little four-year-old boy knelt, whittling a piece of wood.

The father asked his young son, "What are you carving, my boy?"

The boy responded, "I am carving a tray."

"What will you do with it?" questioned the father.

"When Father and Mother are old, I will put them in the corner to eat off the tray as Grandfather does," their son answered.

Then the husband and wife looked at each other. God opened their eyes, and they saw a huge sin of ingratitude because they had scorned Grandfather in his older years. It pricked their conscience through a voice coming from their child's mouth. The husband and wife realized they needed to honor their parents and grandparents, for some day they, too, would be old.

The husband and wife burst into tears and went to the father, who sat in the corner. They hugged him and said, "Forgive us for the way we have been treating you so unkindly. From now on, you will always sit with us at the table, and there you will have the honored place. For now we know one never ought to forget the sacred and glorious fourth commandment, "Honor your father and your mother, that your days may be prolonged in the land which the Lord your God gives you" (Exodus 20:12).

The Winter Saga about Tall Cloud and Bearded Cloud

Vintersagan om Skyhög och Molnskägg

 n the large forest, a long way in Finland's wilderness, stood two old, high pines near each other. They did not look anything like they did when they were young. Their dark tops were the tallest among all the other trees. In the spring, the song thrush sang delightful ballads in the boughs. The small, pink heather flowers looked so humble as they gazed up to the pines, saying, "Lord God is it possible to grow tall, big, and old in this world?"

When winter's snowstorm enveloped the whole area in snow, the grass faded, and the heather flowers slept deeply under the drifts white cover. One could hear the wild storm howling through the pine's crown, sweeping the snow from the eternal green branches. The snowstorm's power destroyed a large house, littering a large part of the woods, while the pines stood like immovable, never bending statues. They did not yell when everything broke around them. They wanted someone to say, "Be firm and strong."

Not far from here, one saw a hill in the forest, and on it stood a little crofter's cottage with a plain roof and two small windows. The poor crofter and his wife rented the land where they had a potato patch and a little piece of pastureland. When the snow was piled high up on the cottage logs in the woods, they walked one mile down the hill to the large sawmill. This allowed them to earn enough money to make bread, churn butter, get milk from the cows, and grow potatoes. They thought it was so wonderful to eat bark bread.

The crofter couple had two small children, a daughter whose name was Sylvia and a son whose name was Sylvester. It was unusual how they were given their names. The family lived in the forest, so they named their daughter, *Sylvia*, meaning *forest*. *Sylvester* is in the almanac. The last day of the year is named Sylvester, so the boy celebrated his name day on New Year's Eve.

On Sylvester's name day, both children went outside to watch snares in the forest, which were used to trap willow grouse. A white hare was seen in Sylvester's snare, and a white grouse was in Sylvia's trap. The hare and the grouse survived.

The animals began to squeak and whine so miserably that the children wondered if the hare and grouse were both saying, "Release me so you will get something good."

The children felt sorry for the animals and freed them. The hare scampered as quickly as possible into the woods, and the grouse flew and hooted, "Talk to Tall Cloud and Bearded Cloud!"

"What will Tall Cloud and Bearded Cloud say?" asked Sylvester annoyed. "They have been so ungrateful, and I do not know how they will react," noted Sylvester. Sylvia questioned Sylvester about Tall Cloud and Bearded Cloud, "What can it be? I have not heard such unusual names!"

"I have not either," agreed Sylvester.

At the same time, the children heard subdued, strange sounds. A strong winter wind murmured through the two high pines in their dark crowns.

"Are you still standing, brother Tall Cloud?" asked Bearded Cloud.

"Certainly I am still standing," responded Tall Cloud. "How are you doing, brother Bearded Cloud?" he asked.

"I am feeling old because the wind broke off a bough in my crown," Bearded Cloud answered.

"You are just a child compared to me," observed Tall Cloud. "You are three hundred fifty years old, and I have stood here for three hundred eighty-eight years."

"Now the storm is returning," noticed Bearded Cloud. "Let's sing a little so that my branches have something to think about," he continued.

They began to sing together in the storm:

Hear our word!
High in the north,
long in time, and deep in the earth
stands our foot toward the storms' snowy winters.
Drizzly summer, centuries of shade for our eyes made.
The cloud comes and goes; like people who
are born surrounded by devastation.
We stand alongside strong and growing
children who search for a light biscuit.
Mountains are fixed, and earth experiences a surge
of growth that hastens to meet in light
toward God's throne.
One's intellect soars to the pinnacle
lifted high up toward heaven!

"Let us now talk with the children," grumbled Tall Cloud.

"I wonder what they will say to us?" asked Sylvester.

"Let's go home," whispered Sylvia. "I am afraid of the tall tree's strange behavior."

"Wait. I see father, the crofter, coming with the ax on his shoulder," observed Sylvester.

"I need a few trees," Father noted as he lifted the ax to chop down Tall Cloud.

But the children pleaded, "Dear father, don't cut down Tall Cloud or Bearded Cloud because they have sung a ballad for us!" cried Sylvester and Sylvia.

"What childishness, as if the old trees could sing! I will look for other trees," Father said.

He went farther into the forest as the curious children stood there to hear what Sky Cloud and Bearded Cloud would say to them.

It did not take long to answer as the wind returned from behind. The crofter ground the tree trunks and branches so that it set off a spark in the stone mill. The pines began to murmur, and the children heard the tree plainly talk again.

"We were afraid for our life! What gift would you like in thanks?" said the tree. The children were at once very happy; however, they were undecided about their present from the tree. They did not wish for anything in this world.

Finally Sylvester said, "I want just a bit of sunshine to better see the hare's footprints in the snow."

"Yes, and I wish for spring when the snowdrifts begin to melt so that the birds begin to sing in the forest," added Sylvia.

"Ridiculous children! We want you to have all the beautiful things in the world, and instead we want for that which shall be; that is, your wish as before. In the sea of our life, we are foolish to wish for a better, more beautiful place. You, Sylvester, and Sylvia, shall receive gifts wherever you go, whatever you see, and wherever the sun shines. When you open your little mouths, there will be spring enveloping you with melting snowdrifts. Isn't that wonderful?" comforted the pines.

"Yes, yes!" shouted the happy children. "It is more than we asked, and thanks, dear trees, for the good gifts!"

"Good-bye now," said the trees. "And good luck!"

"Good-bye, good-bye," said the children as they left for home. While they walked, Sylvester saw the marvelous, usual things around him. The grouse in the trees flew like a ray of sunshine in front of him, glistening clearly like gold over the branches. Astonished, Sylvia noticed the drifts begin to melt on both sides of the path.

"Do you see? Do you see?" Sylvia shouted to her brother. Scarcely had she opened her mouth before the green grass stuck out in front of her feet. The trees began to bud, and the first larch trees' branches began to sing its trill high up in the blue heavens.

"This is wonderful!" the children shouted enthusiastically.

"I can see the sun!" shouted Sylvester.

"I can melt snow!" shouted Sylvia.

"No, no one can do that!" Mother laughed. But it was not long before her eyes were opened. Soon it began to get dark, but it was not darker in the cottage. It was quite light, and soon Sylvester became sleepy, and his eyes gently closed. It was the beginning of winter, yet there was such a feeling of spring air in the stuga. It seemed as if the broom began to get green on its pole in the corner, while the excited rooster became confused, and it began to crow toward evening. All of this took place until Sylvia fell asleep.

"Listen husband, something is wrong with the children. I am afraid they met some troll in the forest," the wife shared with her husband, the crofter.

"You believe only yourself, dear Mother," said the crofter. "I will tell you something interesting. Can you guess what it might be? Tomorrow morning the king and queen will be traveling near our church. Should we take the children with us to see them?" he asked.

"It's a good idea. One does not get to see the king and queen every day," she answered.

The next morning, the crofters and their children were on their way to the church and were so captivated and delighted by what they saw. They noticed how the sunshine floated in front of their sleigh and how the birch budded all around them on the way.

When the crofter and his family arrived, they noticed the

Finnish king was very unhappy because he found the land so deserted and wild. He blamed this on the residents, who should have maintained the area. Meanwhile, the freezing Frau from Finland was downcast during the whole trip. That was obvious to the villagers.

The royalty's sleigh came quickly along the road, and the crowd trembled. The king looked grim, and the queen cried.

"See such beautiful sunshine we get all of a sudden! I am pleased to be in the presence with those who are so happy," the king observed, and he laughed graciously as did the others.

"Your majesty, you ate a good breakfast like me," observed the queen.

"Maybe it was because you ate a good breakfast," the king answered.

"Queen, you slept so well last night," said the king. "Look how beautifully desolate Finland is! See how the sun shines on the two high pines over there in the forest! Here we will build a demesne or estate."

"I agree, my partner and king," the queen consented. "It must be a mild climate here. Notice how the green leaves come out on the trees in the middle of winter!"

At the same time, they noticed Sylvester and Sylvia climbing on the yard fence to carefully see the royalty. The fence had green leaves growing between the posts that encircled Sylvia.

"Children, come to the sleigh," said the queen. The children came shyly with their fingers in their mouth because it took a lot of courage to approach the king and queen.

The king said, "I am totally delighted to see you. Come with me in the sleigh so you can travel to our royal court. You will dress in rich clothing and make everyone happy."

"No thanks, Mr. King," answered Sylvester and Sylvia. "We like to make Mother and Father happy at home. At the court we would be lonesome for Tall Cloud and Bearded Cloud."

"Take Tall Cloud and Bearded Cloud with you," the pleasant queen suggested warmly.

"No thanks, Queen. They need to stay in the forest," the children stated.

The queen continued, "Tall Cloud and Bearded Cloud should not grow in the forest."

"What children don't get in their heads," said the king and queen, and they laughed so heartily that the king's sleigh jumped.

Afterwards, the king and queen ordered a country house be built in the area of the crofter's cottage. They were so happy and grateful, astonishing everyone. The poor villagers had their gold penny, and Sylvester and Sylvia had a large royal figure-of-eight biscuit that the court baker had baked for the trip. They shared the biscuit with all the village children, and yet had so much left over that the crofter's horse barely pulled them through the roads' twists and turns.

On the way home, the old crofter whispered to his wife, "Do you know why the king and queen were so happy?"

"Oh, it was because they saw Sylvester and Sylvia. Do you remember what I said yesterday? 'Be quiet and do not speak about it to the children. It is better they don't know about such wonderful gifts that no one understands.'" Queen answered.

In their happiness, Sylvester and Sylvia forgot the huge royal figure-of-eight biscuit. They did not know how one's heartfelt happiness and warmth for all people could be until they saw the royal couple. After that, they were kind children and everyone believed that was why. Their parents were happy for them with the large wilderness round about the croft. Later it was transformed into a rich and beautiful tilled field next to green pastureland where the spring birds sing all winter long like no one has ever heard before.

After some years, Sylvester was a forester in the new country manor, and Sylvia had the task of maintaining the garden. It was pleasant to see the children delight everyone.

One day Sylvester and Sylvia came to greet their old friends, Tall Cloud and Bearded Cloud. Just then a fierce winter storm arose, whistling and roaring in the high pines' crowns, and they sang an old song:

"I see! I see!
We are so old, we are so gray!
But large and strong in the storm we stay.
For many hundreds of years, in fall and spring,
in the winter chill, in the summer cover, in frost and snow;
in rain and thaw, in night and fog, in morning rays I see! I see!
We are so old,
we are so gray,
but large and strong
in the storm we stay.

Not long thereafter they heard a crack, a crash, and a scrape, felling both Tall Cloud and Bearded Cloud to the ground. They stood for three hundred ninety-three years and three hundred fifty-five years respectively. Their withered roots decayed as heavens' winds were powerfully strong.

Sylvester and Sylvia clapped gleefully as they looked toward the moss-covered pines, speaking to them with loving words. The snow began to melt all around with pink heather growing tall over the fallen trees. Tall Cloud and Bearded Cloud saw their grave amongst the flowers.

It is now a long time since I have heard anything more about Sylvester and Sylvia before they were old and gray. It has been many years since a king and a queen traveled in Finland.

Sometimes I see two good children such as Sylvester and Sylvia with their happy eyes and think of Tall Cloud and Bearded Cloud. There the sun passed by them with overcast heavens, covering the downcast people. The children did not show this expression on their faces. One never saw the children without oneself becoming so happy and empathetic toward the world. It was then the sun melted the ice on the windowpanes, the snowdrifts, and the frost in people's frozen hearts.

Now the spring and the greenery after the cold winter was such that even the broom began to get green leaves, the dry fence supported the roses, and the larch tree sang under heaven's high roof. For this, we have everything to thank Tall Cloud and Bearded Cloud, or more correctly, we all need to thank the good Lord who allows spring and pleasant greenery on the earth.

The Poor Man
Fattiggubben

as someone seen Lochteå, the wooden statue depicted as a poor man? I presume he stands there yet today, just as he stood fifty years ago, dressed in a blue coattail, red vest, and yellow trousers, which is completely too gaudy for a poor man. His hand is stretched out to everyone along the way as the church people come on Sundays. No one can count all the money that fell into the middle of the little hole in the red waistcoat above the old man's stomach. When Lochteå was newly built, there were many respectable farmers' wives with silver money in the corner of a handkerchief who wondered if a large coin would fit in Lochteå's little hole. Sometimes a silver Swedish crown fell in the hole by mistake.

People thought the poor old statue was as rich as the head of the Swedish National Board of Trade, because he had been given a lot of money over the years. He was very faded and washed-out in the face; a piece of his nose had fallen off, and it had been swept away into the rubbish on the church step. It is difficult both night and day to stand and panhandle on the main road with the wind blowing, when it is raining, snowing, and freezing.

The church custodian, Puu-Pietari, came once a month to open the door to Lochteå's back and took out the copper and silver coins that he collected from the parishioners. Lochteå looked miserable and begged for coins from every Tom, Dick, and Harry, only to have all the money disappear from the mischief-maker, Puu-Pietari, who took all the money. Once again, Lochteå was poor in his blue dress suit coat, red vest, and yellow pants.

Lochteå, the poor wooden statue, had a strange adventure that does not happen with all poor people. In the parish lived an old free lodger with the name of *Pietari*. He was usually called *Puu-Pietari*, or *Wood-Petter*. With his jackknife he could carve artistic things such as horses, peasant boys, eagles, dolls, and all sorts of funny figures.

In his heart Puu-Pietari was a greedy, angry, and crafty person who did not think of anything other than to horde money. Once he put more than one hundred Swedish crowns in silver and gold under a stone. He earned this money through begging and woodworking over many years. Being thin and wearing rags, people had compassion for him.

One day when the congregation was assembled at the church for a meeting, they agreed the parish needed to help the poor, destitute Puu-Pietari. However, no one was more content than Puu-Pietari because he thought he could become rich being a poor old custodian. Consequently, he devised the following strategy:

Puu-Pietari had a key, and he knew all the coins were kept in the old man's chest. He withdrew the money through a locked hole in Lochteå's back. On the side of the hole, he made an opening that nobody would notice. Positioning the poor, old statue at an angle, one coin after the other rolled down into Lochteå's stomach.

One cloudy night when the moon was hidden, Puu-Pietari looked into the door of the statue and emptied all the money that had fallen down. The rogue was so wise by not robbing on that occasion, making sure some coins would be left in Lochteå. However, there was no mistake there had been a thief. This continued for some time, and Puu-Pietari's only hiding place under the stone became richer.

One Sunday at the end of the month, the church's treasurer,

as usual, gave a financial report of the offerings. Frowning, the minister reported with an extraordinary serious tone of voice, "Listen, my dear Puu-Pietari, I have every reason to think of you as an upright and honest man. However, I must confess the state of things with Lochteå, the destitute man, appears to be quite strange. With my own eye I have seen people who are dressed in their best clothing, crowd tightly around the poor man and reach in their pockets for coins. However, when you gave an account of how much money had been given in the offering, you stated we had received barely enough for the month. What shall I think about that, Puu-Pietari? You lock the door and then tell yourself, 'From the outside make it look as if there had been burglars.'"

The church's treasurer noted the pastor to be completely correct; and besides, if the poor suspect burglarized the church, he might trip over himself as he held the key in his hand. The treasurer pointed out one needed to confront Puu-Pietari and ask to see if he had an iron tool of sorts. The pastor approved this suggestion, and they decided to carefully inspect Puu-Pietari's tools the following Monday morning.

When Puu-Pietari, the custodian, arrived home, he could not help but tell his wife about the pastor's suspicion regarding the absence of coins in Lochteå, the statue. He told his wife he would inspect Lochteå the following day.

Immediately Puu-Pietari saw himself as the old rogue who thought to himself, "If you are now looking for the poor man, Lochteå, you have found the door latch. Do you understand it is me, Puu-Pietari, who stole money from the man's stomach? No, there is nothing else for me to say other than I need to visit the church immediately tonight, release Lochteå from his place, carry him to the forest's largest quiet area and set him on fire. That will be the end of all the investigation. Who can prove I am the one who ended the life of the destitute man?"

Night soon came, and Puu-Pietari snuck out with an ax and a crowbar that he carried separately as he walked to church. It was

New Year's Day in the middle of a cold winter and so freezing that the snow crackled and squeaked under the old villain's feet. Puu-Pietari was not frightened as he wandered with a full moon in view, and there were no people traveling on the road. Suddenly there appeared a dark cloud over the full moon with the church barely in view.

When he arrived without a soul in sight, he hurriedly began his nightly work. It was not a problem to loosen the hard iron band that kept the lone man on the church road. It was not the first time Puu-Pietari had done such work with success. Twenty times he blew into his frozen hands, and then the iron band finally loosened. With his increased eagerness and amusement, Puu-Pietari seized the poor man firmly behind his neck, shook him a couple of times, and then flung him abruptly down the church steps. Then Puu-Pietari would drag him to the forest, place him in a grave in the snow with dry branches, and set it on fire.

Lochteå's life or death hung by a mere thread. However, an unforeseen thing saved him. Puu-Pietari decided to jump from the church steps in order to accomplish his malicious act. In his fright, he heard the heavy steps of people thumping on the road. The moon was visible behind the cloud and shone with its clear, wintry, snow-dressed beauty over the church and its surrounding landscape. What should Puu-Pietari do now? Should he run? He decided against that thought because he would then be discovered. Should he crouch down and crawl in back of the church wall? Yes, he was able to do that only if the poor man, Lochteå, remained in his place in the snow.

Now Puu-Pietari lay with his nose in the snowdrift beside the steps. The destitute man was gone from his usual place beside the church. Puu-Pietari thought, "It is a good thing I am not wearing a black dress coat, red vest, and yellow pants. The sun has not risen yet as I can barely see the road. I will disguise myself as the poor man for a couple of minutes by standing bolt upright, motionless, and wood-like in the poor man's place until the noblemen pass by."

The noblemen were two robbers from Korsholm's prison who had traveled here late at night to avoid confrontation by the county sheriff and prison guard. Wearing thick sheepskin coats, the robbers were on an expedition near the village church to search under lock and key in the shed and storehouse on a moonlit night.

One of them noticed Puu-Pietari on the church steps and mistook him for Lochteå. "Look! There is the poor man. I think we should bundle his money up before we proceed to the village!" suggested one of his friends.

It was no sooner said than done, when astonished Puu-Pietari was lifted up unexpectedly in the presence of others. He thought someone discovered his trick and came to abduct him. He was so frightened that he wanted to run, but his feet refused to move, and he stood bolt upright as before. Running away was not the answer, so he sat down on the church steps to rest and get a breath of fresh air. He thought about the best way to take Lochteå's money.

"Here he stands, the stingy rascal, yet he was not ashamed year in and year out to steal honest people's cash," said one of the rogues. Trembling with fear and cold, Puu-Pietari was tired of remaining motionless, pretending to beg.

"Well, that should be the end of the beggar," said another thief. "Do you think we should behead him?"

The friend replied, "First, I think we should break his bones and then tear him to pieces in small bits." What? Puu-Pietari thought about their plan.

"That will be enough; we will first tear his stomach apart and then burn him up," noted the other thief.

Puu-Pietari wondered if they knew how to totally break his stomach in pieces, as he stood motionless, pretending to be the poor man, Lochteå.

"Let us seize the scoundrel by the collar," suggested the first robber. Then sneeringly he threw his cold, stiff leather glove in the face of the wooden Lochteå. This really tried Puu-Pietari's patience because now he was grabbed by the collar as the second thief lifted the ax to kill him.

Puu-Pietari yelled and tried to defend himself from the vicious attack. Parishioners watched and listened to see if Lochteå would kick and shout. The robbers sought to look for their prey, but they did not succeed.

In the confusion, the group fell down the church steps, and there lay all three rogues fighting in the snowdrift, shouting at one another. In the process, the two rogues from Korsholm's prison wanted to capture Puu-Pietari. As they were entertaining such evil thoughts, someone arrived.

The county sheriff in the parish came and searched for the thieves, hoping to find them in the area. The diligent sheriff proceeded to wander during the night in the right direction of Puu-Pietari. It was pure luck the sheriff met two hefty men in the neighborhood, traveling on the road in front of the church. The sheriff heard screaming, that made such a commotion in the desolate, quiet, winter night.

Immediately he hurried to the area and could not believe the bandits had assaulted some peaceful residents in the village. The county sheriff found the three rogues in the most furious wrestling match. They tumbled over each other on the church steps, and the sheriff quickly ended their battle. He bound the bandits' hands so that no destitute man in the whole world needed to further fear for the rogues' visits.

Puu-Pietari, who was thought to be an innocent man, was assaulted. His piece of roguery had been discovered, and he prayed to God for help, peace, and forgiveness. In order to escape prison, the old destitute man collected and gave gifts to the needy.

This concludes the history about Puu-Pietari. The poor man still had the same custodial inspector job. No more could unlawful people take his wealth after he returned it. I cannot say what happened to him; however, he continues to be held in high esteem in the parish. One can now and then go past the Lochteå church and see him in his old place at the church door. His nose is probably gone. Maybe someone will see he had an operation at the hospital in Helsingfors. There the doctors make new noses, completely like a pottery maker makes new clay roosters. Nothing is impossible in our days.

Ant Stronghold and Gray Moss

Myreborg och Gråmossa

råmossa, or Gray Moss, was located on the anthill in the middle of the forest near a mountain at the foot of a high one-hundred-year-old pine. The general area was called Ljungamo, or heather with pines, because heather grew there on the plain. Gray Moss was constantly thirsty on the dry mountain because moss did not retain moisture in its roots and on its surface.

Gray Moss stretched its roots between the mountains' crevices. They were firmly rooted, especially for unsuspecting storms, even in the puddles in the areas where it was generally dry. The moss could have died of thirst if the evening sun had not now and then saved a cup of dew. The scant mist swept its white, moist covering around Gray Moss. He sighed and looked up toward the clouds that flew so high over him and toward the ocean, which roared so deep under him.

When Gray Moss was young, he determined to grow up as high as the heavens, but the thought remained remote. In fact, Gray Moss did not grow more in height but only in breadth, creating a pathway from the thirsty earth to the heavens.

Below Gray Moss lay a new anthill, and it was called Myreborg, meaning ant stronghold. The ants thought this was a beautiful name. They felt ashamed to be called an anthill because the word was not flattering in an ant world.

Myreborg was a free society where every ant citizen worked for the benefit of everyone who fought against snakes, dung beetles, and other enemies. The ants were industrious and law-abiding citizens. However, they did not understand why Gray Moss could cover such a large area when the ants were so small. The smallest pine needle that fell off Gray Moss was for them as big as a log. They worked and were determined to build Myreborg.

Some ants had climbed to the top of Gray Moss, and for them it was a day's journey.

When they returned, the ants thought they had been halfway to the moon. "Gray Moss will go up to heaven. How can one be so terribly big and yet not very smart?" they observed.

Gray Moss heard what the small, creeping creatures whispered near his firmly rooted hilly area. In response, he said, "Certainly I want to reach the heavens. Here on the earth I have only the secure mountain and everlasting thirst. Heaven is something I have striven for ever since I was a child."

"Listen to what he says!" The ants and other insects exclaimed. "He should work for his daily bread, pay for his house, and be kind to others. When one has a roof over their head and food on the table, one needs nothing more but heaven. Those of us who have wings want to fly out into the blue. We did not always want to work in this simple earth, but we want to take a pleasure trip now and then toward the heights." When all was said and done, the ants all plopped in the ocean and ate whitefish. "Yum!" they said.

Gray Moss heard the insects with their arrogant speech, thought it was not worth the effort to answer them, and kept his thoughts to himself. He was continuously thirsty, and as spring approached his underside gradually turned to a lush green. The ants proceeded to work and strive for their subsistence on this earth and asked for nothing better.

One day in the middle of summer, children went out from the

closest village to pick blueberries in sandy, hot soil where heather was growing. In the group was a tailor's son, Agapetus, who threw a lit cigarette into the forest. The dry heather and surroundings were soon consumed in flames! What was the children's reaction?

They thought it was very amusing as they looked at the fire increase and flutter from one grassy tuft to another. Then came the wind making the flames behave like a playmate, entertaining the children. The blowing wind engulfed the heather into a large smoky fire, the ladybugs spread their wings, and the frightened children ran away.

The tailor's son, Agapetus, had an unfortunate experience as he was running. He stumbled over a flaming tuft of grass, burning the tip of his nose that looked like the color of lilac. He was self-conscious, and he was called Näspetus, meaning broad nose.

Näspetus turned around, and with a snakelike tongue, he went up a mountain slope on the way to Myreborg. The ants strove and puffed with their persevering work, dragging a blade of grass or a dead grasshopper as they ascended the mountain. Two ants dragged the grasshopper alternately back and forth from one side to the other. Then the flames came with a vengeance in Myreborg!

Gray Moss had seen many forest fires before. However, the heather and moss around him were not burned, so Gray Moss survived, at least for the moment. Quietly he looked around and noticed how parched and decayed he was. The flames enveloped him on all sides, and he wriggled up to the faded branches to his magnificent crown. There was a cloud and a wind that lead him out to the sea in the midst of sooty bleakness. During the three-day fire, Gray Moss lay in the half-decayed trunk with fire surrounding him. Then came a crash, and there he lay in live coals and ashes.

"Now it's the end of me, and I will never get to heaven," thought Gray Moss. Dying, he fell down to the mountain's precipice in the ocean.

"Certainly it is not done!" said a voice above him. It was the reddish evening cloud that Gray Moss saw so often as he looked up with admiration and longing. "I will take your ashes with me and carry them high in the light outer space. There the Lord in the heavens renews the earth and creates a new paradise. You shall then stand at this doorway beside the tree of life and knowledge. Your pines will shine like silver, and you shall drink out of the Garden of Eden. Never more shall you thirst, wither, or perish. Surely the Father of all, who hears the prayers from his creation, understands their requests."

"Do I need to stay on this parched mountain and vainly stretch my branches toward heaven?" questioned Gray Moss.

"Never," answered Evening Cloud. "Your root shall be in everlasting peace and your crown in everlasting light. The paradise bird shall sing in your branches, and Eden's scent will waft out from you. Talk to the Lord, and you will find him, 'for he who seeks finds.'"

"Are the ants coming to heaven, too?" Gray Moss questioned because he was annoyed with them.

"They had their home on the earth and never longed for anything better," answered Evening Cloud. "As it is written, 'they have their reward.'" (Matthew 6:2).

"Let the mountain also come to heaven!" said Gray Moss. It was his last word here in the world as he fell to ashes. Evening Cloud, dressed in its reddest most beautiful attire, took the ashes out in the blue expanse. Gray Moss didn't know about the mountain reaching toward heaven.

When Evening Cloud left, the damp night mist encircled the mountain. Gray Moss no longer needed to water its thirsty branches. The old, dry, moss-covered mountain—standing there alone, naked, and sooty—knew the night fog dropped almost like tears down this rough precipice. It is the mountain that tells me this history about Myreborg and Gråmossa.

A Learned Boy
En lärd gosse

ow can Hegesippus be so wise and understanding? He knows everything, and his brother Knut knows nothing," exclaimed Ms. Justina, gesturing with her hands.

Hegesippus did not have time to answer as he was observing the backbone of a dung beetle through a microscope. He was twelve years old and certainly smart in school. However, poor Knut, a fourteen-year-old junior high school student, had limited understanding.

Hegesippus' and Knut's housemaid, Ms. Justina, was a good-natured person who earned two hundred marks, which included food and a room in the boy's house. The first of May she always received striped boots, and every Christmas she was given a cotton apron. Hegesippus had always been Ms. Justina's pride and joy because she noticed he was much wiser than other children and had more common sense than Knut. Hegesippus was completely convinced he was the most learned schoolboy even though sometimes he was unlearned in English grammar.

Hegesippus teased others with his eyes, ruffled up his hair, and said, "Has Justina seen my egg collection?" Yes, of course she had seen his boring collection about seven or eight times.

"Come here, Justina, so you can see!" said Hegesippus. He showed her a long, cardboard box where small and large eggs were separated and laid in cotton with ordered labels. There were eggs from all kinds of birds, from the large eagle to the little willow warbler: blue, gray, magpie, starlings, thrushes, siskin (finches), chaffinch, and brown, speckled crow eggs. All were blown out of their shell with a little hole on either end. It looked like a bird mortuary with a small coffin for the dead birds.

Meanwhile, ten-year-old Lotta, Hegesippus' sister, came running. She did not understand the rare egg collection. She asked where Sippus (his nickname) had gotten the eggs. He answered kindly, saying he bought some and received other eggs from his friends. "Isn't it a shame to destroy these small birds' dwellings?" asked Lotta innocently. Hegesippus sniffed as he usually had a head cold and often wore an overcoat and boots. He had taught himself to speak through his nose. Furthermore, he was not puzzled about answering such a silly question, and he chose not to respond.

"All the eggs you have painted are pictured in books. Teach yourself to know about the birds' homes and eggs in the forest. Knut knows all the birds by their chirp," observed Lotta.

"Knut is dumb," noted Hegesippus in a condescending manner.

"But Knut protects the small birds and shoots the hawks," Lotta answered in Knut's defense.

"Has he counted the quills on their wings?" Hegesippus asked arrogantly. "I will say to you, Lotta, the birds have somewhat of a different skeleton than mammals, yet there are some similarities. Their extremities have three dimensions: an alimentary canal, a very different skull with a round knob on the head, and they have innate skill to build a cone-shaped dwelling."

Lotta continued, "All birds' homes which I have seen have been round as turnips. They can be cone-shaped or row-shaped. There are passerines that include perching birds and songbirds. Some examples are the wood warbler, swallow, robin, and king bird-of-paradise. There are also climbing birds, poultry birds, ostriches, wading, and web-footed birds and..."

"And the rooster!" inserted Ms. Justina, delighted over her yellow male bird's unusual learning. "Dear Lotta, there is nothing which Hegesippus does not know. He knows everything."

"Hegesippus collects eggs, but he has never seen a bird habitat!" laughed Lotta.

Hegesippus overheard their conversation and was angry. "I do not have a waxwing's egg or a thrush nightingale's egg. I will look for them, and you will see them tonight when I return."

"You never go into the forest. You just strut along the pathway after the doctor said you must get exercise, Hegesippus," Lotta stated.

"No, kind Hegesippus, do not go into the forest because you may catch a cold. Besides there are snakes in there," Ms. Justina cautioned.

"Snakes are reptiles; they have a very long body, and their digestion is a slow process," Hegesippus noted with his flowing knowledge.

"He has never seen a living snake!" Lotta laughed once again.

This annoyed Hegesippus. He dressed himself in his thick winter overcoat, and he took his Lütken's zoology book from which he had gained animal knowledge. He took papa's stick to beat the snakes to death and then proceeded to look for the thrush nightingale.

"Button your coat before you go outdoors!" shouted Ms. Justina.

Hegesippus was already on his way, taking quiet steps by the toll barrier, over the bridge, the road, the ditch, and finally he came to the woods. Here it was more uncomfortable to walk because of the tufts of grass, branches of twigs, stones, juniper bushes, cobwebs, anthills, and mosquitoes. He was tired as he sat on a stone to rest. He was surprised that no thrush nightingale or waxwing had built its habitation on the stone. He soon fell asleep. After he relaxed, he awoke to the whistle of a large goshawk, which flew down on a squirrel sitting on a spruce branch. As the hawk caught its claws in the spruce branches, the squirrel took a leap, fell in Hegesippus' arms, and then hid in back of the stone. There was no greater pleasure than to listen to living nature and fathom this secret.

Everyone can listen quietly to nature, free from babbling after books. Texts can provide wisdom, insight, and understanding, but they are unsuitable if one lacks necessary skills in using them. Now Hegesippus was in the forest for the first time. He gave attention to the animals, the ant's path, and detected the birds' twitters. He came to the forest fully skilled and desiring to know everything he read from Lütken's zoology book. Oh, you know Hegesippus!

He brought his zoology book and looked for some animals that resembled the red squirrel. "What is that bird in the tree? I will look ... is it a parrot or a nightingale? Nightingales have very short bills, and a little tooth inside the head of the upper bill that turns inward. It must be a nightingale." Hegesippus thought to himself. It was so remarkable that he must write about it.

Taking his notebook, Hegesippus hiked farther into the vast forest. After observing his surroundings, he wrote the following in large print:

May 15: "Lotta was mistaken again. I went into the forest and saw a nightingale descending on a hippopotamus. The hippopotamus is a large, rude, heavy, bulging, short-necked animal. It is useful to know many things from books. The vast forest is not as wise as me because it has no books. There are no twigs and animals that know the ABCs. The forest grows and grows and does not know that two times two is four. But I know almost everything. There are some things I do not know, but I will learn more when I am a student. When I become a teacher, I will know everything that exists, even the poor little things in the woods!

The poor things in the woods answered nothing. Hegesippus sought boundless learning with wonder. He stood there so quietly and seriously, wanting to grasp something of wisdom's greatness. Perhaps the pine trees and the bird cherry trees taught him about living to grow. The cloud demonstrated the power of rain, the brook taught him to jump with both feet over small stones, and the nightingale showed him the art of swooping down on a hippopotamus. "Now I must get ready for the bird's nest," Hegesippus mumbled to himself, and he began to walk further until he came to a meadow with a barn.

Close under the eaves above the cowshed door hung something that must have meant to be a bird's nest. It looked like gray paper and was cone-shaped. It must be a nightingale's nest. It is the nightingale!" gasped Hegesippus. With Papa's stick, he began to poke in the gray cone. He had closed the hole in the gray paper cone before something crept out. First one, then another one, ten, and twenty; yes, perhaps a hundred! It was certainly not a nightingale! It was a wasps' nest, and soon Hegesippus felt them stinging on his hand, cheek, and nose. Suddenly, quite an ill feeling came over him. Regaining his composure, he began to run away with force and hit around in all directions with Papa's stick. The wasp's fervor flew quicker and pursued him so aggressively that he neither could hear nor see. He ran with all his might, and in front of him lay in a large muddy ditch filled with water.

Whew! It was just as well because the wasps could not swim. When they saw their enemy lying in the ditch, the wasps began to gradually buzz and return to mend their broken home. If Hegesippus understood their language, he would hear them say to one another, "Hegesippus disciplined us by damaging our home."

Wet and swollen, Hegesippus crept out of the ditch, and he had no thought at all to look further for the bird's nest. Being the wisest, he now would go home. However, this was easier said than done. He was in the woods for the first time and had no idea where to walk. He followed his nose even though it was a poor guide. Hegesippus sensed where he should proceed into the large, deep forest.

The fallow grounds' shadows began to fall along on the tufts of grass. The sun set behind the spruce trees' tops with annoying mosquitoes, and the birds' songs silenced in the tree tops. The song thrush still sang its melodic tones, and Hegesippus heard the grain crunching beneath his feet as he walked in the field ditch. Fortunately, it was not dark as it had been. Hegesippus was tired, hungry, and wet as he walked over tufts of grass and stones. Looking around, he knew he was lost, so he sat down and fell asleep at the edge of the ditch. Perhaps he may have dreamed of how anything like getting lost could have happened to such a smart boy. As he awakened, Hegesippus was thinking about the small red squirrel as a hippototamus came to him and asked, "Why are you crying?"

"I am crying because I cannot find my way out of the vast forest," replied the boy.

"But you must know everything!" responded the hippopotamus.

"I do not know everything but almost everything!" sighed Hegesippus.

"Good-bye to you," said the squirrel.

After a while something in the air sighed, and nightingale asked, "Why are you crying?"

Hegesippus answered, "I cry because I cannot find my way home through the woods!"

"But you know almost everything!" responded the nightingale.

"I do not know everything, but I know a lot more than before," replied the boy.

"Good-bye," said the nightingale.

Now came the stinging wasp, and it asked the same question, "Why are you crying?"

Hegesippus replied as before, "Must I cry for this and that?"

"You know a whole lot," buzzed the wasp.

"I do not know very much, only as much as I want," responded Hegesippus.

"Good-bye to you," buzzed the wasp.

The boy was once more alone, and the whole huge forest appeared to him. He saw the tall spruces, the distressed birch, the enflamed willow bushes, the small European mountain ash, the lingon bushes, the heather, and crowberry. All kindly questioned him, "Why are you crying?"

"Can't I cry? It's so ... so ..." answered Hegesippus.

"You still know a little," the big forest reminded him.

"Yes, but I do not know the way home," replied the boy.

"Good-bye to you," said the forest.

"No, wait a little," sighed Hegesippus in the dream. Will you be so kind and show me the way to the city? My overcoat, boots, and Papa's walking stick are in the ditch, and I might freeze to death!"

"You know something," repeated the forest.

"No dear woods, I assure you I know absolutely nothing," sighed the boy discouragingly.

"Are you really incomprehensibly so illiterate?" asked the forest.

"I am whatever you want me to be; just show me the way home," requested the boy.

"No wait," commanded the forest. "No twists and turns! Admit honestly you know absolutely nothing about nature's straight path and the good quality of life. Truly you babble a lot without a lesson from the books! Confess you know less about things than the ants on the hill or the smallest needle on the spruce branches!"

Hegesippus breathed a sigh as heavy as a log. "It is difficult for one to admit being so unlearned. I know nothing other than which is in the Lütken's zoo," noted the boy.

"Is that so! Out with the truth! Shout loudly, so that everyone hears it, 'Hegesippus is dumb!'" the stubborn forest interrupted.

The perspiration lay on the boy's forehead, and soon he lay there sound asleep with the freezing sweat. "It is certainly true, dear forest, that I am a little stupid," he confessed.

"Out with the truth! Very dumb!" replied the forest.

"No, out of necessity you will know it, so ... I am dumb ... totally stupid!"

"Hegesippus is ignorant!" the echo resounded from all corners of the woods. There was a gaiety like no other. "Do you hear what the boy says?" asked the crow to the bush.

"How can one be so totally oblivious that he talks of it about himself?" said the ant to the pinecone.

Echo sat on the edge of the mountain and repeated every word so that all the twigs, every tuft of grass, and each little bird's nest echoed the same scoffing words, "Hegesippus is dumb…ignorant…stupid!"

"What is this paw?" A voice was heard in back of the field, and Knut stood there with a rifle on his shoulder. "Hegesippus!" he shouted.

Hegesippus awoke. "Is it you, Knut? I am happy to have found you."

"Justina was so troubled when you did not return, so she sent me to look early in the afternoon. I have searched in all the farmyards, parks, and gardens. I did not think you would be stupid to go astray in such a small forest."

"Do not say anything about it, Knut, because the woods know it already! Please help me home because I am stiff in the joints, and I cannot move." Hegesippus sighed.

"Do not try to walk, because I have bones for both of us. So climb on my back," Knut urged Hegesippus.

"It is a long way to the city, and you cannot carry me the whole way," Hegesippus countered.

"A long way? It is barely one hundred steps to the city. If you stepped on the closest little stone, you would have seen the whole city in front of you," Knut responded.

"It really looks as if I would have been a little dumb," sighed Hegesippus when he was up on his brother's back and saw the whole city clearly in back of the bushes. "What is it you carry in your game bag, Knut?"

"It is a bird that robs. I shot him a while ago."

"Oh, I know him. It does not have a very long beak, and it has a small tooth inside that is pointed over its bill. Knut, I do not think you shot a parrot. I have examined the poor thing, and it is a nightingale. I saw him fly down on a hippopotamus."

"What did you say? A nightingale? No, it is a magnificent goshawk and will be placed above the stable door. I saw him chase a poor little squirrel. It is a greedy robber who lives off small birds, but he keeps and eats all he gets including rats, frogs, baby rabbits, and squirrels.

Now Hegesippus did not want to keep his wisdom to himself. He safely reached home on his brother's shoulders, and Justina praised his tremendous intelligence. She whispered in his ear, "Do not say, 'I am stupid!'"

"What does my heart say? Would I be unintelligent if I knew everything?" asked Hegesippus.

Justina replied, "No, of course not!"

The Flax
Linet

t happened far away from here and a long time ago.

A mature man stood at the fence and said, "It appears to be good flax. See how tall it is even though it has not flowered yet?"

"It is God's gift," answered the mature woman.

"Maybe," answered her husband. "Most of the flax is good because every year I drain and plow it thoroughly. I want it to be high up to my waist. I have three shirts, and I want six."

"When it is God's gift to us, we give something to him in return," reminded the woman. "Aren't you satisfied with five shirts, my dear? The sixth shirt we will give to someone who needs it, like our infant son. He is hardly wearing anything, and he is the one who needs warm baby clothes," she stated further.

"God cries for our son. He will not be chilly any more because he has been given a shirt from other poor children," said the man, reminding his wife.

The woman could not stand to see her son go naked. She could only get clothing from some little ragamuffin one sees on the road. "It is good I thought of that because we might be the ones walking on the road," she thought to herself.

The flax grew and grew, and finally, the flowers opened and were bent toward the morning sun. The flax was abundant in the field together with wagtails, bees, moths, butterflies, moles, and frogs in the ditch. The world had rarely seen such beautiful blue flowers.

The morning breeze whispered down from the mountain; the field drank the dew, and the bee buzzed angrily around the flowers' scent. The wren, the smallest of the birds, awoke in its nest at the edge of the ditch and scratched itself in the back of its head with its slender talon. It looked at the flax field with the many thousand flowers blowing in the wind. "Oh, so wonderful! I dreamed something last night," he twittered.

"What have you dreamt?" queried the wagtail.

"I have dreamed that seven times twelve, or eighty-four, of these flax stems should become dressed for God," the wren answered.

"You dream as you have understood, as if God needs clothes. Have you not heard that light is God's garment?" The wagtail questioned.

"I do not understand it, but I dreamt about it," the wren noted.

The bird heard the bee buzzing out over the field and bore quickly into the small flax flowers. It quickly whisked to each one confidently and said, "You shall be dressed for God!"

The flax flowers understood this like the small wrens. However, one believes what one willingly wants to believe. The wren went whistling from stalk to stalk and from flower to flower around the whole flax field and twittered, "Have you heard anything so wonderful that we should be clothed for God?" With this the family walked to their field.

The husband, his wife, and their four-year-old son came to the headland to see the field bloom. "The flax will make splendid shirts! God has dressed them. See how the flax flowers lean toward each other as if they have something to say," observed the husband.

The boy, who recognized all the voices of nature and understood their language, agreed. "They say, 'We have been dressed by God.'"

The old man laughed and answered, "It is right, my dear boy, that flax should be used to make some shirts for me."

The flax flowers quickly grew and flowered. They were already as tall as a man's long beard. The flowers were like shiny, deep, blue-green waves wafting in the breeze. All the flax said to each other, "We should be dressed for God!" However, other field creatures did not agree.

"No, I will not stand to hear such vanity," croaked the frog to the mole. "What is this nonsense talk? The flax has a drooping flower, which shows they have nothing else to do but drink in the sunshine and grow. Will they be gloriously satisfied? No, the flax is arrogant toward me and my mole friends, which creates anxiety for my young ones in the ditch."

"Yes, even me," squeaked the mole. "The whole night I have been incredibly troubled with burrowing many times under the flax roots digging for food. Why doesn't anyone thank me? A small meadow is enough if I just find an angling worm. When I look out from my hole, what do I hear? Nothing but the useless flax that never toils or worries and thinks it is good enough for God. I am disappointed with this dry land. I will discontinue our relationship."

With that, the frog and the mole sat and spoke ill of the flax. A light breeze came out of a cloud and then left as usual in waves over the blooming field. The flowers in full bloom, and the wren sang the following song:

> "*We are so young, so fair, so blue.*
> *We happily benefit from large and small.*
> *Our Father in heaven spins our thread.*
> *Of ourselves we have nothing, but everything by God's grace.*
> *We dress the naked, and he praises our efforts.*
> *We made the bed gently for the freezing child.*
> *We praise our Father who molded us.*
> *We are nothing, and our Father is everything.*"

"Yes, one hears that," croaked the frog to the mole. "They say to have received everything from God. I wonder what we would receive if we laid our legs in the shape of a cross in the sunshine and waited to bend angleworms that travel in our mouth."

After that, they did not feel sorry for the flax flowers. When their stems were ready for the flax, they knew their contribution to the world would be fulfilled. Their use and beauty was all God's gift that they received with thanks and praise.

The older man walked to the field and looked at the flax waving. It was swinging higher and deeper than anything before, and he fell to his knees in wonder. "Mother, it is not six shirts but twenty-four shirts will be woven," the husband stated excitedly. "We received all of this because I plowed manure in the ditch unlike others. So it is when one understands things. The neighbor's flax land is a scrap heap compared with my flax field."

"God gave the growth," answered his wife.

"I should say so wife! When one plows wisely, one gets the harvest. The day after tomorrow I will gather the flax because it is as tall as it will ever be."

"The day after tomorrow as God wills," said the older woman.

The following day the flax flowers said to each other, "Tomorrow we will fall!" None of them were sad, and that is completely as it should be. Their life and beauty is a gift.

The night before when the flax would be harvested, an unforeseen powerful thunderstorm was suddenly seen and heard. The storm swooped down like a huge roller over the field with pelting rain, beating the stalks to the ground, followed by crushing hail that ruined the flax. The blue flowers could not hear each other give a farewell in the rumbling storm. In spite of all this, they were not sad because life and death was a gift.

In the corner of the field was heard a broken, dying flax flower say to the other flowers, "We have not been tenderly dressed by God."

"I have dreamed that with God there is nothing impossible," said the wren that hid under a stone in the headland.

"Thank you, wren," said the flax flower as it folded its petals.

The frog had also hidden in the pasture under a tree stump, but could not keep itself from looking forward, muttering a little bit and croaking, "Proud and lazy! Proud and lazy!"

The mole had its hole near the wren's hiding place and could not look ahead to poke his head out. "Pride and idleness! Pride and laziness!" he uttered dismally.

Soon two hard hailstones as big as a felled log landed on the frog's broad nose, and the other on the mole's snout. There they both lay as their bodies were stretched out, and they had no more to say in this world.

The husband and wife awakened from the frightful thunderstorm. When the sun arose, they went to see their flax field. Everything was ravaged, crushed, and destroyed as if a mountain had just rolled over the blooming plants. The old wife was puzzled while the husband wrung his hands. "My beautiful flax, my working hands, my efforts, my glory, my labor, my reward, everything is gone, and our glory and achievements are reduced to beggary!" he moaned.

"We are not sorry, Father," said the four-year-old boy who followed his parents. "I heard something on the other side of the field saying, 'We should be dressed by God.'"

"It is impossible," sighed the Father. "The boy hears what we cannot hear."

They walked over the desolate field. The earth was plowed deeply in the ground and heaps of hail lay in between the former flax stalks. After some time, the flax straw was upright and unhurt around the edge of the field. Then the flood and hailstorm stopped in the flattened area. Father and Mother looked here and there at the remaining flax stalks with the eighty-four flowers on them.

"I am an unhappy, poor man," he complained. "In my beautiful field stood more than one hundred thousand straight, high, neat, flax plants, and now there are only eighty-four left! Give the ruined plants to the pigs, Mother. Give them to the pigs! What else should we do with these worthless, surviving plants?"

"I will try and preserve them," answered the wife. "Perhaps we can make a little kerchief from the remaining flax for our young boy who lies in the cradle."

The old woman watered and brushed the plants. A small thin bundle of the longest and pliable plant had not fallen. Afterwards, she spun the flax, skeined, wound, stretched, and wove the woof in the warp. To her astonishment, Mother was able to weave a large piece of beautiful, soft flax for the infant boy. It was quite remarkable to see how these remaining eighty-four pathetic, sagging flax were doubled, and a miracle was performed with Mother's hands.

She thought about the fine white linen, and her small fine fabric that had been bleached on the grass. It was so glistening white, unlike what Mother had never seen before. One would have thought the flax was woven by the sun or at least from the finest silk.

"Look what we received from the hardened flax!" Mother stated to Father.

"It is certainly nothing to speak about!" murmured the old man. "We should have woven forty-eight shirts from the flax, which we could have sold in the city!"

The flax was now already bleached as the husband went sullenly away, and the wife began to weave.

Just then a young man came walking along the path, leading a donkey with a young woman and a little child wrapped in sheepskin. They stood at the poor cottage door to rest after their long walk in the hot sun.

The young woman said to the older mother, "It is a beautiful little piece of fabric you have woven. How can one use it?"

The boy who lay in the grass beside the road answered, "The fabric is spun from flax, and the flax said it shall be dressed by God."

"May I have your weaving for my little child?" asked the young woman innocently.

The older mother stood in wonder looking at the very young

mother appearing almost like a child herself, traveling so modestly on a donkey.

The mother was so poor, asking for alms along the way. "Doesn't your little child have any infant clothes?" asked the mature mother.

"No," the young woman replied. "We had infant clothing, but we lost them. We had to leave in the middle of the night because wicked people wanted to kill my little child."

The older woman looked at the fine weaving and thought of her own little boy who would sleep so warm in the flax fabric. The strange young woman looked like an innocent child, yet there was something about her that resembled a queen who commanded attention and who needed to be obeyed.

The experienced mother did not ask any more questions and said, "We had a beautiful flax field, and in my heart I wanted to give something to the needy. This little piece of fabric is all we received from our labor, and certainly your little child cannot travel without infant clothing. I am happy to give this to you! Our flax is clothing for God. I know that those who give to the needy and the unfortunate lend to God."

"That is true," said the young woman, and once more her eyes shone with such an innocent look as one rarely sees coming from someone's eyes. "I wish your next flax field will give a one hundred fold harvest, and your small child who has given its infant clothing to my child shall never freeze in the world."

"Only God can give this," the elderly woman said deliberately.

"Yes, I give nothing, but I pray and receive. Are you sure my child can have your child's baby clothes?"

The elderly mother agreed, and she saw the strange child dressed in its new clothing. The child looked at the older mother with a deeper gaze than its mother did.

"Do you believe your child will never freeze in the world?" The young mother asked.

"I think so," responded the older mother. She did not know this would be absolutely true.

"Good-bye. We must now continue our long trip," said the stranger.

The way to the south wound around the mountain slope. The old woman's eye followed the mother and child traveling as long as she could see them. Their bodies were like a silhouette against the blue horizon.

The older man questioned, "What do you see?"

"I wonder where they were traveling," answered the mother. "They are almost ready to pass the high cedar tree over there, which bows deeply, almost touching the ground."

"It may have been the wind," suggested the husband laughing. "Haven't you seen people roaming around the country called gypsies? Where is the newly woven piece that was here?"

"I gave the flax piece to the strange child," the wife answered.

"What? Have you given away your only piece of weaving as a gift, the only thing we have received from our beautiful flax field? Is it wise of a mother to let her only child freeze in order to warm someone else?" The husband asked.

"Our children never freeze," reminded the older mother to her husband.

"What is it with this silly talk? With my wisdom I did not think my wife would be so senseless," the husband responded.

As the boys grew, the older son no longer heard natures' voices speak. The younger boy was blessed as the sunniest summer, even though it was freezing outdoors. "This is a healthy child. There is a maturity about him resembling his father," said the husband.

Two years passed, and Father now saw a new flax field growing beautifully. As the family looked at the blooming flax flowers, Mother listened and understood her son's babbling speech. "What is he saying?" asked Father while they sowed the field.

Mother answered, "He says the flax flowers say to each other, 'Our sisters will be dressed by God.'"

The husband was irritable and said, "It's the forecaster again. When will we witness the furious thunderstorms that devastate the fruit of my toil and skill?" Reader, do you know what? No thunderstorm came. The flax harvest was saved and unhurt. It produced one hundred fold; yes, more than double the harvest, which the time before was so deplorably devastated. Then the old man noted, "As I always have said, one shall drain deep and plow so skillfully so that the storms do not have power over the crops. Had I not been so sensible and careful, who knows how it would have gone?"

"God gives the growth," said the wife.

"Yes, and we help," laughed the husband. "Look! Who is coming again on the main road? Isn't a man leading a donkey with rope and a young woman holding a child?"

His wife answered, "It's the family who stayed with us two years ago. Before they traveled from the north to the south, but now they are traveling from the south to the north.

Her husband responded, "Should we honor the old superstition? I will go to the stable while you walk toward the highway and sell. Make sure you do not give away your weaving."

The traveling couple stopped at the cottage again in order to relax and eat after the strenuous journey. The woman, who resembled the child, took her little boy to the older mother's son to play. The older woman gave the boy a piece of bread.

"Is your son cold?" asked the young mother to the older woman.

"No, but sometimes he is hungry. Our poor family lives by cultivating flax. Dear woman, will you give my son the gift so that he will never go hungry?"

"I am God's servant; only ask and receive," said the young woman with a queenly look. "I will ask for abundant bread for your boy in the world because he has given my child his only piece of bread. My child has been cold and hungry, even though all the beautiful clothes on the earth warmed him and all the rich cornfields gave him his bread. Does your boy want a large gift so he will hunger and thirst after righteousness?"

Mother did not understand this, but she thanked the young woman, and it was certainly something to think about; that is, thirsting after righteousness.

"We needed to leave our home for a while and now we will return," said the young woman. "Those who were seeking our child's life are dead. May we have a drink of water from your well before we travel?"

"I want to give you the wine which grows from the earth," answered the older woman.

"I am the Virgin Mary," said the young woman with her indescribable look of innocence.

Ride a Cockhorse
Rida Ranka

here is a ballad that everyone knows; however, no one can guess its meaning. My mother sang it when she was a child, and Father heard it when he was just a toddler.

Yesterday Dora sang the same ballad with the little boy on her knee, like a man in the saddle. The ballad was not like ballads of today but was from an earlier period of time. It was more than the babbling tone of a child's voice. In days gone by the more I heard it, the more I listened. Smiling, Dora placed the child on her knee, and she sang the following ballad:

"Rida, rida, ranka … ride a cockhorse …"

More than five hundred years ago, there was a little king's son whose name was Håkan. He was eight years old, handsome, fair-skinned, with the most mild blue eyes and soft cheeks as red as an apple. His father, King Magnus, ruled all over Sweden and Finland; including mountains, forests, lakes, seas, towns, and villages. Sweden had many ships, armies, proud knights, shining swords, warhorses, bows, lances, and shining armaments.

There were also many elegant married women and lovely maidens in the king's court. However, more beautiful and proud than any other was the king's gem, Queen Blanca, little Prince Håkan's mother. One day she sat in her purple dress in the stateroom in the king's castle and held the little prince in her arms. He rode on her knee as children usually do, and the queen sang beautifully.

It was wonderful of the proud queen, who pretended to be a horse for her dear little lad as he bounced on his mother's knee.

> "*Ride a cockhorse*
> *The horse is called Blanca...*"

The prince thought about riding because he had often seen knights and squires guide their snorting, powerful horses in the courtyard and hasten out through the gateway with an energetic gallop. In the summer he sat with his mother when the large jousting event was held outside in the field. The earl and duke rode toward each other with long lances; the trumpets blared, the large feathers waved, the horses neighed, and in a cloud of dust the knights tumbled around each other with banners adorning the field. Prince Håkan could not forget it because he had so often dreamed that one day he could sit in the saddle with a sword, armor, and spurs as other kings' sons. Then he would ride for a long, long way around the world for exploits and adventure! He was now riding on his mother's knee, and she began to sing as Prince Håkan's beautiful blue eyes glistened.

> "*Ride a cockhorse.*
> *The horse is named Blanca...*"

The boy asked in his babbling language: "Where should we ride?"

That was a question! He waited for mother to answer, "Go and play the tower game, or travel to the Holy Land where so many courageous heroes rode before, and then come back."

Or should he ride to Finland's enormous forests where his great, great grandfather, the great Birger Jarl, who in times past fought with wickedness and heathenism? His mother, the queen, thought how the little prince one day would win the new kingdom without a battle.

Then the boy asked, "Where should we ride?"

The mother bent his little head back, kissed him and sang:

> *"Ride away and free*
> *to a little place of solitude."*

There was a little comforting place that the queen thought about as she laid her son in his bed. Queen Blanca was not only a king's daughter, but also an heiress to the powerfully rich. She knew this, but her son, Prince Håkan, did not. Then his mother sang:

> *"Ride away and be free*
> *to a little place of solitude."*

The boy asked, "What is her name?"

This was now a big secret. The queen had not revealed it to some housewife, friar, or knight; not even for the king and his consort. She was concerned for nothing less than the kingdom, and such information one does not reveal because of all the gossiping. It was difficult to find such a bride.

Again the young prince asked innocently, "What is her name?" The queen dared not reveal who the bride was, for fear of all the community gossip. No one in the kingdom should be told including the housewives, friars, knights, or the king and his consort. Again Prince Håkan asked who the bride was.

With her motherly heart and a bowed prince's curly head in his cradle, she took both hands and cupped them around his eyes and whispered, "Her name is Maiden Margareta."

Maiden Margareta was the Danish King Valdemar's daughter and heir to the throne. One day she would win prince Håkan's heart and Denmark's kingdom. People wanted the future wise queen, Blanca, to sing Maiden Margareta into the boy's heart while he was little. Prince Håkan will one day carry the crown for Sweden, Norway, and Denmark.

At the same time, King Magnus stepped into the queen's cottage, and after him followed two chamber maids who awakened the queen. The king loved beautiful ballads, and it was his pleasure to hear the queen sing. When he went outside, he heard the song but not the words. He asked what the queen sang.

Queen Blanca had no plans to reveal her future relationship with the king, who was somewhat uncommunicative toward her and even less so toward the housemaids.

"Please sing another beautiful ballad," said the king.

"It is a little silly song," responded the queen. "It is about a young knight proposing to a maid of honor. It went well in the beginning, but in the end it was bad. Do you wish your majesty for me to continue?"

"Yes, sing!" said the king.

The queen sang:

> "*When he came to the king's garden,*
> *There was no one home; only an older mother…*"

"It must have been troubling for the young knight," commented the king. "Well, what happened to the old dragon who guarded the garden?"

> "*Sit in the corner,*
> *bite the blues away and teach your daughter to spin.*"

"That's right; there is a young woman at home. How did it go then?" asked the king.

> "*Spin, spin, my daughter!*
> *In the morning your fiancé will come.*"

King Magnus laughed. The old man wanted to cheer up his daughter so the work would not be too tedious. What happened then?"

> "*The daughter, she spun,*
> *and the tears did run …*"

"The little poor wretch!" continued the king. But the fiancé never came …

"It is very tender and touching," said the king.

> "*Before the second year,*
> *with the gold band in the hair …*"

"I could believe it, otherwise it could have been too stressful. Consequently, it was totally as it should be. The young knight received his heart's love," the king stated.

"No one understood the queen's song, and the ballad ended."

"What do you mean, my dearest queen?" asked the king. "I thought the romance was very clear and intelligible."

"My lord and king, it is common in such romances. Everything is just fine," the queen answered.

"Of course! As if one cannot understand, there was a splendid wedding. Thanks for the song; it was certainly a pleasant occasion. Now I will take my little Håkan with me. He will now learn to ride on other horses rather than his mother's knee. Will you come with me to the master's farm, little farmhand?" The king asked his son, Håkan.

"Sure," answered the boy. Jumping out of his father's arms, the boy forgot the Virgin Margareta and the ballad.

During that time, King Valdemar's daughter, Margareta, grew up on her father's estate in Denmark. She was a wise little princess with quick, dark eyes and a pleasant disposition. When she was six years old, she had already many suitors who thought more about Denmark's crown than the little princess. It was a wonderful experience; however, the councilor was transferred from the Swedish king's castle to the Danish king's castle in order to plan the futures for the two king's children. Margareta's engagement was discussed twice.

At ten years of age, she presented herself for the engagement. The lofty men did not want to be an adult fiancé to a girl so young. It amused little Margareta to be so sought after by some bearded old princes who came to her father and asked for his daughter's hand. The princess was given twigs from her maid Märta, for at that time it was customary that princes and princesses paraded with twigs. At that time Margareta chose not to become engaged to an older man until she matured.

At eleven years of age on a beautiful summer morning, she went with her friend Ingegerd Knutsdaughter to play in the park at her father's castle by a lake. "Let's play with the bread bits and flat stones," said Maiden Margareta. "I will throw a flat stone for each of my proposals, and the prince who gets the most skips on the water's surface will be my suitor. For every skip there is one piece of bread to be placed in the basket."

"We have many stones here on the beach. I hope Prince Håkan of Sweden and Norway get the most pieces of bread," stated Ingegerd excitedly.

"We will see," answered Margareta as she laughed. "Now I will count as I throw to Mecklenburg. Oh, the stone splashed right into the basket!

"Who is it?" asked Ingegerd.

"Markgreven from Brandenburg," Margareta replied. "I am not satisfied with that," she continued.

"Who will we have then?" Ingegerd wondered.

"Hertigen of Holstein," responded Margareta. "Let's try for the red-headed duke. Three skips and three pieces of bread! I may get to be a duchess."

"Who will we have next? The count of Flanders just sank to the bottom!"

"Do we have more?" asked Ingegerd.

Margareta replied, "The prince of Saxony is the one with a split nose from a sword. Splash! Four skips and four pieces of bread with the stone are the most."

Ingegerd continued, "Let's keep on trying because there might be someone else." Ingegerd chose the right flat and suitable stone.

"Prince Håkan will not get my little finger," said Maiden Margareta. With that she laughed, turned herself around on her high red heels, and threw the stone carelessly without even looking. The stone skipped six times, and Håkan got six pieces of bread.

"Oh!" shouted both girls.

In the confusion, a young, fine-looking knight came riding into the park accompanied with knights and squires dressed in gold and scarlet. His armor gleamed in the sun with his white plumes waving in the light summer wind. With one leap he jumped down and stood beside the horse. He appeared courteous to both girls. He bent his knee to the young Margareta and said, "The most darling maiden, I have now come over land and sea to do my honorable duty. I am Prince Håkan, and with the high fathers' consent, I lay Sweden's and Norway's crowns at your feet."

Maiden Margareta blushed at this word as if she was sixteen years old. As an eleven-year-old, she had the courage to say, "Is it you who received six pieces of bread?"

Prince Håkan certainly did not know how he should answer with such a strange question from his prospective kingly bride. When he looked at her quick eyes, he noticed she was not arrogant as she presented herself. He replied, "Not only six pieces of bread noble maiden, but six crowns. Will you let me place this ring on your finger?" At this word he placed a diamond ring of priceless worth on the prospective bride's childlike finger.

Maiden Margareta let this man of his own free will give her the ring. She thought the young prince was the best bridegroom.

However, she was so young and unwilling to give herself away. She took the ring off her finger, pretended to look and said, "It's a gray stone, isn't it?"

"Oh no, it is a high-class diamond from India," the prince answered.

"I wish it was a gray stone," said the maiden. At the same time she turned and threw the ring as far as she was able out to the harbor. "Did you notice the prince did not take any pieces of bread from the basket?" she added.

Afterwards he took out a large gold coin piece that was suspended on the knight's chain encircling his armor. He threw the coin with all his might out onto the shiny surface of the sea. The heavy piece of coinage bounced and bounced before it finally disappeared under the water. One counted eight skips or eight pieces of bread.

Then maiden Margareta counted what was in Prince Håkan's hand and she said, "You can throw quite well! The next time we should throw with crowns."

Some weeks later, prince Håkan stood with maiden Margareta at the altar. It was the largest and most splendid event celebrated in Denmark's kingdom, including jousting and an abundance of wine and barbecued beef. During the evening of the wedding, the bride received twigs from Märta because she bit the groom when he tried to kiss her.

Eight years after the wedding, Prince Olof was born to queen Margareta and Håkan. He was a quiet, blue-eyed boy who liked to ride on his mother's knee as she sang a Danish ballad to him. It was about the knight, Nils Ebbesen. However, Queen Margareta's solo was not as pleasant as Queen Blanca's.

King Håkan came into the room and listened to the music for a while; then remembering his mother's song, he took the boy on his knee.

"Please sing," urged the queen. "There is more iron in me and my voice than in you."

King Håkan sang:

> "*Ride a cockhorse.*
> *The horse is called Blanca...*"

"It was your mother," the queen noted.

"Yes," responded the king as he continued to sing.

> "*Where will we ride?*
> *Ride away and free*
> *To a little piaffe.*
> *What will she be called?*
> *Maiden Margareta...*"

"It was me," said the queen.

"I do not know if you understand the remainder of the ballad because it was sung in order to blend with the beginning:

> "*When we came to the king's castle,*
> *there was no one home,*
> *only an old woman...*"

"The ballad concluded with the fiancé approaching," noted Queen Margareta.

"Yes, he came," repeated King Håkan.

Little Prince Olof brought order to the world on his father's knee, just as his father rode on his mother's knee. Much more can be said about them, but enough was said in the ballad. The little boy who rides a cockhorse today does not know anymore of Prince Håkan who rode away to be free, and the little girl who sings to her doll about Maiden Margareta. Kings, queens, princes, and princesses die, as everyone else. However, beautiful and happy stories ride on the ballads' tones from generation to generation.

Tom

o you know Tom? He was a white set-
ter with a silky coat and long brown
hanging ears. He always waved his
white plume-like tail. Many children
in Finland had played with him, while
other children a long way away in
Sweden and Denmark had listened
to sagas about Tom's wisdom and the
strange tricks he could do. He was a beautiful and kind dog, and
everyone wanted to hold him in spite of his faults.

No matter what people wore, he would tug at their clothing.
This cost Tom many gentle taps with the rattan cane as he ran into
the kitchen. Sometimes he thought his frisky behavior deserved a
gentle tap.

In the neighborhood there was a swarthy, sulky, blacksmith
who usually soldered tin in the yard of a short-tempered man
whom Tom did not like. One day the blacksmith brought home
a shiny saucepan and placed it in the kitchen. Tom rushed in and
pulled at the blacksmith's trouser leg. He did not like to threaten
Tom with a rattan cane. In spite of the threats, Tom remained
quite loving and watchful.

He faithfully guarded the yard night and day, looking for
persons with mischievous intentions. The police were constantly
on the watch sleeping with open ears and eyes. Not one sound
could be heard even on a sandy plain but that Tom could hear it.
He stood vigilantly so the neighbors could sleep in peace.

Tom thought it was his obligation to keep his eyes on all that
happened during the night. When a boat rowed on the lake, if a

dog yelped from a long way in the village, or if the moon shone on the quiet water, Tom took great delight.

"Why is Tom barking?" the servants asked among themselves as they looked outside.

When Tom was two months old, he was a little pudgy, straight-haired, disobedient puppy, resembling a pig that ate sweets. One day he saw a fishing rod in the yard with bait attached to the hook. He took one bite of the bait, and this unfortunately went through his lower lip. The hook had a barb, and it did not come out of his lip the same way it went in. There was no other alternative than to cut off the fishing line and pull the hook through the lip.

When Tom was four months old, he wandered from his home, following a young lady to the city. He saw a lathe operator who had a cat with kittens. There was uproar when the cat jumped on top of Tom as he stood at the door! The garden door stood open to the street, and Tom decided to leave and take a longer walk by himself without the cat. No sooner was he out on the street before a large, rough, killer-dog dashed toward the unfortunate wanderer. Tom got out of the way, and seeing a cab at the corner, he took a leaping stride inside.

"Oh really!" said the hired driver quite surprised. "Do you have something with which to pay me? I usually do not drive anyone without payment." Poor Tom climbed down from the cab. At the same time, he saw once more his fierce pursuer, and he ran as fast as he was able. He ran up and down the street until he did not know where he was in the large world because as he had been four days in the city. He only knew his yard where he lived, his kitchen where he slept on the rug under the table, and his kind friends who always cared and caressed him. What or who in the wide world would be cruel to Tom? His family called for him, "Tom! Tom! Tom!" The police were phoned, the children cried, the mother who provided food for Tom ran around to the city to look at all the white dogs, but he could not be found. It was a dark evening, and Tom was still missing.

The following morning an article appeared in the local newspaper about a missing dog, including the description. Just when the news alert appeared, a noise was heard on the kitchen floor. It was Tom patting with his paw! Where he had been they could not say. He looked like a sad pig, barely able to wag like a swan, and he was completely full of soot on one side of his chubby body. Was it dirt from the ground? Who knows? He steered his steps to the water bucket and was now content. There were other mischievous antics that were part of Tom's nature.

He was a frisky puppy toward people and beggars. For example, when he saw schoolboys throw a ball in the garden during recess, he was quick to catch it in his mouth as he chased a dozen shouting and laughing students. During the winter, he nibbled the boys' caps on a toboggan run.

Tom often ran to a bakery where he was given food, including Russian biscuits. He was known to take peasants' hats from the lunch counter and carry them triumphantly into the kitchen.

Once when small girls were playing with their dolls on the steps, a kind imaginary wolf licked the dolls on the face and then put them in his mouth for fun. Fortunately, someone grabbed a doll's arm and pulled it out of Tom's mouth. Nothing could be evil in Tom because he looked happy and everyone knew he meant well.

Setter dogs are great bird hunters, and Tom knew this was his gift. He had never gone to bird-hunting school because this skill was natural for him. During opening season, he chased and grabbed the innocent victims in his sharp teeth. He often came home with blackened legs from the beach mire with a mallard in his mouth.

Then he was given the responsibility to watch over the hens by standing immovable for a lengthy time with sharp eyes and one forepaw lifted. One unfortunate hen had been forbidden to wander in unprotected territory. Tom grabbed the hen zealously about the neck and carried her to the kitchen steps. That was the end of the hen.

A similar unfortunate fate happened to the children's smaller dog who entertained them, including Tom. On a sunny morning the puppy took a forbidden journey to the park. As the master went out for his morning walk, he met arrogant Tom gently carrying the poor puppy in his mouth. Playfully, Tom took the puppy leap and restrained himself from meeting the rattan cane. In spite of this mistaken occasion, Tom wanted to behave in this beautiful world. However...

One afternoon a fluttering, despairing hen's cackle was heard in the yard. Old Greta, the hen watcher, ran and found a sick hen struggling with Tom. They searched around them and suddenly the rattan cane administered justice. The servant girl, who at a distance had been a witness to the event, said that a big horned owl had flown down onto the hen. Tom hurried to the hen's defense, and the horned owl unsuccessfully received its plunder.

Now everyone turned to the innocent one, Tom. They praised his heroism as he looked forward to the best bone and rusks from the pantry. Now composed, he saw himself as the day's hero and a prey for an unfair suspect.

When Tom knew for sure he had done something wrong, his conscience bothered him. He could not be happy until he was forgiven. Often the hens hatched and hid their eggs in quiet, strange places, and then appeared proud with a whole flock of chicks. They could not avoid Tom.

One day he looked very depressed and put his nose on his mistress' knee. "What have you done?" the mistress asked. Tom lifted his head up onto the mistress' dress where he left a big egg yolk stain! Where had he been? Tom knew he had misbehaved. The next time when he discovered the hidden hen house, he ate an egg and a sudden warning came. Carefully he carried the last egg home, and fortunately it did not leave an egg yoke stain on his sharp teeth.

Tom was never idle in the summer. When he hunted with a piece of rope in his mouth, he dug diligently in the ground. There in the gardener's desperation, a thousand grayish-brown field mice walked under the vast grassy pasture. They had done incredible damage by gnawing the fruit tree's bark, by eating up the potatoes, gooseberries, raspberries, and rosebushes. Tom decided to end this nuisance.

One day a man saw Tom busily digging for field mice. He sniffed with his nose along the grassy area, and there he discovered something suspicious. First he bore his nose into the sod in order to make sure he was at the right spot. Afterwards he began digging with his forepaws and then with the hind paws until he scratched up the earth and dug a hole so big he could put his head in it. He continued tirelessly until he found living space. The whole field mouse family, including father, mother, and children, looked quickly and went down in Tom's wide mouth. He did not have time to use his teeth. When his stomach was not able to hold more of the field mice family, he had no recourse but to use his teeth as long as he lived. That was the end of the mice pranks.

In back of the greenhouse, Tom had his storehouse of supplies. There he buried his bones and covered them carefully with earth. One day an unwelcome hungry, rough, mongrel guest named Mirka appeared with a horse and carriage from the train station. Mirka was discovered at an unfortunate time. Tom's storehouse of goods was available for persistent looting. He did not notify even the great conqueror, the horned owl, about exposing Mirka's broad teeth.

One cold winter night when the frozen thick ice was over the hidden treasure, Mirka proceeded to rob but returned without success as the ice was too harsh for him. If Tom could laugh he now had good reason, but he had other ways to express his satisfaction. He wagged his longhaired tail in contentment.

"Was Tom sensible?" That was the question a hired driver in the city asked. Then Tom ran by with a basket in his mouth to buy bread from the baker.

"Give me the dog, and I will teach him to speak!" the baker

demanded. Tom understood everything the man said to him. He sensed with his eyes to follow the conversation as he walked. Tom came when the man laughed or when the setter heard lively voices. Tom was the happiest among the cheerful ones participating in the gaiety.

The driver talked to Tom and asked, "What does the dog say?" Tom barked roughly. "What does the cat say?" Tom yawned as he went along meowing indistinctly. Does a dog think about its mistress? Didn't Tom think about anyone else? He growled gently like thunder in the distance. "Go and see if Isak is nervous!" the driver commanded. Tom ran to the window and looked out. Then he laid himself down and waited patiently. He was smart and could do other things as well.

For example, he could do many tricks such as bowing slightly, and then people shook his right paw. The mistress commanded, "Tom, lay dead." Tom placed himself immediately on his back with his paws raised up in the air.

If someone showed him two identical large lumps of sugar, they would say, "This is my piece, and this is yours." Tom never misunderstood the words, "yours" and "mine." His greatest pleasure was to carry baskets, bags, and sticks, like a valet. In addition, he was great at retrieving things.

For example, once when the mistress' hat blew into the lake, she shouted, "Get the hat, Tom!" He swam out and grabbed it with his teeth. No one knew better than Tom how to play a hiding game. He covered his head with a towel while others hid themselves. Then they commanded, "It is daylight!" Tom threw off the towel and began to look. He sniffed in every nook and cranny and soon he discovered something. It was not long before he was waving a plume and revealed the most secretive hiding place.

Tom enjoyed receiving presents, especially on Christmas Eve, including a cake, a collar with a metal tag, and a leather ball. There were other things Tom liked as well.

Tom loved the cupboard, and there he stood longingly

scratching on its door. The ball was hidden in the most impossible places, including under the heavy rug, on top of the cupboard, and in back of the cushion on the sofa where the women sat knitting their socks. He looked eagerly and untiringly in the canary's cage and the fireplace. Always at the end he sniffed the air with his keen nose and detected the location of his beloved rubber ball.

Sometimes Tom discovered it in the most inaccessible places like the top of the cupboard or on the chandelier. No one showed any inclination to help him take it down. He thought for a while, pondered the situation, and had an idea. He noticed the family usually used a stick for such purposes. He ran out in the hall where the master's sticks were located. He fetched one of them, barking and bowing. He enjoyed other games too, including Blind Man's Buff.

Tom's mistress tied a towel over his eyes and threw the ball out on the floor. Getting his attention she said, "Look, the ball!" Tom groped around cautiously with his nose toward the chairs and table, but he made no attempt to free himself from the towel before retrieving it. He was proud of his achievements because he ran around for everyone to praise him. It was easy to teach him; however, being strict was of no use. With a caress and an encouraging word, he could prevail like a Pagliacci. He understood an impatient word with ease, but with a harsh word, he was as oblivious as wood shavings.

Tom was in various poses. Once a praised French sculptor molded Tom in plaster. The best image of him, however, was Tom lying so peacefully and awake on the steps.

Tom was a full four years old when he died. He was ill and was sent to the veterinarian in the city. After three days he longed for his beloved home and his good friends who took care of him. At home his grave was placed between a mountain ash and a spruce on a hill toward the east. There the sun shines most clearly in the summer morning. All of the neighbors were at the funeral. There was a brief speech:

"Thanks little Tom for all the happiness you gave us!" All the assembled thanked one another for being kind to Tom.

Tom's young mistress can never forget her faithful friend and servant whose name was placed on the gravestone. The children played quietly where it was so beautiful. When they learned to read they said to one another, "Do you remember Tom? Yes, Tom was a kind dog!"

The Withered Leaf
Det vissnade lövet

It is now fall, and darkness is seen out through the window. The storm whistles, the rain patters toward the door, and the high seas' waves are seen. Oh the dark, gloomy, roaring ocean, thundering and storming after its prey, lying buried in the autumn night like the living dead! It is still the same sea at midsummer, lying happily around its flowery beaches. The white sails blow as the gulls fly overhead, and children at the wharf's edge run to their bark boats.

Now it is dark and threatening, and no one can dismiss the unforgiving waves. Darkness lies like a curtain in the uncertain distance. The beautiful thick forest was green, the sun shone as the birds sang, and young girls saw a three-leaved trefoil. Its enticing birch leaves have dropped and cease to blow. The autumnal wind breaks the spruce branches. The birds sleep, flowers lie withered, and wolves step quietly over the mossy tufts of grass.

I know an ordinary, historical story about a withered aspen leaf. It was a young, strong aspen that had stood somewhere in Finland's forest. May came with its fresh, beautiful, light green budding leaves adorning the most gentle, softest, highest aspen. The spring winds surrounded the aspen in the night and sang the following ballad,

> "*A thousand, thousand leaves has my young aspen;*
> *every leaf is woven from the sun and dew.*
> *Every leaf is a tongue, and with a thousand thousand tongues,*
> *my aspen praises God's endless goodness.*"

"It is a pleasant ballad. Wind, teach it to me!" the chaffinch twittered as it built itself a nest in the aspen tree. So, the wind did.

What will it say in praising God? thought the little young thing with aspen's full-blown leaves. The aspen leaves thought about the song, but they did not understand exactly what it meant. "I have never seen God," thought the leaves. "How will I praise him whom I have never seen?"

The following day the wind changed directions, and the aspen and young leaves began to whisper their thoughts. "What are the leaves saying? Are you not God's created work? Yet you say you have not seen your Creator," the chaffinch chattered.

"It is certainly possible," remarked the young leaf, mournful and trembling. "It is so difficult to understand his creation."

"Perhaps you should live a little longer until you comprehend it better," suggested the chaffinch.

The summer came; every leaf grew big and green under heaven's sun, and all the thousand leaves praised God. The same young leafed aspen thought to itself, *I do not understand what they mean, because I am not old enough to understand everything.* Then the leaves mourned in their innocence because they understood so little.

The summer was long, beautiful, and warm. Then came autumn with the first frosty night and leaves turning a golden yellow. The wind continued to sing the following ballad in the trees' crowns:

> *"A thousand, thousand leaves has my young aspen;*
> *every leaf is woven from the sun and dew.*
> *Every leaf is a tongue, and with a thousand thousand tongues,*
> *My aspen praises God's endless goodness."*

The nights were long and dark. The ripened lingonberries were harvested, and the migratory birds traveled away as the leaves began to fall. All the leaves continued to praise their Creator as if they understood, being this was their responsibility in the world. The aspen leaves at the top of the tree wanted to understand this, but they could not because their leaves were already turning golden.

One fall night in the north, rushing winds swept the gold, dry leaves that remained. The leaves remaining at the top were toppled in the forest, and there lay a thousand dead leaves in a pile while hunters were seen carrying rifles. It was a clear frosty day, with leaves rustling under the hunter's feet with yelping dogs and hopping rabbits. The air was like a refreshing, damp, fall feeling with the fragrance of flax when it is taken up out of the water and hung in sheaves to dry in the fenced fields. The green aspen leaves lay there intermingled with dead and living plants. They mourned the possibility of dying before fulfilling their mission in the world.

After the beautiful day, it was a stormy night with the rain falling heavily, and the leaves dispersing here and there in the forest. The aspen leaves scattered a long way away to the beach, swirling from the seashore out into the dark waves.

Amidst the debris was a lost ship with the snow falling over it in high drifts. In the nearby cliffs lived a fisherman and his wife and children in their poor house. The children looked out at the tree branches that had drifted toward the beach. Upon further searching, they found part of a tree and dragged it with delight to the little house and shouted, "Father! Father! Come and see the nice old piece of oak we found at the beach under the snow!"

The fisherman looked at the piece of oak timber and replied, "It is from a beautiful hard wood tree. It is part of the stern of a large vessel, and it will give us good fire in the stove. Mother, put on the porridge pot so we can have something warm to eat!"

The fisherman scraped the snow from the oak trunk as it lay in the fireplace, and suddenly a large gold leaf fell from it. The little girl picked it up and turned it over and over with wonder, for she had never before seen the forest or leaves. With a delightful find she showed it to her mother and asked her what kind of leaf it was.

"It is an aspen leaf. Let me see … it is an unusually large and gorgeous leaf with a green stem still on it. It lay in the snow for a long time. We should dry it carefully and place it in our Bible as a bookmark because I want to know where I read last," Mother answered. Mother read her Bible, God's Word, every day.

The following day was Sunday, and Mother took her Bible from its usual place in the fisherman's cabin, and began to read loudly from King David's Psalm 103:15–18, which is one of the most beautiful love songs that had been sung in God's honor. She read the following passage:

"As for man, his days are like grass;
As a flower of the field, so he flourishes.
When the wind has passed over it, it is no more,
And its place acknowledges it no longer.
But the loving kindness of the Lord is
from everlasting to everlasting on those who fear Him,
And His righteousness to children's children,
To those who keep His covenant
And remember His precepts to do them."

The fisherman and his children listened reverently to the beautiful words. The winter storm roared over the sea, and the cold, night darkness spread itself over the solitary cliffs. In the poor cabin it was peaceful, happy, warm, and light in God's presence.

When the woman closed her reading she laid the Bible down, and between the pages she placed the aspen leaf as a marker and said, "See, the leaf is golden yellow!"

"It is golden from the warmth," the fisherman continued as he turned it over in his hands. It seemed to have been transformed because it shone like clear gold, glistening happiness.

The aspen leaf now understood namely that it was meant to praise God. It had seen spring, summer, fall, and winter. It had seen the clearest sun, the darkest night, the most delightful beauty, the bitterest distress, and yet it did not understand that in everything nothing is known but God's will. The aspen leaf always had been miserable, anxious, and trembling yet beautiful and soft in its spring days. Now it understood everything. It no longer mourned because it was happy and willing to die. It shone like clear gold, so how could it be anything else?

The leaf continues to lie between the Bible's pages. Even the ring around it faded long ago, and yet it could praise God. Soon the May wind will sing in the aspen's crown,

"A thousand, thousand leaves has my young aspen;
Every leaf is woven from the sun and dew.
Every leaf is a tongue, and has a thousand, thousand tongues,
My aspen praises God's endless goodness."

The thousand, thousand trembling leaves know what it means to love its Creator.

This is the story of the withered leaf.

The Red Cottage
Den röda stugan

Setting: Aina and Rosa are playing in a green pasture by the country road.

Aina: "Today is the first of May. Look at the shiny piece of silver I received from my grandmother. It is so unusual!"

Rosa: "My father also gave me a silver coin."

Aina: "What should we buy for our grandmother and father?"

Rosa: "Should we buy pepparkakor?"

Aina: "Or maybe sugar rosettes because that is the custom the first of May. I know what we should do. Let's buy ourselves a little red cottage by the country road."

Rosa: "Okay. We'll move there tomorrow."

Aina: "I do not know if I will have time so soon. I have a lot of homework, and my dolls must have new summer clothes. Maybe the day after tomorrow."

Rosa: "Okay, the day after tomorrow. Then we should buy a little cow."

Aina: "Let's buy a calf."

Rosa: "We will milk the cow."

Aina: "Then we will strain the milk to make soured whole milk and coffee cream."

Rosa: "I agree. We will serve food to Father, Mother, Grandmother, and Grandfather."

Aina: "Let's buy fresh rusks from the baker."

Rosa: "No, we will bake them. I wonder if there is a baker's cottage?"

Aina: "If we cannot find one, we will knead and bake them in the kitchen.

Rosa: "We will roll the buns with a little flour and then we will bake them."

Aina: "First they must ferment."

Rosa: "Yes, I know. We will knead and roll a little knäckebröd, and then bake it. What do you think?"

Aina: "That seems reasonable. I will churn the butter until we have sour milk."

Rosa: "I will help churn also. I received a blue painted churn for Christmas. Listen! Do you hear a mouse in the kitchen?"

Aina: "We should have a little kitten."

Rosa: "Maybe we should have a little dog and name it Azor. He will wear a red collar."

Aina: "We must also have a hen and a rooster. When we get eggs, we will bake pancakes and invite guests."

Rosa: "Aina, do you think we should have two roosters?"

Aina: "I think it is best we should have only one rooster, some chickens, and ducks."

Rosa: "Let's buy some doves too because they are so beautiful and tame. Don't hawks prey on the doves?"

Aina: "Yes, but Frans will shoot the hawks with the bow and arrow. Also, I think we should have a riding horse."

Rosa: "Who will take care of it?"

Aina: "The farmhand will do that."

Rosa: "I think we should have a small lamb."

Aina: "And some little pigs who will eat out of the little pail."

Rosa: "What should we do when the pigs grow up?"

Aina: "We will slaughter and preserve them."

Aina: "We will have checkered rugs in the winter, four chairs and a table, and two dressers and a bed. You and I will sleep in the same bed."

Rosa: "That's okay. Who will wake us in the morning?"

Aina: "Oh dear one, the rooster will awaken us, and we will make coffee. We will not need a maid. Father always says I am Mother's maid."

Rosa: "Do you know, Aina, it is so tiresome to work and scrub. Who will wash our clothes?"

Aina: "We will send them home to be washed. Stina will do that for us."

Rosa: "Where will we get food?"

Aina: "Dear Rosa, don't you understand we will buy our food and cook it ourselves."

Rosa: "Where will we get the money to buy it?"

Aina: "Where will we get money? Wait. We will make brooms and sell them in the city."

Rosa: "Will that be enough?"

Aine: «Certainly. Besides, we can also teach small children to read."

Aina: "That will be pleasant to read with the children. They like to play with our dolls, so we will take the doll cupboard with us."

Rosa: "On Sundays we will go to church."

Aina: "When it rains and we have bad weather, we will stay at home and read the sermon."

Rosa: "Then they will all come and visit us in the afternoon along with our fathers and mothers, grandfathers, grandmothers, Mimmi, and Julia."

Aina: "It shall be a feast. We must get a waffle iron."

Rosa: "And a doughnut pan to make crown pastries."

Aina: "Or we can put whipping cream on the cakes."

Rosa: "You know, Aina, I enjoy Uncle Adam's wonderful history tales."

Rosa: "I agree with you! I remember when we made tarts with strawberries and milk during the war and that was the big news."

Aina: "Let's make raspberries and cream, porridge with lingonberries, and arctic raspberry/cloudberry jam. I certainly can set a good table."

Rosa: "I have a copy of *The Doctor's Cookbook,* and it has a recipe for roast bird with cucumbers."

Aina: "With luck we should also have a little spinach and poached eggs."

Rosa: "Let's prepare a dish with radishes, beets, parsley, and tarts with meat soup."

Aina: "No, let's make raisin soup with a lot of raisins in it."

Rosa: "That will be really pleasant!"

(Two poor children approach from the main road and stand at the enclosed pasture.)

Aina: "Perhaps they would like to have some meat soup. Let's ask them. What have you eaten for dinner today?"

The Poor Boy: "We haven't had any dinner."

Rosa: "What have you eaten for breakfast then?"

The Poor Girl: "We have not eaten any breakfast either, miss."

Aina: "That is terrible! Haven't you ever dipped anything into coffee?"

The Poor Boy: (Pondering) "Coffee?"

The Poor Girl: "We have never seen coffee, miss."

Rosa: "We have rusks you can dip in milk."

The Poor Boy: "Last evening someone gave us a little bread in the village."

Aina: (Looking at Rosa) "Last evening they ate dried bread!"

Rosa: (Looking at Aina) "Everything fresh tastes best!"

Aina: (To the boy) "Look, here is money for some bread!"

Rosa: (To the girl) "I will give you a few coins for some milk!"

The Poor Children: "God bless you, girls!"

Rosa: "How is our red stuga coming along?"

Aina: "Oh, you. Sometime we will get a stuga. I have read in the Bible that those who give to the poor loan to God."

Little Genius
Lilla Genius

 nce upon a time there was a learned man who was known as the Book of Advice. He had many books in his library from which he sought information. I don't know if you have heard about such a title given to a person. It was a very awe-inspiring title. This book of counsel was for those who learn much from books but know little or nothing about the practical things of life. The Book of Advice was a text about rules of behavior. This learned man would put a needle through a winged insect and place it up in a corkscrew because he was a bug collector. He was very intense with his work. No one ever saw him so content as when he struggled with a needle.

One summer morning the sun shone into the study, and the Book of Advice, dressed in his nightgown, began to perspire. He lifted the glasses from his nose and the nightcap from his moonlit forehead. He managed to crouch under the curtain to see the sun shining. "Hmm ... today is insect weather," he said to himself.

The Book of Advice took his gold helmet, tan-colored lightweight coat, woven bag, bottle, various rare insects, and walked outside toward the street. In the process, he tore a hem on a piece of his clothing, nudged a little girl who carried a milk pitcher, and quarreled a little with a streetlight that was in the way.

Finally, he came to a park outside the city. There was a scent of summer with greenery, flowers, and birds singing. However, there were no books about plants and advice. He placed his woven bag on the white cow parsley, the yellow buttercups, and the green osier bushes. He shook the bird cherry branches because they were a good place for insects, particularly when the bird cherry branches bloom and are worm-eaten. "All trees live to be worm-eaten. There is much to do in the old decayed stumps, the fallen crown, and dried branches," thought the Book of Advice.

It was difficult to hunt the flying beasts, *hymenopteran*, in the beautiful park. They had such swift wings, and the Book of Advice did not have much information about them except they could cause death. However, he did know about other insects, including spiders, because he caught them in their web. Everything the insects did was gathered, because he desired to know different insects' purposes and lessons.

Hunting for insects was not always enjoyable because he already had a few hundred. He was tired and rather irritated as he sat at the edge of a pond, where a large, white water lily had just opened its beautiful chalice-like blossom toward the morning sun.

"Aha!" exclaimed the Book of Advice with sudden delight. He had found a strange being hidden between the water lilies' petals. The wretch was a scant one-half inch long, as fine as a peduncle. It was like a very small child, transparent with glistening butterfly wings and snow-white shoulders. The Book of Advice was known to be totally enveloped with happiness when he found an unusual insect.

He separated the poor thing in the bottle from among the rest of the flies and walked contentedly back to his study. Here he stacked up the new insects on a needle. He fastened the needle onto the circular cork and began to study his unusual find under the microscope.

"It was very odd!" he thought to himself. "I have never found such an insect. It must be a homunculus minimus, the microscopic anthropoid! He struggles too much. I cannot count the tears on his hind paws. He dies on the needle while I search in my books for the genus, homunculus," mused the Book of Advice.

The miserable thing was placed on a needle in the corner of the study, and the Book of Advice went to search in his books. When he could not discover anything related to *homunculus,* he proceeded to the largest library where there were one hundred thousand books stacked on the shelves. He began to search in them from cover to cover until he found the description that was over one-half inch thick. It was terribly long and laborious work.

The Book of Advice searched and searched for seven whole years, seeking anxiously with an ashen face. In fact, his tan-colored coat even began to look like a blooming potato field. However, no *homunculus* was seen; at least nothing like that which lives and is seen in the water lily's flower cup.

After the seven-year lapse, The Book of Advice gave his one and only text about the new insect, *homunculus,* to his student. He wrote the following in his book: "The homunculus lives on the scent of flowers and usually discharges in a pond or a park during a certain time in the summer."

The Book of Advice looked up once more at the old cupboard in the corner with the dusty box. There the corkscrew and *homunculus* had been forgotten for seven years. The poor thing sat to the left in the needle, lifelike, cheerful, and struggling as before. It had grown to an inch long. The Book of Advice and insect liked it so much that they laughed.

He was not a negative person, but it annoyed him that an insect would laugh. "Is it right that you laugh? I will teach you!" He took his large iron mortar with the heavy iron prod, laid the brute in the mortar that was broken in small pieces. "Now, you keep quiet!" ordered the Book of Advice.

The Book of Advice looked in the mortar and saw the little thing sit in the bottom with joy and more lifelike than before. It was not a bad thing to attempt to push him asunder. He had now grown two inches long.

Afterwards, the Book of Advice made a big log fire in the fireplace, threw the beast into it, and closed the fireplace doors. "Ah ha! You are of the type who does not look after the welfare of others; now burn yourself up! You will not trick the villain anymore," he thought.

When the fire was extinguished, he was curious and opened the fireplace door. There sat the little happy dwarf unhurt in the ashes. He was now three inches long and could speak.

"Here it is certainly fine and warm," said the little scornful creature with his fine voice that was not more powerful than a mosquito's peep.

"Reach for Jupiter!" noted the Book of Advice and clapped his hands together with surprise. "You are the most tenacious scarabeus I have ever seen." He then took the beast out of the ashes, went away into the woods, and dug down deep into the earth with his hands and arms. To conceal the opening, he rolled a stone over it, and the beast lay down in its grave.

A week later he went out to the woods to take a look. The woods and stones were left, and the unsavory creature was now four inches long, and it sat unharmed and happy on top of the stone. "Here it is beautiful and cool in the forest," said the little one. The Book of Advice was frightened. His thinning hair was combed around his moonlit crown, the green eyeglasses moved up and down on his nose, and the tannish-brown coat reflected on the silvery buttons.

Sometime after, a hen was seen running through the woods, and there was a little human creature sitting on a stone where the Book of Advice left him. "Poor beast! Come and warm yourself in my cottage with the other chickens!" invited the Book of Advice's wife. Cautiously taking the little creature between her bony fingers, she carried him home in her apron.

The old woman had a woodshed where she placed the human-like creature. Neither the woman nor the hen was enamored with the newly arrived guest with its eye cut out. "It is nothing," said the little one. Immediately after, he sat back with shining eyes and smiled broadly at one of the chickens.

"You will live with the pigs!" ordered the old woman to the dwarf-like human. "Pigs, if he gives you trouble, just climb under the trough!"

No sooner said, and it was done. The creature settled in to live with the pigs, but unfortunately a pig ate him up in one gulp!

The old woman was so astonished and frightened that she wanted to kill the pig. She stood ready, and it should have been the end of the pig's young life if the old woman had not heard a tender voice say, "What are you going to do little mother?" The little creature laughed behind the pig's back.

"I am okay," Mother responded. "Now I had better keep him," thought the old woman. She put the *homunculus* to bed in a pail with hay inside the door. The old woman's thirsty husband came inside as he had been outside cultivating their field. He took the pail and put it down into the deepest well. "What in the world have you done? You have drowned my best beast!" the old woman yelled.

Her husband was afraid and dumbfounded because he had a lot of respect for his wife. Before he answered anything, the tender voice was heard to say, "It is nothing little mother, as I feel quite well." Once more the little creature sat and laughed at the pail.

The old woman had a strange facial expression and with eyeglasses around her nose, she looked at the little creature from all sides and asked, "Who are you?"

"I am a creature," he answered.

"Hmm … Where is your home?" asked the woman.

"Everywhere and nowhere," answered the creature.

"Oh, really! You are very intelligent. What is your name?" she continued.

"Call me Little Genius."

"Are you in the almanac?" she asked.

"Look it up!" he suggested.

The old woman looked without her eyeglasses, but there was no listing in the almanac about the saint, Little Genius. "I understand the creature is a girl because the first name is Little and the last name is Genius. It is a wonderful name because people in earlier times gave their children that name. When I consider things, as the trough knows, the creature was once a humanlike child. Answer child, where is your minister?"

"Minister? What is that? Who is that?" Little Genius asked.

"Listen. The beast does not have proof of who one's minister is. I am quite well-behaved in a way with the Little One. The reverend must have some advice for you. I will not have any sorcery or magic in the house." Following this, the old woman gently placed the Little Genius down in a basket, tied a towel firmly around it, and brought the basket to the rectory.

As the Old woman entered the building, she thought to herself, "I will ask the minister what I should do with the creature, if it is a person or what it is."

"Pastor, here is a wonderful beast I found last Wednesday in the forest. Then it was four inches long but has now grown to five inches. Do not drink, eat, sleep, or consider anything strange, cheerful, or difficult. Nevertheless, it looks as if the human child has butterfly wings on the shoulders. It can speak and calls itself, *Little Genius*. I think it is a girl. What shall I do with the creature? Is it a person or what is it?"

The pastor thought about this thing and finally requested to see it.

"Here, I have it," the old woman said as she read the minister's thoughts. She opened the basket, but Little Genius already was sitting on her shoulder.

It nodded with complete confidence and responded, "Here I am, pastor!"

"Hmm, hmm," the minister said to himself as he took the double glass eye and began to look at the little creature from all sides. "My parishioner, where were you born?"

"The sun is my father,
The air is my mother,
The world is my cottage,
Freedom is my way,

Power is my life,
Light is my food,
Warmth is my drink,
Awake my sleep …"

"I admit," said the pastor after some deliberation. "This is quite an unusual certificate of baptism. What do you think of my fly swatter?"

The little one laughed and answered:

"Power does not shatter me,
Steel does not cut me,
Fire does not burn me,
The earth does not bury me.
Out of the air and water,
Out of predatory animals' teeth,
Out of human hands,
I go completely,
Without fault,
Overly bare,
Smiling happily,
As the spring's leaf,
What is it you want,
little pastor?"

"I do not want to have anything to do with you, little disrespectful scamp," scolded the minister. "Go your way. You are not part of my congregation. I do not know you."

"Once you knew me," noted the mischievous one as he lifted his small index finger.

"When was that?" The minister asked.

"I do not remember," answered the mischievous one.

"When you were a lad, I ran with you to catch the parks' butterflies and read stories about their wings. Then I rowed with you on the clear lake and wrote letters of the alphabet on the streets. I stood with you under the heavens and saw God's eye shining in the night," the little one noted.

"When you were in your youth as a student, I sat with you alone, friend, and drew the moon's beauty on your outside icy window. I wrote your most beautiful thoughts about honor and heroism, and about love of one's native country. I wanted to make you a great person like a minister, and in time you will be," sighed Little Genius.

"Youthful dreams!" sighed the minister.

"These dreams will be the best of your life. You have worked for bread, for parishes, for titles and dignity. Had you worked for God's kingdom, Minister Father, then I would not venture to joke with you. Now you will hit me with the fly swatter because you ate and slept away the imperishable in your soul. It is not kind of you, Minister Father!" the small one noted.

Fortunately the pastor did not hear the last disrespectful word. He sat quietly and self-absorbed in his youthful memory.

"The minister should send the disrespectful person to the county sheriff because of his unkind mouth," reminded the woman on behalf of the minister.

"Let it fly. Look here, Little Genius, freedom is your way; fly to freedom!" urged the minister gently as he opened the window.

"Thanks! I will do as you want, Minister Father!" It flew away like a sunbeam toward the blue summer heavens.

The woman had not understood a word of what Little Genius had spoken because it did not show respect for the minister. It was this that made him so exceptionally meditative, resembling almost like repentance and sorrow. Both the woman and minister stood at the window and wondered about the disappearance of the little creature.

As they looked outside, they saw an old man dressed in a tannish-brown coat and a green helmet walking and panting over the grassy hillock and fences. "What in all my days!" exclaimed the woman. "Is it not the Book of Advice who stomps harder than someone who measures land?"

"There they can stomp only because Little Genius had beat him with his hands. When one does not know him, one gets frightened, as the Book of Advice knew. It may never be dangerous for me but for many others. Will you do me a favor, Mother? Burn up the fly swatter! I might jump to conclusions if the little creature comes again."

"Keep watching and praying that you may not enter into temptation; the spirit is willing, but the flesh is weak" (Matthew 26:41).

Tuttemuj

Tuttemuj

uttemuj was only a little small, brave, four-year-old boy. He had two brothers, nine-year-old Micke, and eleven-year-old Nicke. The brothers were given a white woven birch bark canoe with paddles that were as light as a pea pod dancing in the water.

One day Micke came home with the canoe from the long trip to Spain's gulf. He left the canoe untied at the walking bridge where the boys usually sat tending to the boats. Tired and hungry, he ran up to the house and said to himself, "After this long trip to Spain and back, I am hungry for a sandwich rather than waffles."

The next day Tuttemuj was wandering and enjoying his precious freedom. Was anyone else there other than he? He quickly looked for any police who might be guarding the boats and canoes, but they were nowhere to be seen. He came to the bridge where he saw the untied canoe. Observing others, he knew how to paddle with the oars. Before the police caught sight of him, Tuttemuj was out on the lake. The calm water's reflection was seen on the surface, and for the first time, a young boy of four years old found himself alone on the huge lake. How gentle and beautiful the water was! The paddle went into the water like a spoon in a bowl of soup. Should he begin paddling? It would be tempting. He and his brothers had gone on the ice late last fall like flies in soured milk.

Tuttemuj dipped his hand in the water, and it was wet like the big bowl he used for bathing. He thought to himself, "I could gently place the oar into the water like I step into the bathing bowl." He carefully dipped the oar, and then lifted it higher, and then to the left as he saw his brothers do. The canoe moved.

A little mosquito flew closely over the surface of the water, while Tuttemuj watched it with wonder. "Can you fly like a bird?" Tuttemuj asked the mosquito. Then another insect and a fish caught his attention.

A curious smile appeared on his face as he eyed a fly. Smiling to himself he asked, "Can you swim being so little? If you can, who taught you? Micke and Nicke can swim, but I am too little. When I grow up, I will swim to Spain," Tuttemuj declared.

"It is not an art at all to swim; in fact, it is harder to go on dry land," the fly said smiling.

"I can do that," answered Tuttemuj.

The fly did not notice a large perch was behind him. "What are you?" asked Tuttemuj.

"I am nothing. I am just eating my breakfast," responded the perch.

"We usually fry fish," Tuttemuj informed the perch.

The perch had not noticed a large northern pike near him among the reeds. In a flash, the northern pike was alongside the canoe and devoured the perch for breakfast. There was a whirl in the water when the northern pike hit the canoe with its tail, and the canoe jerked.

"Are you playing a joke? Do you want to eat me up like you ate the perch?" questioned Tuttemuj to the northern pike.

He briskly hit the pike with his paddle in the water, so that the oar flew out of his hand and floated away. A little breeze arose, and the canoe drifted aimlessly on the lake. Cupping his hands in the water, the canoe leaned to one side and then the other. Tuttemuj did not notice a white angel sitting at his side, protecting him. If his mother only saw him now!

Time went by and Tuttemuj wondered if his little blue cap could have blown into the water. Yes, it floated like the oar. Could he scoop water in it? Yes! Was it possible the boots would float? Maybe. Besides the canoe, he had three boats on the lake, the hat and both boots. It was a total fleet! (Micke and Nicke only had one vessel and that was a steamboat named Thor.) The hat and boots followed the canoe for a while, but were soon lost in the waves, floating away like the oar. Tuttemuj's small hand reached out after them, but it was too short.

For a while he sat in stocking feet and later was happy to be barefoot. He dragged the stockings in the lake and tried to pour water in them. However, it ran right through the socks, and they did not float! Tuttemuj threw the socks into the water with one sock falling into the lake and sinking. The canoe continued on its journey south.

The wind blew the canoe toward Spain, and eventually, it was drawn to the Spanish harbor, docking on Spain's coast. Embarking from the canoe, Tuttemuj saw something moving among the alder shrubs. Was it Näcken, the evil spirit of the water? No, Näcken does not live in Spain. Tuttemuj stepped on a large stone not far from the beach to balance himself; then he kicked and said goodbye to the canoe and went his own way like the oar, his hat, and the boots.

He stood barefoot on a large rock in the water and attempted to get on land. "I will swim," he said to himself. However, he forgot he could not swim.

At the same time, three cows and an ox came out one at a time from the brush. They were thirsty and wanted a drink from the lake. When the cows saw Tuttemuj, they said, *Moo,* and the ox uttered, *Ugg!* Did they think Tuttemuj was a dog? At least they thought he looked like one, but dogs usually bark at cows and nudge them in the leg.

Tuttemuj was not afraid about anything because he was always armed with a weapon. He and his weapon were certainly suitable for each other because he thought to himself, "Do the cows and oxen want to eat me up? If they come near, I will hit them." He pondered as he aimed to threaten the enemy with a reed.

After Micke had made himself a sandwich, he set out to look for his brother along the pier where he always tied the canoe. However, he discovered it was gone.

"Where is my canoe? Where is my brother, Tuttemuj?" Micke ran along the shore looking for him. "What is that floating on the waves? A boot! Whose boot is it?" He continued asking himself. Upon further examination, he recognized it was Tuttemuj's! Then there was a little blue hat partly submerged. "Whose hat is it? It is also Tuttemuj's!" he continued. Micke knew his heart was in his mouth. He rowed to Spain and found the canoe together with the oars lying in the reeds. If Micke had been Mother, he would have swum at this sight. Being he was Micke, he rowed farther and discovered a courageous war hero who was barefoot without a hat, standing on a stone troubled by his enemies.

Freedom and liberation is beautiful. Perhaps Tuttemuj's heroic resilience benefited him in the long run. "If the enemies had come, I would have hit them so ... so!" he thought.

"Where are the oars?" asked Micke.

"The paddles you mean?" replied Tuttemuj.

"Yes. Where are the paddles, your boots, and stockings?" Micke continued.

Tuttemuj looked embarrassed.

"Are you so negligent?" questioned Micke.

"Moo," responded the cows.

It Is Most Beautiful in the Forest

Det vackraste i skogen

You can believe it was a beautiful early morning about 5:00 a.m. The sun was still low in the horizon, and the birch trees' shade had long, green grass growing underneath. We did not sleep long in the mornings because there was outside noise from the neighbors.

There was an old fisherman who always called outside when the clock struck four in the morning. "Up and go! Up and go!" The sailors shouted at one another when the wind blew in the darkness. Like an arrow we were out of bed. At first it was hard to awaken so early, but we got used to it.

Like older people said, "The early bird catches the worm."

One does not live to sleep away summer mornings with radiant clearness, while the dew lies in the grass and the birds sing. One wastes away many beautiful hours of one's life; however, there comes a time when one cannot help but sleep. I do think we must do as nature wills. Certainly sleep is a priceless gift for the tired, distressed, and sick. One should not be lazy during the glorious morning, and hear the old fisherman standing outside the window shouting, "Up and go! Up and go!"

Let me share with you about how it was during the morning hours in the forest. It was green, fresh, and very delightful. There were many different kinds of trees such as the high pine that at one time said, "I want to be a straight tree."

The small, knotty, juniper bush consoled itself by thinking it was also a tree and thought, "If only I was trimmed and tied to a post to stay upright."

The juniper bush continued, "It does not bother me because I think more about my freedom. Just think, if I was a tree, the children would not be able to reach up to me when they come to cut juniper twigs for the bedding on their cottage floor Sunday mornings!"

"It is the only thing you can have in the world," said the spruce which stood so dignified beside the juniper bush. "You are right to tramp on, you pixie," the spruce meant.

"What does that matter? It is enough that I give people happiness from my fresh scent in the forest. Besides, the odor will be good enough to smoke out the mosquitoes. Then the boy will cut a juniper branch, cook the berries in water, and make syrup from it," the juniper bush said.

"Now it is quiet," said the mountain ash. It sounds dreadfully conceited to list all of one's qualifications. "What tree or shrub is the most beautiful in the forest?" asked the mountain ash. The question shook the mountain ash pleasantly on its thickly wooded white branches because it now stood at the height of its midsummer flower.

"Yes, that is quite a question!" shouted the bird cherry. "My gift is my white blossom as if I had been in a snowball fight. Well... who among us is the most beautiful?" Suddenly a pungent scent from the snow-white bird cherry blossom was noticed.

The silver birch thought this was a very intelligent conversation. It had fixed its long, green hair with curlers, and now he shook his hanging corkscrew curls in the gentle morning wind. "I am decidedly the most beautiful," he thought, glorying in himself.

The alder tree stood at the shore of the lake, noticed its reflection, and thought it was bluish-green and charming and that nothing could be more beautiful! Reflecting on this, he nodded and commented, "Yes, it is a question to think about!"

The aspen stood beside him and quivered from fright, knowing that something could be more beautiful than he. This poor aspen always trembled, knowing it soon would be tall and big with a rather timid heart and brittle branches. The linden nodded, not thinking ill of itself. The willow tree and willow bush stood beside quietly and kept their thoughts private.

The flowers asked about spreading their cool, thick-foliaged, leafy roof over the grassy hillocks full of anemones and cloudberry flowers.

Arrogantly, the pine stated, "It is totally not necessary to be beautiful, large, and strong. Look at me. I am not stately. When I shake myself, thousands of needles fall to the ground, and the ants gather and use them to spear when they walk as if in war. Being stately and huge, I will not deny them my needles," the pine stated arrogantly.

The oak, alder, aspen, and linden stood very quietly and listened to the pine. The oak reflected with a beautiful thought saying, "It is ridiculous to judge one's own concerns. Each one of us may think that we are the most beautiful. Let us ask the chaffinch in the birch tops because he is not biased to say who is the most beautiful in the forest," the oak observed.

This said and done, the trees, shrubs, and flowers asked the chaffinch who was the most beautiful in the forest. He thought for a while and did not want to chirp the truth. Then two children were seen walking.

They saw a boy and a girl who lived in a little cottage nearby. When they went out in the early, beautiful, summer morning, they clapped their hands and shouted to God saying, "Heavenly Father, your forest is so beautiful! Dear God, your world is beautiful! Lord God, let us poor small children grow up in your wisdom, testifying and praising your might and mercy all of our life's days!"

When the trees, bushes, and flowering plants in the forest heard the children's prayer, they marveled and waved quietly in the slight breeze. With their gentle murmuring, one could clearly hear the chaffinch twittering its song in the top of the birch tree:

"Beautiful, beautiful is my green forest and all of God's creation throughout. I say to you, what is the most beautiful in all the forest that God allowed to grow in this part of the country? There is nothing so beloved, good, and innocently sweet as these two small children who praise God's goodness in the clear summer morning. Beauty, power, and grandeur are completely nothing. One needs a humble heart that gives all honor only to God.

The tree stretches its arms toward heaven, the flowers loan their colors from the sun, and the birds sing nature's love song. The same eternal spirit lives and speaks to all of us. We all grow out from the clear sunshine of God's grace. The children's prayers to God are better than the bird's song, the tree's greenery, and the flower's scent. God himself sees you, loves small children, and grows small flowers in life's vast forest. He allows you to grow in wisdom and grace eternally!"

How God Created Finland

Hur Gud skapade Finland

hen God created the world on the third day, he said, "Gather the water under the heavens out in the open sea so that the dry land will be seen," and it was so. God called the ground "dry earth," and the water he called "the sea." God saw it was good.

The sea was huge with broad lands rising up out of it. However, the earth is not the same today as it was then because dreadful earthquakes, floods, and glacial periods shifted along the earth's surface. Large pieces of land sank in the sea, and other landforms arose out of the sea bottom.

In Europe there unfolded a large, desolate sea from the North Pole and south to Germany. In the more elevated area in the north, there was a deep valley. The highest mountain in the south arose from the bottom of the sea, here and there rising up over the remote area.

The sea raised its ocean floor one-quarter to one half-inch over thousands of years, according to God's expected creation.

The old fisherman said to his son when he rowed out with

the net at the seacoast, "Here I have sailed in my youth, and now our boat barely floats through the channel. When I was young, the grain was used as bait while we dragged the net. This point of land had been an islet; now it has grown together with firm ground.

Everyone wondered if the large sea would eventually wear away and finally dry up. However, it is not the sea that dries up, but rather it is the sea floor that rises. When this occurs, the sea flows a long way away from the beach. Even the river's course was dangerously steep, and it sucked out the water from the inner lakes. There had been deep streams, floods, and shallow lakes; however, after a period of time, they gradually dried up too.

Natural occurrences that are God's glorious instruments continue their work in his plan to this day. Near the large, dark, and desolate sea nearest the Arctic Circle exist many islands and shoals. Where Finland lies, a large archipelago of islands existed two thousand years ago. Gradually the islands merged, and the furrowed ground created pools of water that remained in sunken places. Green growth began after God's order and spread itself on the sunny side of the ridges.

Bear, elk, reindeer, and many other animals began to move about on the forested islands. We called it Ladoga Lake because it had a broad sound. It joined the Arctic Ocean with the sea and is now called *Saima Päjäne Näsijärvi*. The entire sea was enveloped with water. However, it did not go through behind the mountain, *Maanselkä*, and unite with the waters surrounding the large peninsula that we now call Scandinavia.

God saw this new, unknown land emerging out of the deep sea, and saw that it was good. "I will give it a name so that it may fulfill my will on the earth," God commanded.

Two pieces of firm land were created, which before then was closed to the eastern region. The broad bridge is now water-rich land between Hvita Sea and Ladoga, and the narrow bridge links Ladoga Lake and the Finnish gulf. Over these bridges many people come from eastern countries. God created this beauty out of the sea and called it *Suomi Finland*. The people's runic poets looked back in time to study the country's origin called the *Suomensaari*, or Finland's islands.

Finland was so wonderfully created that no other country like it was formed on the earth. One-half of many lands before had been in the bottom of the ocean, and the other half sank into the deep sea. The northern part of Sweden continues to grow out of the sea. The many thousand lakes, the wide sinking mosses, channels, rivers, and brooks rising from the bottom over the whole country flowed out gradually and abandoned the dry land. Finland has continued to gain a large piece of disjointed land both within itself and at its seacoasts. People from other countries obtained a vast amount of land from Finland, but its people cleared it and said, "We plow, and God grants us enough land, and we hardly understand why."

What will God do with such a miracle that he does daily right in front of our eyes? He must have a special love and affinity for this land because he never does anything without a purpose. God's ways and purposes we do not know, but his creation we know: "God saw that it was good." We understand that gradually God chose this land from under the earth, so he has also elected these people as his instruments for some good in the world. In addition, he gives us that which is yet hidden. When he called his servants to do his work, he chose them from among those who have unique needs so that the glory shall be His.

We must praise God because we received such a beautiful country, and we must also love the other countries on earth. Finland's children, God has given you this land so that you will grow in body, soul, wisdom, and grace.

For example, when you receive your parent's inheritance, remember God's will by doing everything better than they have done before you. You will receive a portion of this world from them to maintain. In doing so you will reflect performing God's will, and you shall do it well! When someone does work better than those before, everyone benefits. For example, every new skill, knowledge about the country's wealth, happiness, and prosperity, benefits the country's development.

God desires that everywhere you will discover a wilderness, and you shall provide care in creating a Garden of Eden. There you will see something that can become useful, but you will think it to be useless. Seize and use it so that it will be of benefit to others. When you see evil on the horizon, turn that which harms you into something good. For example, someone may be poor and helpless, and you will help them. Or you will see someone who is uneducated, and you will teach them.

Many people do not think about the betterment in improving our communities. They ruin the country and leave it uninhabitable for future use. There exist so many lazy and ignorant people who think, "What concern is it of mine how it was then as long as it is good now?"

Beloved children, let us rather fulfill God's will on the earth! Let us be careful with the prophetic word until the morning star arises in our hearts. The Lord says to us, "Trust in the Lord and do good; dwell in the land and cultivate faithfulness" (Psalm 37:3).

"So we have the prophetic word made more sure, to which you do well to pay attention to a lamp shining in a dark place, until the day dawns and the morning star arises in your hearts," 2 Peter 1:19.

Pikku Matti
Pikku Matti

way in the forest hillside stands a cottage where one sees a blond, chubby, curly-haired little boy's face filling an entire window. The adults who lived there included the old, blind soldier, his wife, and the little boy's parents. The blind grandfather could neither work nor build, and they would die of hunger if the old man did not busy himself by tying seine or fishing net. I will describe the stuga, or cottage.

The little house had a brick chimney, red-painted walls, a nice fenced-in sheltered area, and a large potato garden. Four or five years ago the home was in better condition. However, it was now unkempt as the interior was dark and smoky from a hole in the grass roof, and the fence had been broken for a long time. The old woman made brooms, and every year the church gave them three barrels of corn to bake corn bread.

One Sunday morning the large boat that took everyone in the village to church, capsized because of a storm in the middle of the lake. Pikku Matti's parents and many others perished. Fortunately on that Sunday, the grandparents did not attend the service. They decided to remain at home and care for the children. The huge church bell was heard over the lake welcoming people to worship and honor those who God so suddenly called to everlasting worship in heaven.

The grandparents were now alone in their little home with

their sorrow, poverty, and little grandson, Matti. When he grew up, they called him Pikku Matti. He was chubby and rosy-cheeked as a ripe apple with clear blue eyes and hair as yellow as gold. It was the only gold Pikku Matti owned in the world.

Have you seen the fire glistening clearly from the fireplace in the poor cottage? There you would see Grandfather Hugg mending his fishing nets while Pikku Matti's grandmother read loudly out of the Bible. She read how the poor and blind that lived in the dark land would see the shining light of Jesus Christ who opened the eyes of the blind. (*See* Mark 10:46–52.)

Pikku sat on the fireplace ledge in front of the blaze with the cat on his knee and listened so devoutly as if he understood what Grandmother read. Finally, sleep came so sweet in his round, blue, beautiful eyes as he sank down toward his grandmother's knee.

There is confidence in God who comforts all of life's adversities. This home is rich. Do you think Grandfather, Grandmother, and Pikku Matti will change their wealth of reverence, innocence, and peace for palaces of gold?

On a green summer day one saw the cottage with the front gate. Pikku Matti's hair fluttered in the wind as he ran toward the cottage, running over a log and a stone. Approaching the gate, someone threw a shiny ducat to him. Pikku Matti did not think any longer than the length of his nose as he threw himself full-length over the glittering coin. As he did so, the gate fell on his horse's muzzle.

In spite of some of the family's physical needs, they did not lack for basic food. Pikku Matti ate hard and soft bread most every day, but sometimes he was treated to a feast of potatoes and sour milk. For that reason, he grew to be rather stocky.

He could not read. He could pray, and he knew the Ten Commandments given by God as recorded in Exodus 20. He could stand on his head, do somersaults, and throw open-faced sandwiches over the clear lake's surface from the shore; while Grandma went to wash his shirts, and drive on the smooth road with the neighbor's horse to get water. He could carve out a grouse from a log wedged in the snow, whittle a sleigh, and use green spruce for horses and cows with heron bone for the legs. This was Pikku's special skill, and it was a difficult task for one so small. However, it was not enough. I do not know if I should speak about it, but he did not have any long pants to wear.

There were two reasons: First, Pikku's grandparents were very poor, and secondly, he lacked clothing that fit him. He was the most courageous among all the small boys in the village to go without long pants. Recently however, he became very worried about wearing his grandfather's long shirt. One Sunday morning something happened as everyone gathered at the beach to take the boat and depart for church. Pikku said he wanted to attend the service also.

"The boat will not take you to church and back home dear child," noted Grandmother. "Besides, you do not have long pants to wear. However, I have an old skirt to loan you, but everyone will think you are a girl." Grandmother reminded him.

"I will not be a girl! I will be a man!" Pikku stated.

"Everyone will notice. A man is a man if he is not bigger than a five penny coin. You will be fine at home, Pikku!" Grandmother continued.

He saw many people congregating to board the boat to church, and he decided to join them to hear and see the vast array of jokes and stories from the great Wipplustig, who told stories about a cupboard, Napoleon Bonapart, Mogul, Princess Lindagull, Ahriman, Bumburrifex, and the goblin. Everyone wanted to look inside the cupboard to see Napoleon Bonapart with his gold crown and his long saber and the large Mogul with his hoop around the waist and his unkempt beard. Princess Lindagull led the tiger, Ahriman, by the collar, the giant Bumburrifex, and the goblin into Åbo castle.

"You cannot just go here and there, dear child," noted Grandmother once again.

"Why not?" questioned Pikku.

"There are well-known people around such as the judge, the scribe, the county sheriff, and the lay assessor. You just cannot go anywhere without long pants."

Pikku Matti fought with himself for a while, with Wipplustig playing in his thoughts. Finally he said, "If you would just loan me the skirt …"

Grandmother laughed heartily when the little namby-pamby wearing the skirt walked on the cottage floor. "Now you do look like a girl!" Grandma observed.

"I look like a girl, so I will not go there. I am a man!" Pikku stated firmly.

"You certainly look like a girl, but you can say to all you meet on the way you are a man," suggested Pikku's grandmother.

On the way he met a traveling man who said, "Can you tell me, little girl, where the court sessions are held?"

"I am not a girl. I am a man." Pikku confirmed.

"You do not look like a boy," the traveler observed.

Pikku Matti did not answer anything, but when he came to the courtyard, he shouted so loudly that everyone heard, "I am not a girl! I am a man!"

All the men and women laughed while all the boys and girls made a circle around him, clapping their hands and shouting, "Look at little Maja who has such beautiful clothes!"

"It is Grandmother's skirt and not mine! I am not Maja; I am Pikku as you see," he firmly said.

Then the largest and cruelest of the boys took Pikku Matti by the neck, carried him in front of the game closet, and shouted loudly, "Who wants to see a man in a skirt?"

Pikku Matti was angry with the taunter and shouted, "It is not my skirt! It belongs to my grandmother!" he cried.

The arrogant comrade continued to shout, "Who wants to see a man in a skirt?" He continued by pulling Pikku and shouting all over the courtyard. Never before had Pikku been so humiliated! He cried, shouted, and scratched. When he was finally let go, Pikku ran quickly and stumbled over the skirt with tears in his eyes and crying. He got up and ran further until he fell again rolling over and over.

He came home breathless and sobbing to Grandfather's cottage and yelled, "I will not wear a skirt! I am a man!"

"Don't cry my, Pikku. When you are are grown up, you will see you are as good as any other man," Grandmother responded consolingly.

"The next time you can borrow my trousers," Grandfather suggested.

The grandparents felt sorry for Pikku. Next to God, Pikku was their only happiness on earth. They should have made gold-embroidered velvet pants for him. As he sat in the corner of the cottage eating a sandwich, he did not think anymore of the humiliation.

Sometime later on the dusty road there was a man who was driving twelve horses hitched to a gold carriage. Everyone who gathered nearby admired him, and they commented about the wonderful things he did. He was dressed from top to toe in silver and brass. The people observed the tall man carrying a birch bark knapsack filled with silver coins and licorice pieces on his back, which he threw to the children on the road.

Pikku Matti heard about this event, and immediately he wanted to be with the other village children. However, he often sat alone and preferred to be with the family's pigs.

"Grandmother, never in all the world do I want yours or anyone else's skirt! I want Grandfather's dress pants!" shouted Pikku Matti whose face was as red as a raspberry at the recalling of the disgrace and embarrassment he suffered with that piece of clothing.

"Put Grandfather's pants on, and let me see how they look on you," Grandmother said. Pikku Matti could not have been happier! He flew like a cat up on the ladder so that Grandfather could hardly follow him.

The man on the road had a large green painted wooden chest. It has always been an object of Pikku's admiration. The first thing to be seen with Pikku's little eyes was a large saber with a glistening sheath.

"I would like to have that!" he shouted.

Grandfather nodded and responded, "You can have the saber while I get the uniform out of the chest." Grandfather patted Pikku kindly on the cheek saying, "When you are a man, you will be able to carry a sword and fight for your native country. Would you like to do that, Pikku?"

Facing his grandfather he said, "I want to take revenge on those who teased me."

"No, no, Pikku, they were not cruel to you. You now have trousers with a waistcoat," Grandfather reminded Pikku.

"Yes, Grandfather, with a saber and hat."

"You will get it on one condition. Do not go to the gate by the road when the tall man comes," Grandfather reminded him.

"Yes Grandfather," Pikku answered.

Quickly Grandfather and Pikku descended the steps from the attic as a snowstorm came beating on the road. The county sheriff was seen, and people said it was unusual. Grandfather's trousers dragged on Pikku Matti with the suit sleeves hanging down and the tails sweeping the floor. Grandmother folded and pinned up the arms and tails with sewing needles. The suit was heavy, and Pikku looked like a dwarf in it.

He thought this was unnecessary fuss. The large soldier's hat was piled on top of his head that had fallen down over his shoulders. The heavy saber hung on his back, and the little rider was ready. Never had a hero been so proud from a battle as Pikku Matti when he wore trousers for the first time. His small, roundish shape disappeared in the oversized clothes as one looked at his blue eyes, the rosy cheeks, and the pug nose looking out from the narrow, small space between the dress suit and hat. Reader, can you picture Pikku in your mind's eye?

Looking so magnificent and well equipped, he marched as one heard the sword clatter on the small stones. The hat leaned to the left, and all the knights were ready for his leadership. It was not very long before the older folks laughed, especially Grandfather. He swerved the little one around, kissed him on the nose and said, "God bless you, little Pikku. You will never be a worse man even if you wear the old bear bourgeois uniform."

"At-ten-tion!" ordered Grandfather. "When the country gentleman comes, you will salute him like this." He taught Pikku to stand erect and self-assured like a stick with his left arm alongside and his right hand at the forehead, saluting.

Quickly Pikku stood at the gate post before the tall man came driving so that the wheels emitted sparks over the stones. The man was almost near . . . in a flash he came so quickly!

Then Pikku placed his left arm straight down and the right hand was at his forehead, saluting. Then one heard the driver suddenly pull on the horse's reins with a *ptrrroh!* Immediately he shouted, "Raise the gate quickly!"

A man placed himself at attention by the gate as a reminder that everyone should go by properly. The gate flew open on a given command that gave the tall man an advantage while giving orders on the road. When the carriage approached like lightning speed, everyone bowed correctly, and a plump Pikku stood at attention. The farm foreman who guarded the gate was so puzzled he did not think to open it without the head foreman's order to unlock it correctly.

The carriage was forced to stop, the tall man looked surprised, and the driver quickly shouted, "Open the gate!" Pikku opened it and saluted perfectly as Grandfather had shown him, almost as when a trained puppy is taught to sit. The driver cracked the whip, the horses whinnied, and subsequently the man in the carriage shouted, "Keep quiet!"

"Who are you in a bourgeois uniform?" shouted the tall man to Pikku Matti. The tall man laughed so heartily that the carriage shook! Pikku did not notice anything. He only thought what Grandfather said to him and saluted correctly. This amused the tall man more as he asked about the boy's parents.

The sheriff told how the boy was a fatherless and motherless lad who lived with his grandfather, a shabby-looking, miserable, poor, and blind soldier by the name of Hugg, along with his grandmother. The sheriff said this in a contemptible tone of voice, which he used sometimes when a person of authority speaks of a pauper or beggar in the company of others. Stepping out of the carriage, the tall man proceeded to the summer cottage.

Grandmother was frightened, and she almost fell off the chair when the haughty sheriff stepped inside. Grandfather now had more courage and showed courtesy by offering the sheriff a bench on which to sit.

"God's peace, my friends," the tall man greeted the older man cordially and shook his hand.

"I am pleased to meet you again, my friend," continued Grandfather.

"Aren't you Hugg from my former business?" asked the tall man.

"I am, Mr. Captain," responded Grandfather with a great deal of surprise because he recognized the tall man's voice.

Recognizing the grandfather, the country gentleman said, "It is amazing that I, who am so forgetful, recognized you. Do you remember in the greatest battle you placed me on your shoulders and waded over the stream when I was wounded, unconscious, and almost fell into enemy hands? Perhaps you have forgotten, but I have not. After a period of peacefulness, I searched for you at length and finally concluded you were dead. Now I have found your family!" The land master lifted Pikku Matti from under his arms and kissed him so energetically that his huge hat fell off. The sword clanked and all of Grandmother's sewing needles came loose from Pikku's suit jacket and pants.

"Leave me alone! You made the hat to fall on the floor, and Grandfather is upset!" Pikku shouted to the land master.

Totally embarrassed by Pikku's behavior, Grandmother defended her grandson by saying, "Do not take my grandson's behavior personally, as he usually does not socialize with others."

The land master responded, "Grandfather will get a better hat, and you, dear grandmother, are unconcerned about the boy's little mouth. Listen Pikku, you see me on the outside, and in time you will be a strong man. Do you want to be a brave soldier like your grandfather has been?"

"Grandfather says the time will come when I will be a brave soldier," Pikku answered.

"You are like a rock which has courage," the land master observed.

"Captain, for the first time I am wearing long pants and courage follows," Pikku added.

The land master noted, "Courage follows with the uniform because there is a lot of honor left in it. Such memories are passed from generation to generation. You will be strong as a bear when your arm reaches full length. Will you follow with me, eat soft bread, and drink milk every day? Perhaps from time to time there will be some licorice and kringlor (twisted biscuit), if you are good," said the man, smiling.

"Will I get a horse to ride?" asked Pikku.

"Yes, of course," responded the land master.

He wondered about his conversation with the land master. His small blue eyes flew from him to Grandfather, from Grandfather to Grandmother, and from Grandmother back to the land master. Pikku crept behind the old ones' backs and said, "I want to stay with my grandparents."

The old, blind soldier said in agreement, "Dear Pikku, with us you get only hard bread, water, and soft salt. Didn't you hear the gracious land master wants you to have soft bread, milk, and other foods? You will even get a horse to ride!"

"I want to be with you, Grandfather; I will not leave you!" shouted Pikku Matti, choking back tears.

"You are a good boy," said the land master also with tears in his eyes and patted the little boy's red cheeks. "Stay with Grandfather and Grandmother. Visit me when you become a good man in the world. I will give you earth to plow, the forest to cut, and you will be a farmer or a soldier. Either way you will be an honorable and faithful person for your country. Right, Pikku?"

"Yes," responded the boy, standing erect, steady and ready.

"God bless you child!" said Grandfather and Grandmother whose hearts were touched.

"God bless our dear country and give it many such loyal sons, like you, little Pikku," continued the land master. Many cease from eating the coarse hard bread, and they eat soft biscuits. Then they will know God and their conscience.

"Like it says in the ABC book," remembered Pikku Matti.

"Yes, but it's not in everyone's heart," answered the land master.

The key to societal stability is reverence and respect for parents and their authority. Exodus 20:12 says, "Honor your father and your mother, that your days may be prolonged in the land which the LORD your God gives you."

How the Forest's Small Children Taught Themselves to Read

Hur skogens små barn lärde sig läsa

 forest fire had burned all the old trees leaving a desolate area. As far as the eye could see, about a mile in each direction, one saw nothing but rough stones and dark tree stubs. The main road went through the forested area that was not at all scary. People saw the whole waste filled with strange trolls who stretched out their bony arms with horses' heads, horns, and six legs like flies. One also saw oddly shaped stumps in the deep darkness.

The only tree spared from the fire was a very tall, old pine. The fire singed it a little at the roots. It stood there alone like a king without subjects, and his kingdom was all a large waste. What should the pine do with stumps and stones surrounding it? I will tell you.

There was a little house almost entirely in the road. It had been built when the forest was all green. Now the cottage stood alone and looked at the pine, and the pine looked at the stuga. After all, one must have some association or connection in this world.

In the little house, lived a poor woman with her granddaughter, whose name was Esther. In the whole wide world, they had no other relatives. Esther seldom saw anyone other than her grandmother and an old peasant man, who used to deliver flour, salt, and flax for the elderly as he passed by in his wagon. In exchange the grandmother gave him the most beautiful white yarn she had spun on her spinning wheel.

The grandmother and her granddaughter noticed thirsty, small children in the summer as they traveled in the wagon. When the wagon stopped, the children jumped out, and they asked for a bowl of fresh water. It was like the main road's wine because it flowed as clear as crystal out of the mountain king's spring near the old Norway pine. Esther was paid a copper coin even though she didn't ask for it. She thought God had given the clear water for nothing.

One day in July, a wagon stood on the road, and a man stepped out, leading a little boy by the hand. "May Ahasuerus have a drink? He is thirsty," he asked.

"Esther, get water out of the spring!" Grandmother asked her granddaughter.

"Is her name Esther?" asked the traveling man.

"Yes sir, she is named after Esther in the Bible," responded the old woman.

"Is the boy's name Ahasuerus?" the woman asked the gentleman.

"Yes, his name is from King Ahasuerus who took Esther to be his wife. My boy might become a king over a large kingdom." Upon returning with the water, the gentleman gave Esther a coin as she bowed in thanks. She had never seen gold and did not know what the gold metal meant, which was so heavy, even though the coin was so small.

"You are a kind girl, Esther. Some day will you marry my son, Ahasuerus?" asked the strange man.

Esther curtsied again. No man had asked her to marry his son.

"Will you be his bride?" the stranger asked again.

"Thanks," she responded humbly. She did not understand completely what he meant. The strange man laughed and patted the girl kindly on her long, blond hair.

"How can you live so alone here in this disgusting desert waste?" he asked Esther's grandmother.

"Some time ago when we moved here, there was a large green forest, and I tied up all the nicest birch and willow roots to weave baskets. One summer night a peasant on the road made a fire while we slept. The dreadful fire and smoke went out of control for three weeks in the large forest, and no one could extinguish it. Everything was so blackened and deserted as you now see it. I was poverty-stricken, so where could I go? Here I had at least a roof over my head," Grandmother answered.

"Why didn't the fire burn your stuga when the flames surrounded you?" asked the man.

"Listen. God's four white angels stood at each of the four corners of the house and woke me so that not one spark fell on it. I did not see the angels, but Esther saw them, and I am sure they protected my little cottage for her sake. I am a poor person, and my little Esther is as innocent as the angels themselves."

The strange man was totally serious and deep in thought. Finally he said, "Dear mother, will you take care of my Ahasuerus for one year? I am wealthy, and Ahasuerus is somewhat spoiled. It would be wonderful if he could spend a little bit of time with you poor, God-fearing people. I must travel to a foreign country on business, and I cannot take my son with me. When summer comes, I will return to get him and bring you a roll of cloth for payment."

The older woman agreed to care for Ahasuerus, even though it astonished her that the man would leave his son with a stranger. The father patted her on the shoulder and said, "Take good care of the boy, and do not deny him anything; however, do not spoil him. God bless you. Good-bye my boy, and be kind toward the woman and Esther. We will see each other next summer!" With this he stepped in the carriage and began his journey.

At first little Ahasuerus was so surprised that his father left him with strange people; however, he did not say a word. When the carriage rolled away and he was alone with the unfamiliar people, he began to cry as he ran after the wagon. When Esther and her grandmother followed Ahasuerus to bring him back, he hit and kicked Esther and the woman. After running so hard after his father, Ahasuerus was tired, and he fell asleep on the grassy hillock near the road. Then the older woman took him to her humble home. Upon arriving to the cottage, he continually cried for sugar bread, and finally he fell asleep until the following morning.

In less than three weeks, five-year-old Ahasuerus soon forgot the carriage, the horses, begging for sugar bread, and his continual shouting. He was a little obedient boy whose behavior improved

Four-year-old Esther and little Ahasuerus played well together. Esther led her friend to the old pine tree that she called Gröningen because it was the only green tree in the desert-like waste both winter and summer. There the children found water from the huge mountain spring, the castle, and the garden of stones. They brought the burned greens and tree trunks home to the stuga to use for wood. When they were dirty from the soot, they washed their clothes.

Ahasuerus worked hard for Esther's grandmother. At summer's end he and Esther picked lingonberries from among the stones. In the fall the children were given turnips from an old peasant man who ground flour. In the winter they built a snow castle and Ahasuerus taught himself to carve a bow and arrow for hunting. Pulling on Grandmother's goats, he commanded, "Male goats, bow! Bow low so you get your sugar!"

When spring came the snow melted away from the rough rocks. The dark stumps, Gröningen's dark branches, and the mountain king springs began to murmur between the stones. Other plants stuck out like straw in the bare wasteland. The wind blew the birch, ash, and mountain ash seeds, which took root in the burned ground. The children thought the land was much greener in spring than in summer.

Summer came and the old woman began to wait for the strange man to return. However, summer, fall, winter, and spring came and went. Ahasuerus' father was still gone one year after the other. Grandmother was older, the children were bigger, and still the strange man did not return. Fortunately, Grandmother had most of the strange man's polished coins because she needed the money to spin cloth on her loom and sew clothes for she and the children. She taught them to read the Bible, and they grew like two healthy beautiful flowers in the wilderness.

The wasteland continued to change, and God's blessings shone like the sunshine everywhere. Everything before was dark, desolate, and devastated. The small trees had taken root from the wind blowing, and they were growing tall. A young forest arose with equally tall peaks as high as the eye could see. Gröningen was pleasant again.

When the wind sighed in its dark crown, someone heard it say to the small tree, "It is right of you, child, to grow up under God's gentle sun! Grow straight and tall to achieve honor."

The small trees heard this and grew quickly with delight. The birds began to sing in their delicate tree pinnacles.

Esther and Ahasuerus enjoyed playing school in the trees, and they read their Bible in the midst of the young forest. The woods heard them and began to whistle with its leaves like a thousand tongues. As the children increased their reading skills, the forest sighed even more.

Esther and Ahasuerus were content as they kept the Bible on their knee, and in front of them lay another book about God's nature. They learned a lot about creation through reading his Word. The trees were so hardworking, the small flowers nodded happily, the birds sang beautiful psalms both morning and night, old Gröningen heard meditatively, and the grimy rocks thought silently.

The strange man still did not return. Ahasuerus who was now a big boy went to school in the city; however, he did not like being away from Esther, Grandmother, and his beloved wilderness. A year passed, and he called himself Ödeman since he was used to being in the wilderness. He was now twenty years old when something remarkable happened.

One beautiful summer day exactly fifteen years from the beginning of this tale, came an old man traveling on the main road through the former wasteland. In astonishment he looked around and observed everything was different and more beautiful than before. The young forest was green everywhere with the little cottage in the distance between the tree leaves' branches. He walked with trembling steps toward the house.

Esther, now a tall beautiful girl, met him; however, he did not know her. She took the old man to her grandmother who now was quite old, gray, and blind. Grandmother sat next to the fireplace as the strange man began to ask questions of his son, Ahasuerus, and where he lived. Then he pulled out a big silk handkerchief from his pocket to wipe the sweat from his forehead.

The old woman understood it was the father who came to get her dear boy, and she began to cry so hard that she could not answer. She said Ahasuerus had gone into the woods hunting, and he would return soon.

The stranger was Ahasuerus' father who was a businessman. He traveled a long way to a foreign land on the other side of the earth and had fallen into pirates' hands and was held captive. He could not come back before now when he finally was set free. While he was away, he earned a lot of money, and he intended to live in peace with his large sum. With tears in her eyes, Esther kissed the strange man on the forehead, and thanked him for allowing Ahasuerus to live with them.

Soon Ahasuerus came home from hunting with a bag full of

black grouse and rabbits. One can imagine there was delight and astonishment when he unexpectedly found his lost father, whom he thought he would never see again.

The strange man stayed for three days in the cabin, and there was much thought about what he should do. Now you will hear the results.

That same summer the strange man bought the former wilderness. He hired more than one hundred workers who began to break boulders, dig a foundation, and build a house. The next year stood a large beautiful home that could well resemble a princely castle. Nearby was a small red painted stuga. Custodial workers who maintained the property lived there with their wives and children. In the large house, the strange man moved in first, followed by Grandmother, Ahasuerus, and Esther, who now were man and wife. Everything was much warmer, better, and more comfortable than before.

Ahasuerus was now the king over the large wilderness realm. However, this wasteland was now blooming with oaks, meadows, and villages that gave joy to the wanderer's eye. Old Gröningen changed from being sullen and gray to the beautiful Mountain King spring, with a young, green forest that grew up with Esther and Ahasuerus.

So stands God's large book opened for us in the summer's greenery. His holy Word stands written not only in the Bible, but even in the trees' leaves, in the spring's clear water, in the lake's small waves, and in the heaven's sailing clouds.

The Tailor Who Joined Finland with Sweden

Skräddaren som tråcklade hop Finland med Sverige

 ikka was the competent village tailor who sewed buttons onto clothing. He was a decent, industrious, well-behaved, and levelheaded young man. One could not wish for a better tailor. He was the smallest man in the village; so small that he barely reached to Pietari's knife belt and weighed as much as the farm dog. He was an honest and good-natured person who laughed when one told a joke. However, there were those who had other thoughts about him.

There were two people who were not patient with Tikka. The first person was Harjus Mårten, a strong man who had at one time accused Tikka of stealing two homespun pieces of cloth that was to have been a jacket for Mårten. Nikku, the violinist, also was impatient with Tikka. He wanted to be the village's master of music rather than Tikka, who played the harmonica.

Tikka bought his instrument in the city for three coins. He taught himself to play by ear as he listened to ballads and dance music while the village boys rolled a wheel on the main road on

Sunday afternoons. From time to time, he was also seen sitting on the tall stumps near the beach, playing and singing near the juniper bushes while the Wittalatorpare red rooster spread out its wings as if to fly.

One summer evening at the age of thirty, Tikka sat and played for the Wittala village girls. They admired him because he treated them kindly. He had two women he could marry; either the shorter woman or the taller woman in the village. I will tell you what happened.

Wittalas' small, brown-eyed, kind Maju was the shortest woman. She was not taller than Tikka himself. They had been good friends since she was seven years old when he sewed her a Sami doll with a vivid red skirt and silk hat.

Light-haired Nilla was the tallest woman in the village. When Tikka stood straight, he was able to touch the hem of Nilla's apron. They had been good friends for a long time. He had saved five hundred marks by sewing with his quick tailoring needles, so he could now support a wife. Why should he not marry?

Tikka made his choice, and he decided to propose to wealthy Nilla because she was someone of whom he could be proud. One Sunday morning a friend of Tikka's arrived at Leivonmäki's cottage. Nikku, the violinist, owed Tikka thirty marks for the new homespun jacket Tikka made for Nikku. Then Tikka gave a long lofty speech as others listened.

At the conclusion of the presentation, Tikka tapped his pipe on the fireplace, laughed heartily, and announced he would propose to tall Nilla.

Tikka did not want to be rejected, so he went to Nilla and discussed the possibility of marriage. She looked at him like a church tower looks down on a haystack. Nilla patted him on the shoulder like he was a little boy.

Tikka asked, "What would you like from me as a sign that I am serious about my proposal and marriage to you?"

"Everything!" she answered. "I need a soft fox skin rug when I go to church. Go out into the forest and hunt fourteen foxes, sew me a good skin rug, and I will think about it."

Tikka was quick. He took out the scissors and set the bait. In a short time he caught fourteen foxes, sewed a rug from them and took it to Nilla.

"That is good. Now I need a very thick bride's comforter. It must be extra fine with brilliant bird feathers. Capture three hundred woodpeckers because your name, Tikka, means woodpecker. Sew their tail feathers to the quilt, and I will think about things," Nilla requested.

Tikka hunted and caught three hundred woodpeckers, sewed their tail feathers to the long pile blanket, and gave it to Nilla.

"This is not too bad," observed Nilla. "You understand I must dress myself well when I am a bride. Look for pearl oysters on the oars and make me an authentic two strand pearl necklace, and I will think about things."

Tikka looked at Nilla like a haystack looks up to the church steeple. He thought about her request because this demand was more challenging than previously, and he proceeded at any cost.

For two summers the small tailor disappeared from the village. He was as slippery as an eel on oars in mud. He searched like a gold-digger through the lake's sandy bottom, and finally he had collected the authentic pearls that would be enough for a double strand around Nilla's neck.

"What do you think of this?" he asked Nilla.

She lifted the pearl necklace into her hand, placed it around her neck, and finally answered, "Now I will ask father."

Nilla and her father, the innkeeper at Anttil, discussed how they should respond to the unrefined tailor. The innkeeper asked, "Tikka, you are not just an ordinary man because you are a persevering person who can accomplish big things. I have a married sister in Sweden, and I need to hear how she is doing. Since you are a quick tailor perhaps you can connect Finland with Sweden across the Gulf of Bothnia. Then I will be able to speak with her without making the troublesome trip. Perhaps I will consider giving Nilla to you as your wife."

Tikka considered the challenge, clenched his teeth like a haystack looking up at the church steeple, and answered that he wanted to make the attempt.

He did not waste time arranging his plan. He went to all the elderly women in the village and asked if they would spin several huge bundles of fishing line. The women spun and spun the whole winter. Finally they had spun so much fishing line that no boat could carry it all and Tikka needed to charter a ketch.

One beautiful summer morning Tikka tied each end of his long fishing line to a pine tree on the coast of Finland and Sweden. Certainly no one would go to all this useless trouble tying the fishing line and, in addition, buying fifteen thousand salmon hooks and Baltic herring for bait! His long line and bait should give a good miraculous draft of fish.

Tikka sailed out with his ketch and laid out his long line. The weather was pleasant, and the whole week was as cool as a cucumber on an otherwise stormy sea. He tried so hard to unite Sweden and Finland. However, on some days he caught other things on his long pine tree line. During the journey back he occasionally used his long line to catch many salmon, flounder, pike, perch, and bullheads. There was a big fish market in Björeborg where Tikka brought his vast catch.

Then he went to Anttila's landlord and said, "Hello, father-in-law. I have joined Finland with Sweden. Now give me your daughter, Nilla, as a housewife!" Anttila's landlord was a little astonished and somewhat hesitant.

"It is good you linked us with Sweden, but there is still something lacking. May I ask your long line how my sister is?" Antilla asked.

"What is her name? Where does she live?" Tikka questioned.

"My sister, Mrs. Olsson, lives in the city of Öregrund located on the opposite side of the sea. Set out a hook for her and perhaps she will bite on the long line," suggested the landlord.

"If I bind Finland together with Sweden, then you can ask how your sister is. Perhaps I will get an answer to the question about having Nilla for a housewife," Tikka continued.

"It will be Mikael's Sunday next week," Antilla reminded Tikka with a contented grin. He was now certain how to lure or entice the tailor.

Tikka asked Nilla's father about having some people witness the engagement.

"Invite twenty people if you want," said Anttila. "The cottage will be full of members who will come from the church, including Harjus Mårten, a man who is also looking for a wife."

Harjus Mårten had an eye for Nilla, and he said to Nikku the fiddler, "Let us watch when Tikka comes to propose to Nilla on Mikael's Sunday. Then I will take her to the middle of the room while you play the wedding march." Reader, you understand Nikku wanted to play a funny trick, and Tikka's enemies stopped at the cottage to meet at the appointed time.

Tikka went into the pasture and thought about what he should do. He heard someone speak about a new device called a telegraph where people could converse at long distances through a wire. If he could lay a piece of wire over to Sweden, he had won the task. "Nothing was impossible for me, a courageous tailor, who joined two countries with a fishing line with just one stitch too!" Tikka thought to himself.

Tikka traveled to Åbo, Björneborg, and Raumo to ask all the tailors he met what a telegraph was. Some tailors said, "The telegraph must have a hollow pipe."

Some answered, "It is a piece of witchcraft."

Others responded, "It is a dark ball that one raises up on a pole."

(During this period of history when an Englishman came here

as an enemy on his ship, one would hoist up a dark sign on a pole along the coast to signal the enemy's arrival.)

Tikka traveled farther and finally came to Nystad, and asked his tailor friends what he should do.

One of them answered, "Go to the harbor because there is a steamship leaving in the morning with a telegraph on board."

Tikka went to the port where he saw the steamship with a large wheel and a taped copper wire which men prepared before going out into the harbor.

"May I travel with you?" asked Tikka.

The captain of the steamboat happened to be in a cheerful mood as he looked at the thin tailor and answered, "I think you are able to float to the wire like a cork."

"I am a tailor, and at one time I linked Finland and Sweden," answered Tikka.

"Great! Follow me, and you will be able to do a lot of work again," continued the captain.

Tikka followed the vessel and unwound the wire. The steamship steered out west in smooth weather with high waves now and then. Light telegraph wires extended from the wheels down into the harbor. It was not easy work because a capable and skillful tailor like Tikka was needed. The boat went forward slowly and gently. Occasionally storms came, and rolls of wire cracked from the heat and almost tore off. Tikka was tireless as he took the opportunity to use his tailor-making skills. It went as smooth as an English sewing needle going through a shirt lining. Sweden was so firmly sewn together with Finland under the harbor that the stitching continues to this day.

"It was a good thing we had the strong tailor with us," observed the steamer's captain. "What do you want for payment?" he continued.

"My only reward is to be the first one to telegraph from Nystad to Öregrund," replied Tikka.

"Granted, one such modest request cannot be refused," the captain said.

Tikka went to the port where he saw the steamship with a large wheel and taped copper wire that men prepared before going out into the harbor.

The captain ordered the steamboat be returned to Nystad. Tikka telegraphed the following message: "The innkeeper at Anttila asked how his sister, Mrs. Olsson, is getting along in Öregrund."

After a while came the response, "Mrs. Olsson greets and thanks you. Recently a salmon bone caught in her throat, and she just returned from the doctor. She is now better and has invited Mrs. Rörstrand for coffee."

"Give me the document, and I will attach it to the telegraph," requested Tikka.

The certificate was received and Tikka sauntered back to Kartanonkyla. As he passed Wittala's summer cottage, Maju was washing herself in a milk dish. She looked so industrious, cheerful, elegant, and delightful, with warm kind eyes in her less than acceptable attire.

Dusty and sweaty, Tikka was seen walking on the road. Running out to him, Maju asked, "You look so tired! Do you want some milk to make you feel better?" Maju ran to get the shiny pot with the refreshing milk. "From where have you come?" she asked.

"I have come from Nystad, and the connection between Finland with Sweden is completed. The announcement of our forthcoming marriage will take place on Sunday with Nilla from Anttila," Tikka announced.

Maju sighed and answered, "I know and good luck, dear Tikka. You will get a rich bride."

"Maju, if someone planned to propose to you, would you want a fox skin, a long-pile rug made with bird tails, and a necklace of authentic pearls from your fiancé?" asked Tikka.

"What would I do with all the frills?" Maju questioned.

"If someone should propose to you, Maju, would your mother send him out into the world as a fool to weave together the grand duchy kingdom?" questioned Tikka.

Maju laughed. "Mother would tell him to make himself presentable," she said with flippant humor, alluding to Tikka's less than acceptable appearance after the long trek.

"Good-bye, Maju!"

"Good-bye, Tikka! Good luck!"

Tikka went to his lonely stuga where he did not sleep a wink because of his forthcoming proposal. The next morning was Mikael's Sunday. Dressed in proper clothing, Tikka put the certificate in his pocket and went to the Anttila farm.

Harjus Mårten and Nikku were there and the violin was ready for the bride's march. Everyone was happier than usual when Tikka played the suitor's number. Nilla was unhappy because her father wanted her to marry Harjus Mårten with whom she could not get along.

Tikka tread bravely into the cottage and shook hands with Nilla's father, Anttila the innkeeper. "Good morning, Father! I am here to seal the promise. All the church people are my witnesses that Nilla shall be my wife."

Anttila had a crafty facial expression as Nikku played the violin. "My sister in Öregrund has presumably bitten the hook, and she will see and hear how people are," Antilla noted.

Tikka took the telegram out of his pocket and read the following: "Mrs. Olsson greets and thanks you. She had a salmon bone caught in her throat and has just returned from the doctor. She is now much better and has invited Mrs. Rörstrand for coffee."

"What did you say?" shouted the red-faced Anttila, the innkeeper, who was annoyed. Nikku was forced to make a mistake as he played the violin because the fifth string broke. "Are you trying to make a fool of me?" asked Nikku.

"Here is my certificate," answered Tikka as he went in front of the railing with his document. Everyone crowded around him to see the remarkable piece. Yes, the certificate was quite correct, citing that so and so had the tailor, Tikka, weave together both countries with telegraph thread through the sea. Tikka and another person asked how Mrs. Olsson felt after the verified document, and they received the following response:

"The shrewd host from Anttila was caught in his own snare. He could not dispute his vow in front of so many witnesses. He must admit that Tikka owned claim to Nilla. Nikku hid the violin quickly under his arm and slipped away. Harjus Mårten declared strongly he did not intend to yield to the little woodpecker, Tikka, even though he could not read the document.

Nilla wanted to have a word with the tailor. The church tower looked down with the softest eyes on the haystack and the flagpole. The haystack might fall on Tikka's throat; however, Tikka took a step back and declared the following:

"Thank you very much, Anttila, for wanting to give your daughter, Nilla, to me as a housewife. However, I have been a fool for her and you. She is completely too tall for such a small man as me. Give her to someone better who can expand your business around the world! "Good-bye, Father! Good-bye, Nilla! Let us remain good friends," Tikka said as he departed.

Soon the haystack vanished from the wind, and the church steeple stood in its solitary grandeur. The congregation whispered and laughed a little which so angered Anttila that he tapped his best pipe in pieces on the side of the brick stove.

The whole village knew that Tikka proposed, but not everyone knew he had given his bride the basket. The week after Mikael's Sunday, many people wondered about the tailor's honesty while listening to the pronouncement. These persons included Tikka together with the crofter's daughter, who was the honest and virtuous Maju Wittala.

"Now it is hemp seed with hemp seed," said the people and nodded. No hemp seed and pinecone is suitable in the same bird's nest.

Tikka and Maju were a happy, industrious couple. They were the same height, for neither one had to physically bend down to the other. The old dilapidated stuga was repaired. When one saw Tikka and Maju, small and clever, skipping over to the church hill people were heard to say, "Just like children playing at their best!" Meanwhile Finland and Sweden gloriously slept together with the mountain in the north, Tikka's thread, and many other things.

The Troll's Christmas
Trollens jul

ne Christmas Eve there was a beautiful faintly lit house on the corner by the street. In a corner burned a large Christmas tree with brilliant stars, sweets, apples, and lit boughs. The children were kept quiet when someone or something rustled in the hallway.

The Christmas goat arrived and asked as usual if the children were good. "Yes," they said.

"Is that right?" answered the Christmas goat. "Have the children been kind? This year I have only half as many Christmas presents to give them."

"Why is that?" asked the children.

"I came a long way from the north where I left the door open at many poor cottages. I have seen many small children who do not have even a piece of bread to eat for Christmas Eve. I have given half of my gifts to them. Don't you think it is right to do that?" the Christmas goat asked.

"Yes, yes, it is right and kind," shouted the children. At first Fredrik and Lotta were silent. On previous Christmases, Fredrik had received twenty gifts, and Lotta was given thirty presents. Now they were unhappy because they only received half the number of gifts as before.

"Don't you think I did the right thing?" questioned the goat again.

Then Fredrik spun around on his heels and answered curtly,

"Why are we having such a bad Christmas this year? The troll has a better Christmas than we are receiving!"

Now it was Lotta's turn to cry, and she said, "Will I only get fifteen presents? It's a much, much better Christmas in the evening with the troll!"

The Christmas goat replied, "Is that so? I will immediately take you into the forest." He took Fredrik and Lotta each by the hand as they trudged along with all their strength.

In a flash they went quickly and stood in the midst of the deep snowy trees. It was frighteningly cold, and the snow whirled so that one could hardly see the high fir tree branches, which stood in the darkness. All around in the forest one could hear the wolves howling. The Christmas goat went immediately away again and left the children in the forest. He had no time to wait as he looked for many kinder children than Fredrik and Lotta.

Both children began to wail and cry with several wolves surrounding them. "Come Lotta," said Fredrik. "We must try to find a little cottage in the woods."

"I think I see a little light over there between the trees. Let us go there," suggested Lotta.

"There isn't any light, only icicles shining in the darkness on the trees," answered Fredrik.

"I think I see a large mountain in front of us. Can it be Rastekais over there with Sampo Lappelill, the champion wolf, on Christmas Eve?"

"What do you think?" answered Fredrik. "Rastekais is about four hundred twenty miles from our home. Maybe we should climb up there where we can have a better look around."

It was no sooner said than done. They hiked through the high snowdrifts and over bushes and trees that had fallen over. Finally they came to the mountain. There was a little door through which was shown something like a light. Fredrik and Lotta went toward it and immediately noticed to their amazement, it was Rastekais the elf with the wolves peering through the door.

Fredrik and Lotta stopped in their astonishment because directly alongside the door was a large hall where thousands of small, agile, eighteen-inch trolls were seen dressed in gray wrinkled clothing, celebrating Christmas. They stood to read the saga about Sampo Lappelill. The trolls were not afraid of the darkness because they had almost frozen to death like a glowworm. The decayed tree stumps illuminated everything. Then they saw a large, sparkling, dark cat along the back of the mountain. Many elves shouted, "No, wait, wait! It is too light; we cannot stay out here!"

It was quite strange for all the trolls in the world to shun the light and feel ill at ease when someone got to see them as they were. The trolls celebrated at the big party because the days were shorter when it came to the year's end, and the nights were always longer. They always thought every Christmas would be only night and not day. In addition, they were very happy as they danced toward the mountain and celebrated Christmas with amusement in their own way. The trolls were mostly heathens; however, there was nothing better than Christmas.

Fredrik and Lotta noticed the trolls were not very cold. They treated each other with ice candies in the cold winter nights, and blew on them so the candies would not be too warm when they put the delicacies in their mouth. One of the small male trolls was seen mimicking the Christmas goat.

The gigantic, cruel, mountain king was not with the troll this year because ever since he emitted sparks at Enare's rectory, no one knew what happened to King Mundus. Many believed he moved to Spetsbergen to govern the pagan land and flee as far away as possible from Christians. The gigantic mountain king left his kingdom in the north because of King Mundus' evil spirit. In the midst of Rastekais sat King Mundus with the troll's queen at his side exchanging Christmas gifts.

King Mundus gave Queen Caro such a high pair of stilts that when she stood on them, she was the highest and finest woman in the whole world. Queen Caro gave king Mundus a pair of unusually large snuffers, which he blew and then extinguished. He was grateful for the gift.

While ruling, king Mundus revolted and courageously kept a number of trolls together and announced to them the light would soon end. Darkness would be forever over the entire land and trolls would rule the world. Suddenly the elves shouted, "Hurrah! Hurrah! For our great king, Mundus, our beautiful queen, Caro, for the evil, darkness, and everlasting kingdom!"

The king responded, "Where is my colonel spy whom I sent up to the pinnacle of the mountain to investigate some ray of light that was still left out in the world?"

The spies came and answered, "Master king, your power created complete darkness!"

After a while the king asked, "Where are my spies?" Soon thereafter they arrived.

Observing the heavens the troll stated, "Master king, far away a small streak of light like the stars, are twinkling when they come out from behind the dark cloud."

The king commanded, "Go back to the mountain peak and look for my spies!"

"The troll continued, "Lord king, heaven is overcast with heavy, snowy-like clouds, and I no longer see the sun."

The king answered, "Return to the mountain peak! Look for my spies!"

Soon the trembling, blind spies appeared, and they answered, "Master king, half of the cloud disappeared and a large, clear star, larger and clearer than all the other stars, shone in half of the heavens. We were so frightened and trembled that the sight of it made us blind!"

The king further questioned, "What does this mean?

All the trolls stood around in quietness and shook, with no one answering.

Finally, someone in the group said, "Lord king, two human

beings are standing at the door. Let us ask them if they know more than us."

The king answered, "Call Fredrik and Lotta."

The children appeared before the king with a fearful expression on their faces, thinking they had done something wrong. The queen noticed their uneasiness and said to one of the elf women who stood around the king's throne: "Give the children some dragon blood and some dung beetles to refresh themselves. They must open their mouths!"

"Eat and drink! Eat and drink!" said one of the elf women. With that the children had no desire at all to eat and drink.

Then the king said to the children, "It is in my power to transform you into crows or spiders. However, I will place a riddle before you first, and if you can guess it, I will allow you to go home without harm. What do you desire?"

"Yes, yes, what is the riddle?" asked Fredrik and Lotta.

"Well… what does it mean when the light streams up in the middle of the year's darkest night, when all the light is past, and the darkness and elves govern the world? A long time ago out east a star was seen, which sent a ray of light over all the other stars. It threatened my power with destruction. What did the star mean?" the king asked the children.

Lotta replied, "It is the star that arises on Christmas night over Bethlehem in Israel and shines over the whole world."

The king further questioned, "Why does it shine so brightly?"

Fredrik answered, "At night our Savior was born, and he is the light which lights up the whole world. In the night the light begins to increase and all the days in the year are longer."

The king began to violently tremble on his throne and said once again, "What is this light called who is both Lord and King who has come to save the world from the power of darkness?"

Both children replied, "Jesus Christ, God's Son."

No sooner was it said before the whole mountain began to shake and tremble, collapsing. A gale wind was blown through the big hall, and the king's throne was thrown. The stars shown over the darkest ravines, and all the trolls dispersed like shadows and smoke. Nothing was left, including the Christmas tree with ice on it. The angel voices began to resound like harps. The children covered their faces with their hands and did not dare look up. It fell over them like a sleep when someone is very tired. They certainly did not know what happened on the mountain.

They both lay in their bed sleeping, as the fire burned in the kakelugn or tiled stove. Kajsa, who always awakened them, stood beside the beds and called, "The sun is up, and we must get to church on time!"

Fredrik and Lotta awakened and looked at Kajsa with amazement. She stood eighteen inches tall and had a beard. The children noticed the coffee table was set with fresh Christmas buns and coffee they could drink on Christmas Day. People saw the beaming lights inside the sanctuary and heard the bells ring outside as they walked to church.

Fredrik and Lotta looked at each other and did not dare tell Kajsa they were with the trolls at Christmas. Perhaps she would not believe them, laughing and saying they had slept the whole night in their bed. You know, I know, and now you know I know. It was pleasant to know what you know, even if you know more than I know.

The elves' Christmas had magnificent lights with Bethlehem's star coming down, and it shown in all the children's eyes. Fredrik and Lotta certainly noticed it, but they dared not look up. Have they kept their promise? I do not know, but when you meet them you can ask.

The Boy Who Heard the Silent Speech

Gossen som hörde det tysta tala

nce upon a time, there was a boy with a hearing impairment whose name was Paavo. He often wished he had the skill to hear and speak, but he could not. He looked at other children move their lips as they understood each other, but Paavo used sign language. His father knew what Paavo said, his sister and brother understood him better, but mother understood him the best. The village children did not understand signing. They imitated and teased him with their hands.

Penttu was the worst taunter in the village. When Paavo saw the boys on the road, they bleated like a lamb, *bä bä*. The village children thought this was quite funny, but little Lisu did not. Wanting to express kindness to Paavo, Lisu invited him to her cottage and served him a bowl of soured whole milk. There were other ways people spoke with Paavo.

For example, Mother used sign language to communicate with her son telling him about God in heaven. "He is good toward all his created work, especially toward unhappy children," she said. Paavo knew God willingly would help those who are kind and make requests of him. Paavo observed when someone helped Father or Mother or when the person helping wanted payment for their work. Then Paavo thought to himself, "If I had something to give to God, then I would ask him to teach me to hear and speak."

Paavo was six years old and had never been in church. What would he do in God's house? He would not understand the minister's sermon, nor would he be able to hear the service and the hymns. One Christmas morning Mother thought it was not right that Paavo stay home alone and not attend Julotta, the early morning Christmas worship. "Do you wish to come along?" Mother asked.

"Yes," he replied excitedly. Certainly Paavo wanted to attend Julotta on Christmas morning. However, he wondered how he would place his money in the offering bag because he had never been to church before. He thought to himself, "I will watch the children put their ten penny in the collection bag." Mother forgot to tell him how the money should be spent. The ten-penny was a large, heavy coin much heavier than a five-penny. He thought the ten-penny was far too much money. Now he could pay God and the Lord will help him speak.

On the way to church Paavo wondered how he would talk to God and others. Perhaps he should ask, "Dear Lord, I want to hear and speak with other people. You are so good and wise. Will you help those who pray to you? Will you help me hear what the minister says? You will get paid for it, dear God, with a ten penny."

Then he thought again, "Certainly God must live in the church, but how will I get to speak to him when there are so many people? Will he understand when I sign with my hands?"

Paavo was worried because he could not ask other family members as it was dark, and they could not see him signing. He watched Father drive the quick horse, Vallacka, who wore bells that echoed in the mountains and hills. It was a half Swedish mile or five kilometers to the church, but the horse and wagon went like lightning on the main road. All the magnificent snowy birch and spruce trees seemed to run toward Paavo with the full moon alongside. When they arrived to church, many horses and sleighs stood outside. The doors opened, and it was completely lit inside looking like God's heavenly kingdom. A stream of people's breath went out from their mouths as if they were burning incense to the Lord.

After a while there was a large crowd, and Paavo became separated from his family. He was little and squeezed between all the people and then proceeded forward not knowing where. Soon he stood in the front and center of the altar where there was a white cloth, the burning lights, and the beautiful, large portrait showing the Savior on the cross. Behind the altar wreath stood the minister in his white alb or long vestment that was embroidered with gold. Paavo, poor lad, thought the minister was God. He went to the altar where he laid his coin on the altar wreath, and made the sign of the cross with his hands wishing so fervently to be loved by the Lord.

As the minister sang the liturgy and read the prayers, he did not notice Paavo. Seeing Paavo at the altar, Mother went forward and took him by the hand to sit with her in the pew. There was another person who looked at Paavo and understood his signing. It was the invisible Lord in heaven, who sees everything, and he certainly knew that Paavo did not understand better.

As Paavo sat beside his mother on the bench, he looked at the lights, the minister, the parishioners, the tall ceiling, and the beautiful pictures. Because he could not hear anything, he fell asleep on the bench. While he slept, God sent an angel to him in a dream. The angel spoke to Paavo not with words but with thoughts. He remembered when a good thought arises in one's heart, it is an angel who speaks.

The angel called, "Paavo!"

"Here I am," answered Paavo in the dream.

"God has heard your prayer. You will get to hear the silent speech and know that no one can pay God with money because He is rich and owns the whole world. When you leave the church, take your money from the altar and give it to the poor man sitting at the door. If you pay God a little for the goodness he has given, you will love Him more than anything else on earth. You need to obey His commandments, and be kind toward all people and animals. If one gives a coin to the needy from the goodness of their heart, he or she gives to God."

Just as Paavo awoke, the Julotta service was ended, and the congregation began to leave the church. Then Paavo remembered the angel's words and asked his mother if he could go before the altar. She thought he wanted to look at the beautiful portrait. However, Paavo took his ten penny out of the offering bag and instead gave it to the beggar at the door as the angel said.

When they left the church and sat in the sleigh, there were many people in a hurry. They believed if they drove past all the other sleighs on the way home on Christmas morning, they would have the tallest summer flax in the field. Many lashed their horses while Paavo heard the horses' say, "Why do you hit me? I am running the best I can!"

Paavo thought it was strange he understood the horses' language with his inside voice. However, he did not understand the gift he received—that is to hear the silent speech.

It was soon eight o'clock in the dark morning; the air was frosty, and the stars twinkled clearly in the heavens. Paavo's inside voice heard the most beautiful music as they traveled over the icy roads. It reminded him when the shepherds heard the angels singing on the first Christmas morning in Bethlehem. What could it be? Paavo did not know it then because he never heard music, but he understood it afterwards. It was the morning stars that sang and praised God.

The stars rang through the air coming through the heavens, bending down to earth on the snowy mountain, the frozen lake, all the trees in the forest, the squirrels in the spruce, and the tit mice on the fence. The sleigh slid like glass over an icy roof. All said to each other, "Hear how the stars praise God because salvation has come into the world! Let us sing our most beautiful praise song with them!"

Paavo heard this, but did he understand it? No, he was hungry. He only thought of the freshly baked Christmas biscuits that smelled so wonderful in the oven the day before. He wondered if he would get to eat a lot of pork for the Christmas dinner. When they came home, Mother fried yesterday's porridge for breakfast. Paavo heard the porridge say to the wooden spoon, "Do not eat all of it; leave some for Father!"

This amused Paavo because he understood it better than the morning stars' love song. He laughed so hard the porridge could barely stay on the spoon, and he signed to Mother, "The porridge says, 'Leave some for Father.'"

"This was wise of the hot cereal because Father is hungry also," replied Mother.

Paavo wanted to put the spoon in the bowl when he heard his inner voice saying, "Father got up so early and has driven you to church. How can you eat up his meager breakfast?"

Paavo was embarrassed and put the spoon away. He understood that he had almost done something wrong, but he did not quite understand who had warned him.

A little while later, Paavo became more aware to hear the silent speech. He heard the plough say to the stone on the field, "Make room so my patch of tilled ground will be fruitful!"

The willow bush said to the cloud, "Why are you hiding the sun? I cannot see out of my catkins."

The fence asked the Scotch pine beside him, "Loan me a stake because I may fall down."

The well warned the bucket, "If you push me aside, you may not be able to get up again."

The blue anemone reminded Paavo, "Be so kind, and do not trample me to death!"

The cranberry said to Paavo's hand, "You have picked enough of me. I am not so sour that you cannot make a little syrup from me."

His cap commanded him to…"Throw me in the brook so I can run away from you."

When it was summer, Paavo heard the grass on the meadow say, "Now I will really grow! Paavo's land is large and wide." Turning to the sun, grass continued, "Dear sun, read your evening prayer when you set in the horizon. Pray to God in the morning, and you will get to shine warmly, giving the greenery and the harvest to my beloved children!"

Paavo was so experienced with all of this he did not like to be thought of as being something wonderful at all. There were those who wondered about him when he heard his conscience speak. One time when he thought to do something negative, his conscience said, "It is wrong!" When he was obedient he humbled himself, and his conscience said, "It is right!"

At one time he wanted to lie, and then he heard his conscience cry. When others were good to him and he was ungrateful, he heard his quiet, inside voice sobbing. He could not stand to hear this. He must be truthful and good to everyone. He had no peace with that continual, everlasting voice which was a warning to either punish or approve of things he had done.

Paavo wondered if even other people heard their strange inside voice, that is, their conscience. He almost thought it was the same with everyone which lay so deeply hidden. One early spring day, an unusual event occurred.

Penttu threw a cat into the well and leaned forward looking down to the drowning animal. Then Penttu fell into the well and almost drowned. He was in a lot of trouble. With great difficulty, Paavo lowered the heavy bucket down to rescue Penttu and the cat in their utmost distress. This time Paavo thought he heard Penttu's conscience say, "Remember how often you teased the boy with a hearing loss, and now he has saved your life." In spite of everything, Paavo grew up to be a strong young lad.

One day God sent the minister to the village for the annual reading examination. He met Paavo, who was deaf. Soon a school for children who were hearing impaired was built in the city, and the minister sent Paavo there to be educated. He learned to read, write, and to better understand his heavenly Father. He believed he could speak to God with the ten penny. Paavo also learned to do carpentry and wood carving in the parish vicinity. No one in the area could carve such beautiful chairs and tables as Paavo. Everyone liked him because he was an honest person who always was compassionate and truthful. He praised God for this gift because the conscience is God's voice in a person's heart. This gift continued into his adult life.

Paavo and Lisu eventually married. Paavo had his own workshop, and he could never have a better wife than Lisu. They had two children, and were very happy together. Lisu usually said to the small boys when she served fried porridge, "Didn't you hear about the porridge talking to the spoon, 'Do not eat it all up; leave some for Father!'" Then Paavo laughed and signed to his family as his mother before had signed to him.

What more is there to say about Paavo? Well... when people sincerely ask something from God and pray in Jesus' name, as God's Word teaches us, so shall they always be certain God hears their prayers. God does not always grant us what we ask. Instead, he gives us something better. If a person is hearing impaired, they can ask the Lord to help them hear and speak. There are two large gifts God has given for all who receive them. We must thank and praise the Lord. God gave Paavo something better than hearing and speaking. He gave him the gift of listening to the silent speech that means one needs to constantly listen to one's conscience. Listen to the Lord's voice through his Word, the Bible.

In spite of his hearing impairment, Paavo learned to hear the woods, lakes, stars, and everything else in the world. This is not unusual because almost all children hear His creation. When you play with dolls, stones on the mountains, pine cones, sticks, rocks, snow, straw, and the unfamiliar, all are your sanctuary in the quietness of your heart.

Between the Sandwiches

Mellan smörgåsarna

other cleaned the hallway near the large table while Vick sat barefoot on a stool and ate a smörgås, or an open-faced sandwich. His wet muddy shoes were next to the kakelugn, or the tall tiled stove, as he waited for the sunrise while conversing with his mother.

"When I grow taller than you, Mother, we will ride in the carriage so your feet will not get wet on the road. Will you let me drive the carriage?" Vick asked.

"Yes, of course," she replied.

"I will build a golden castle for you with four windows, and I will pretend you are my little child. I will wash and comb your hair so you will be really nice," Vick added.

"But Vick I have already been little at one time in my life, and where were you then? You did not comb my hair, drive me in the carriage, or build a gold palace for me. How could you forget yourself? No, I did not see my boy then. He must have been in the woods picking berries."

"Mama, why didn't you look for me? Was I big then?"

"I don't know if you were big or small because I did not see you. I didn't know there was a Vick in the whole world. When I was little, I had a mother who cared for me like a china doll."

"When you grew taller was your mother little? Did you build a castle for her?" asked Vick.

"How could I build a castle when I am a girl? When I grew my mother was so little, and I did not see her anymore. I saw the vacant sofa where she usually sat when she held me in her arms. I saw her beautiful blue dress that hung in the closet, and her hymnbook that she usually carried to church. Her name was written in it with large letters. I could no longer feel her arms around my neck, her kiss on my forehead, and her warm eyes looking at me. I did not hear her read the evening prayer with me, "*Gud, som haver barnen kär...*" or, "God, who loves the children dear ..."

"Did she leave you?" asked Vick.

"One day she slept and then died. No one has held me as she did," continued Mother.

"Oh, no. Do you remember the tale of Robinson and Sampo Lappelill who cared for a wolf? When you grow up, you too will marry and have a wife to care for; then you can build her a gold castle!" Mother said.

Vick's thoughts went in circles that were heard in the forest and echoed back exactly at the same place where they began. "When I am big, I will sail to Africa and shoot all the tigers and snakes. I will let the lions live because they will be my sporting dogs. I will build a stall as big as a church for all the animals. The elephants will be my horses, and I will ride them so they will trample down the forest like grass. Have you ridden on an elephant, Mother?"

Mother answered, "No, I haven't. Why don't you ride a horse?"

"I would rather ride an elephant and destroy all robbers, wolves, and Turks," Vick stated.

"No, no, that is not the way we treat animals and people! You should send the Turks to school to become Christians," Mother urged Vick.

"When will I go to school, Mama?" he questioned.

"When you have learned all the letters of the alphabet," Mother reminded him.

"I already know A, B, D. I can count to fourteen. One, two, three, five, six, thirteen, fourteen," Vick responded.

"What kind of work would you like to do when you grow up?" asked Mother.

"I would like to be a prince, a minister, a bourgeois, a farmer, a beggar, or a vagrant. Sit down, Mama. Would you like a sandwich?" asked Vick.

"Yes, please. What work interests you?" Mother asked again.

"I want to be a king because we have such little butter for the bread," he observed.

"Be satisfied with little! Why do you want to be a king?" Mother continued.

"Then I can do and have whatever I want," answered Vick.

"Is that so? Do you want me to tell you a tale?" asked Mother.

"Yes, Mama, a long story."

"I won't tell a long story this time. Well … one evening boys and girls were sitting on the meadow during a midsummer night. They decided to choose a king so they could do whatever they pleased. Some chose the lion as their king, but they thought the lion would eat them. Others wanted their king to be an eagle. Others thought the Christmas elf would be suitable as a king; however, how would he be suitable as a king on a midsummer night? Everyone was hungry, and they unanimously chose to give the open-faced sandwich to their king," Mama stated.

Vick looked very surprised, and he could not answer because he had a mouth full of food. "The sandwich was crying out to the king only in triumph around the meadow as it was being eaten. It was just as the king wanted because now he and his court could do as they pleased," Mama continued.

Vick knew Mama would tell a long story, and he was a little disappointed with the sandwich king saga. Mother continued with the following tale …

"I knew three young pine trees on the mountain top where they slept in the ravines. The pine trees were named Goldtop, Silvertop, and Woolytop. The stars had given the pine trees these names, and the cloud queen was their godmother. All three were happy, hoping they would be successful in this world. After a period of time, they grew quickly after having drunk the cloud queen's morning milk. The pine trees' hanging twigs looked down on the little people in the valley who thought the pine trees were quite elegant.

"One evening the north wind drove the cloud queen's carriage over the mountain, and the horse's harness became entangled in the three bushy pine trees' crowns, which hung over the road on which the queen was traveling. One would have thought there was a sort of being on the mountain!" The juniper bush twigs observed as they clung to the pine tree's branches.

The wind howled, the moon cried, and the juniper bush twigs said to the crowberry, "Nowadays one sees the young trees along the edge as if they were following us. Hurry neighbor, run to the tailor and borrow a pair of scissors so I can cut the pine's tall head!"

"Out of the way, you creep! I will help myself!" shouted the north wind. He blew so hard at the three pine trees' crowns, enabling him to drive his horses in the right direction. However, Goldtop, Silvertop, and Woolytop stood embarrassed.

"Courage boys!" shouted the Cloud Queen to the horses when the north wind galloped away with her. "Everyone shall get to choose what he or she will be in the world."

Believe the king's word! The three pines continued to drink the cloud's water and sip on the mountains' nutrients. Soon their crowns' branches became more mature and leafier than before. This allowed the eagles to build a nest in the high pines. The thunder thought about recharging its cannons. The stars heard the Cloud Queen's word about courage and were curious to know what the three pines wanted to be when they grew taller.

As the west wind drooped its wings to the mountain, it said, "Dear mountain, did you ask what the three pines intend to be when they mature?" The west wind shook the pines' crowns and sang:

> "Hulevi, cut in,
> seventy-seven kilometers past!
>
> What would Goldtop like to be?"
>
> "I would like to be the highest because the Moon Queen
> is my godmother," answered Goldtop. "Is that so?" answered
> the west wind.
>
> Hulevi, cut in, seventy-seven kilometers past! What would
> Silvertop like to be?
>
> "I want to be the biggest because I have grown out of the
> mountain," answered Silvertop.
>
> "Is that so?" answered the west wind. Hulevi, cut in, seventy-
> seven kilometers past!
>
> What would Woolytop like to be?"
>
> "I want to be the most hardworking
> because God has created me to
> benefit the world," Woolytop noted.
>
> The juniper twigs replied,
> "Those who live get to see."

Mother was quiet as if it was the end of the story.

"What does it mean?" asked Vick curiously.

Mama continued, "Earlier in my life, I traveled abroad. When I returned, I wanted to see my former friends, the pines, but only found their cut off stumps on the mountain. The sun shone high and low as before; the winds hopped like crows on the cliffs, and the clouds sailed quietly on the evening heavens. What in the world could have happened to Goldtop, Silvertop, and Woolytop?" Mother wondered.

The little, piercing juniper bush's voice was heard in the mountain slope, "Goldtop had the tallest spire with a rusty weather vane that constantly quarreled with the winds. One beautiful day the vane was angry toward the north wind, and the whole tower fell in minute pieces. Silvertop also fell and was now only three quarters of a meter high. The other eight trees surrounding Silvertop were then reduced to one-half of a meter because a ball came rolling down on the path hitting all eight trees. Near a shed, Woolytop stood to the left and shouted to the boy cone as loudly as he could; in order to get a little money, 'Hurrah! Hurrah! To our great king!' "

"And Woolytop? What became of him?" asked Vick.

"Woolytop was not the tallest but the healthiest," noted the juniper bush twigs. A roughly-hewn log wheel was needed for the axle at a large mill located by the rushing stream. There was nothing better in the whole forest than Woolytop because the large mill wheel turned around it. "I ground mill grain for people's bread," it said quietly and looked back very cautiously.

"Now the story has ended. What did you think about it?" questioned Mother.

"I would like to be as healthy as Woolytop because it has purpose in life. The mill wheel turned around it, and ground grain for bread," Vick noted. "I think I would like to be a miller, and you may live with me in the mill room," stated Vick to his mother.

"Will you build a golden castle for me?" asked Mother.

"Mother, the whole area will be beautiful when I build a golden castle near the mill," promised Vick.

How Scandinavia and Finland Became a Peninsula

Huru Skandinavien och Finland blefvo en halfö

 ave you ever been on a lush island look-
ing along the sea's flowering beach?
There are no storms, foam, or heat from
the sea but rather the bluest heaven
with the greenest landscape. It is the
place where I want to live, build a red
painted cottage, and anchor a white,
painted boat with a light blue sail in the
bay. It would be something to live and die
there with one's closest friends!

However, I choose to not live there because it takes a long
time to sail from one place to another. As long as it is a calm and
pleasant sea, I enjoy rowing. There is a story about this that came
from my grandparents and parents who heard it when they were
small. Others have remembered this tale about Florio and Unda
Marina. The story is as follows:

The pleasant island was called *Skandia* and was located in the
North Sea between the Atlantic Ocean in the west and Asia's
large mainland in the east. The Finnish people called the island,

Suomensaari, or Finland's Island. Between the island and Asia, there was a wide channel. Asia's king had a son named Delling, meaning aurora, and the king on the opposite side of the ocean had a daughter named Atalanta, meaning sunset glow. The two kings gave the pleasant island to Delling and Atalanta, so they could meet and play there undisturbed with shells and butterflies. At the red light of dawn (aurora), and the sunset glow (Atalanta), Delling and Atalanta met every season on this glorious island.

On the iceberg at the North Pole lived Dark Whale and White Whale. They saw Delling and Atalanta play on the pleasant island and felt envious in their dark hearts.

White Whale asked, "Why should these children be so fortunate? Why should they play above the northern or southern magnetic pole with butterflies, while we freeze on the iceberg?"

The envious Dark Whale blew darkness and cold over the beautiful island as if it was an iceberg. However, she did not have very much air in her black lungs to blow the whole summer away, succeeding only half way. She blew during the six months in winter, but the remaining six months were divided between spring, summer, and fall.

"What have you done?" asked White Whale sadly. "For three months the children will be lost in the darkness, and for six months they will see the hems of each other's clothing in the cloud without seeing one another. The last three months they will reunite and play as before on the sunny, happy island."

Dark Whale replied with her ice-cold ridicule, "Yes, why should I be so close-minded? I want to blow darkness everywhere so the children can play 'Hide and Seek' the year around."

White Whale thought this would be too difficult for them, so she comforted the children by singing a new ballad that blew to all the murmuring winds on the glorious island:

"Our lengthy island is the most beautiful
island in all of God's wide earth.
Its pleasantness is short, but its love is genuine as the whitest snow,
and it is the children's happy island."

Dark Whale heard the dancing ballad on all the waves' beaches. After hearing it for one thousand years, she thought it was boring and old. She proceeded to search for her father, Old Giant, in the earth's interior. The Swedes and Norwegians called the giant *Fornjoter,* and the Finns called him *Virokannas.* Dark Whale complained, and the wind and sea waves sang an improper ballad that kept her from sleeping on the iceberg. "Such a worn out ballad for pleasant children!" she said to herself.

"What will it say, fortunate children?" mumbled the giant in its mossy beard. He had never heard his children speak since the creation of the world!

"Children, one usually thinks all kinds of small blunders are like a constant trickle. Now jump on the two wretches on the glorious island," noted Dark Whale.

"Drive them away!" shouted the giant.

"I cannot, Father, because the island is theirs," replied the younger son.

"Surt!" called the giant.

Surt came. He was the giant's eldest son, the fire prince and blacksmith who had his forge in the volcano's crater.

"Go break apart the lovely island! Dark Whale, your sister does not get a good night's rest because of the foolish ballads."

Surt left and prepared a volcano under the pleasant island. Then he lit the opening and … ugh! There flew a little corner of the island out into the harbor, and it was called Iceland. However, the largest part of the island stood unmoved in its granite base.

Surt came back with the report that the beautiful island stood firm.

"What now?" the giant asked. "Your sister, White Whale, finally needs to get a good night's rest away from the silly ballads. Build a rampart and tower around the pleasant island so that no beast will crawl out of the ocean! I think that will be the end of all the ballads."

Surt went back and forged bricks from the mountain creating the delightful island. It was long laborious work, and the coal in his forge was gone before he finished his bricklaying.

Delling, the aurora or the red light of dawn, came in through the sound and Atalanta, the sunset glow, floated over the mountain in the west to play as before on the glorious island. Dark Whale, who was sitting on the iceberg constantly, heard the same romantic song and went with the dark night into the heart of his father in the nether regions of the underworld.

"Father, Surt has deceived you, and he has left a hole in the wall. The children swam to the island through the strait, and the romantic song keeps me from having a good night's rest," Dark Whale complained.

The giant answered, "Surt, you made a brick with a hole in the southeast. You have breathed your hoarseness with your wretched volcano. Go to Iceland, creep under Geyser, and cough out mud and sludge for one hundred years!" Surt fluttered away, and the giant called his other son Kare, the wind prince, who was as shrewd in his feebleness as Surt was foolish in his unruly power.

The giant continued, "Kare, the frogs swim through the sound to the beautiful island, and Dark Whale, your sister, does not get a good night's rest. Go fill the strait, the bricks, and the bridge with sand! If you are not more successful, then I will remove the feathers."

Kare flew off quickly and came to the broad side of the strait uniting the Arctic Ocean with the sea, which is now called the Finnish Sea. There Kare shook up the highest pines on the beach and measured the great strait's depth like one finds in Ladoga. "How will I build a bridge of sand over the length and breadth of this strait? No one is strong enough to pick up this mountain and heave it!" Kare thought to himself.

Being tired and perplexed, Kare sat hunched up in a crevice and observed two boys, Kase and Svase, who stood on each side of the sound. They played on the rocky ledge and threw smörgåsar or open-faced sandwiches over the water. Immediately Kare had an idea.

He said, "Kase, the whole world says Svase can throw a stone to Lofoten, but you cannot throw even to the middle of the sound!"

Kase was annoyed with Kare's accusation. Taking a rock from the cliff, he threw it into the middle of the strait.

"That's not too bad; maybe it was perhaps a stroke of luck," Kare remarked jokingly.

"A stroke of luck?" shouted Kase who was more provoked than anything and continued to throw rock after rock into the sound.

Kare went over on Svase's side and said to him, "Svase, the whole world says Kase can throw a stone to Jenisej, yet you cannot throw a stone to the middle of the channel!"

"What? Oh, can't I?" With that, he threw a stone to the middle of the strait.

"You were just lucky," joked Kare.

"A stroke of luck!" shouted Svase. Then he threw one stone after another like Kase into the sound. Kase and Svase competed for manhood's highest praise and threw all the rocks on the beach out to the channel. After they threw stone after stone equally as far, they were so tired that they could not lift even the smallest stones any more.

Then Kare noticed to his great delight there was a huge bank in the middle of the channel that he created. "Now I will begin my work," he said to himself.

Taking a deep breath, Kare jumped far out into the Arctic Ocean and breathed out the worst northerly storm he had ever seen. The waves rolled as high as the mountains, tearing down to the bottom of the sea and rolled the sand into the sound. There he gathered all the surrounding gravel and mud, widening out both sides. He built a wide, secure bridge between the main land in the east and the pleasant island. The strait no longer existed because the northern bay was the only remaining part and was called *Hvita hafvet,* or the White Sea. Lake Ladoga was in a bay to the south. The beautiful island united with the continent in the east and is now a peninsula.

Reader, this is only a saga telling about the beginning of time. In the midst of the sea and hovering heavy mist, people may have seen the island's blooming beach as they rowed and sailed, but the island was always far away.

Dark Whale and the old giant in the earth's interior thought they had always separated the aurora or light of dawn and the sunset glow, but they deceived themselves. The power of light and love is known to be dark for a while but never dies. For three months of the year, the two king's children could not see each other, but they continued to search. For six months they saw the red edges of each other's hem on the clothing over the mountain. They had renewed courage to look once more in the clouds, and finally they saw each other at midsummer.

There they met as in times past on the glorious island where the clouds' colors returned in rose and yellow, and the children sang again the old song which was so dear to them:

> *Our island is the most beautiful on God's vast earth.*
> *We yearn for it; however, its happiness is short-lived.*
> *Its love is as pure as the whitest snow*
> *and the children's island is the most glorious.*

The Holy Night
Den heliga natten

 e are all familiar with the red-clad bearded one known as Santa Claus. However, do you know about the Christmas goat? He was the children's good friend when his four feet bounded into the hall on Christmas Eve dressed in a bushy fur coat with his long beard. His horn was made from a wooden spoon, and his basket held the most delightful presents. His goal in the world was constantly to be on the go, go, go. Times change and now the happiness at Christmas is celebrated in many ways.

Have you read the Christmas account in the gospels? I believe you have or how would you otherwise know what Christmas is? Christmas is not presents, it is not the lit decorated tree, it is not lutfisk, porridge, and cakes, or one's freedom from all the cares of school and homework. It is not the many lights and beautiful hymns sung in church. Christmas is something much, much more, which one finds in the gospels.

The meaning of Christmas is so vast there is not enough room in this little saga to tell the significance about this holy night. At this time of year in Sweden and Finland, the winter in the north was wrapped in snow and freezing cold. However, in the warm land of Judah there was a winter night like Sweden and Finland have in October.

The flowing spring was murmuring, and the trees stood with lush foliage. High on the mountain peaks one could see snow, but the straw in the valleys remained for the grazing flock. This nature child had thrown its blanket off, and yet it did not freeze.

A wonderfully quiet and peaceful night had come quickly, as night comes in the south without hesitation and without twilight. The sun sank in the horizon after a full day and soon everything was totally dark as one saw stars shining like candles lit in the heavens. All the stars were shining at the same time from the largest to the smallest. It was like a curtain rolled up, and one gets to see a glistening illumination. On the mountains, the sky was a deep blue and more transparent than the finest glass. The stars were in their splendor and so beautifully quiet, shining over each other.

The weakest fixed stars twinkled as if they were cheerful, like the large, secret solar systems in the vast distance. Sirius blinked at the light mist on the winter streets as if it was saying, "Watch and do not sleep, for we all must glory in worshiping and adoring God!" The huge full moon sailed and snuck around so proudly over the heavens' ocean. It was afraid to obscure a single star behind the golden shield.

The shepherds awakened their herds on Bethlehem's mountainous valley and viewed new large and splendid stars arising, located right above them. They had often awakened in the night out in the hillside where the stars were like their intimate friends. The shepherds did not know the new star. They wondered what it meant as it came to them with the angel's song, proclaiming Jesus' birth as written in the gospels.

On the poor donkey sat Jesus' mother, Mary, carrying her unborn child with the beautiful gleaming stars shining overhead. After traveling from Jerusalem to Bethlehem, Mary gave birth to Jesus. God's beaming angels hovered over them with lit wings singing heavenly, glorious music praising the child. Tears of joy ran down Mary's cheeks. Through the sparse room, a light night wind blew, and the baby Jesus was very cold as he lay on his mother's knee. Donkeys and a male sheep with a warm, thick coat of the softest wool were in the stable. Mary asked the sheep, "Dear friend, please give me a little wool from your thick coat so it will warm my little child who is freezing!"

The stingy sheep replied, "I need my coat to keep myself warm." He did not give Jesus' mother so much as a little strand of his abundant fur.

Then the selfish sheep heard a voice speaking to him: "Poor sheep, don't you know what you have done? You have denied God's Son a piece of your thick fur the night he was born. You shall spend Christmas night wandering aimlessly around the world freezing, and your fur will not be enough protection."

Immediately the sheep ran around on the mountains, and then he fell in a trance. He slept until the following Christmas when he meandered all around the world again on Christmas night. He heard natures' voices say to each other, "Tonight is the holy night when no one does anything mean to someone else!" He heard this and could not escape the voices because they were heard everywhere on the mountains, in valleys, in the forests, flat lands, high over the lakes and oceans, and down along the harbor.

He had broken the holy night's peace by isolating himself and freezing along the way. He sought to find the child so that he could ask forgiveness for what he had done to the one who laid in the feeding trough. The sheep wanted to give the Christ child the most beautiful Christmas gift—his wool.

Glossary of Terms

A

Agapetus – Agapetus' name was derived from Pope Agapetus I.

Agricola, Mikael – Mikael Agricola (1510–1557) was a Finnish minister who became the founder of written Finnish and one of the prominent advocates of the Protestant Reformation in Sweden and Finland. He is often referred to as "the father of Finnish written language." Mikael Agricola was consecrated as the bishop of Turku in 1554 without papal approval. He translated the New Testament, the prayer book, hymns, and the mass into Finnish. He accomplished this in three years. He died upon returning from Russia after negotiating a treaty with the Russians.

Ahasuerus – Ahasuerus was the father of Darius the Mede; a Persian king, probably Xerxes I (486–465 b.c.) See Ezra 4:6 and Esther 1:1ff. The Greek name is Xerxes.

Ahriman – Ahriman was the personification of the devil in Persian religion.

Ahtola – In Finnish mythology, Ahti or Ahto is the god of the sea and fishing, portrayed as a man with a mossy beard. He is the husband of Vellamo, and they dwell in the undersea palace of Ahtola. Vellamo is the lady of the lakes.

alder – The Alder is any tree of the genus, *Alnus*, related to the birch with catkins and toothed leaves.

alimentary canal – The alimentary canal is the passage where food is passed from the mouth to the anus during digestion.

almanac – The almanac is an annual calendar of months and days with astronomical data and other information.

alms – a charitable donation of money or food to the poor

anemone – The anemone is any plant of the genus, *Anemone*, akin to the buttercup with flowers of vivid colors.

archipelago – Archipelago is a group of islands.

Arctic Circle – The Arctic Circle is the parallel of latitude 66 degrees 33 minutes north, forming an imaginary line around this region.

ash – The ash is any tree from the genus, Fraxinus, with silvery-gray bark and hard wood.

aspen – The aspen is a poplar tree, (Populus tremula), with tremulous (trembling) leaves.

aurora – Aurora is a luminous electrical atmospheric phenomenon, like streamliners of light in the sky.

B

barb – A barb is a secondary, backward facing projection from an arrow or fishhook.

bark bread – During famine times in Finland and Sweden (1596–1598), people ate leaves, husks, hay, straw, moss, and bark from trees. Bark meal contains more zinc, magnesium, and iron than is found in rye and wheat.

base viol – The base viol is the lowest pitched member of the violin family.

baste – To baste is to sew loosely in preparation for sewing.

Bethany – A town on the Mount of Olives—Luke 19:29 NASB; Hometown of Lazarus—John 11:1 NASB; hometown of Simon the Leper—Matt. 26:6 NASB; Jesus visited Bethany—Mark 11:1, 11, 12 NASB; Ascension—Luke 24: 50–51 NASB

bilberry – Bilberry is a hardy dwarf shrub, *Vaccinium myrtillus* of Northern Europe, growing on heaths and mountains, and having dark blue berries.

birch – The birch is any tree of the genus *Betula,* bearing catkins and found in northern temperate regions.

birdcherry – Birdcherry is any of several cherry trees, especially the *Eurasian Prunus Padus.*

Birger Jarl – The jarl was a "mayor of the palace" and chief military officer of the kingdom. Birger Jarl was the founder of Sweden and the greatest ruler of Medieval Sweden.

Björneborg – Björneborg may be the Swedish name for *Pori* in Finland. Björneborg is also located in Värmland, a province in western Sweden.

blindman's buff – Blindman's buff is a game in which a blindfold player tries to catch others.

Bonaparte, Napoleon – Napoleon Bonaparte was the Emperor of France from 1799–1814.

bourgeois – Bourgeois a person of the middle-class.

brig – A brig is a two-masted square-rigged ship with an additional lower fore-and-aft sail on the gaff.

Bumburrifex – Bumburrifex or "Grymme jätten" was a ferocious giant.

buttercup – Buttercup is one of various plants of the genus *Ranunculus,* with shiny, bright-yellow flowers.

bäck – Bäck is the Swedish word for *brook* or *creek.*

C

cadet – A cadet is a young trainee as in the armed services or police force.

caress – To caress is to stroke gently.

chaffinch – The chaffinch is a common European finch, *Fringilla coelebs.*

chicory – The chicory is a blue-flowered plant, *Cichorium intybus,* cultivated for its salad leaves and its roots.

chignon – A chignon is a coil or knot of hair worn at the back of the head.

chive – Chive is a herb plant, *Allium schoenoprasum,* with purple-pink flowers.

cloudberry – The cloudberry is a close relative to the raspberry, *Rebus chamaemorus,* and is an amber color.

Coccinella Septempunctata – The *Coccinella septempunctata* is a seven-spotted, oval and dome-shaped lady beetle.

condescending – being on equal terms with someone with an attitude of superiority

councilor – an elected member of a council

cow parsley – Cowparsley is a tall, hedgerow plant, *Anthriscus sylvestris,* with lace-like flowers.

crevice – A crevice is a narrow opening or fissure in a rock.

crofter – A crofter is a person who rents a small piece of land.

crowberry – The crowberry, *Empetrum nigrum,* is found in bogs in the prairies. It is a creeping vine-like shrub.

D

daler – The Swedish riksdaler was the name of the currency of Sweden until 1873 when it was replaced by the krona.

decipher – to convert a text into intelligible script or language

draft – the drawing in of a fishing net

dragonfly – any of various insects of the order odonata, having a long, slender body and two pair of transparent wings

ducat – The ducat is a gold coin formerly used in many European countries.

duchy – Duchy is the territory of a duke or duchess; each with certain estates, revenues, and jurisdiction of its own.

duke – A duke is a person holding the highest title of the nobility.

dung beetle – Dung beetle is any of a family of beetles whose larvae develop in dung.

E

earl – An earl is a British nobleman ranking between a marquess and a viscount.

empress – An empress is the wife or widow of an emperor.

epilobium – Epilobium is a genus of about 160–200 species of the flowering plant family, Onagracae.

Esther – Esther is the seventeenth Old Testament book. *Hadassah,* or *myrtle,* was the Hebrew name.

Estonia – Estonia is a Baltic republic.

Euphrosyne – Euphrosyne is the goddess of joy and one of the *Three Graces* sculpted by Antonio Canova (1757–1822). She is the happy one bubbling with laughter and the goddess of joy in Greek mythology.

Exodus 20:12 – "Honor your father and your mother, that your days may be prolonged in the land which the LORD your God gives you."

F

fallow – Fallow ground is plowed unsown land.

ferment – Ferment is the breakdown of a substance by microorganisms such as yeasts and bacteria.

Fjäder Harbor – Fjäder Harbor means *Feather Harbor* in Swedish.

flax – Flax is a blue-flowered plant *Linum usitatissimum*, cultivated for its textile fiber.

fortress – Fortress is a military stronghold; especially a fortified town.

frigate – Frigate is a navel vessel between a destroyer and a cruiser in size.

G

gaff – The gaff is a spar to which the head of a fore-and-aft sail is bent.

Genghis Kahn – Genghis Kahn was a skilled general who led a Mongol nation; born 1162 and died 1227.

goshawk – Goshawk is a large short-winged hawk; *Accipiter gentiles*.

granite – Granite is a coarse, granular crystalline igneous rock composed of quartz, mica, hornblende, etc.

Greek – ('Ελληνικο'ς) Koine Greek was spoken by those who wrote the New Testament. It was a vital part of Greco-Roman culture in which the New Testament and Christianity had its origin.

grouse – any of various game birds of the family *Tetraonidae,* with a plump body

Gustav Vasa – Gustav Vasa was born in 1496 or 1497 and died 1560. He was a generous transformer who was the foremost innovator in restoring Sweden's independence, securing the constitution and developing its social structure.

H

hare – The hare is any of various mammals of the *Leporidae* family.

headland – Headland is a promontory that is a point of high land jutting out into the sea.

heather – Heather is an evergreen shrub *Calluna vulgaris* with purple bell-shaped flowers.

hemp – The *Cannabis sativa* fiber is extracted from the stem and used to make rope and strong fabrics. It is an Asian plant.

Hercules – Hercules was the most popular of Greek heroes who was strong and courageous.

heron – The heron is a large wading bird of the family *Ardeidae* with long legs and a long S-shaped neck.

hewn – cut with an ax or sword

hoarfrost – Hoarfrost is frozen water vapor deposited on vegetation in clear, still weather.

homunculus – Homunculus is a little man.

horned owl – The horned owl or *Bubo virginianus* has horn-like feathers over the ears.

hymenopteran – The hymenopteran is any insect of the order hymenoptera having four transparent wings including bees, wasps, ants, and yellow flies.

I

iceberg – An iceberg is a large floating mass of ice detached from a glacier and carried out to sea.

Iceland – Iceland an island in the North Atlantic.

iron mortar – Iron mortar is a vessel in which ingredients are pounded with a pestle; a club-shaped instrument.

islet – An islet is a small island.

J

Jenisej – Jenisej is a Russian river 4092 km long that arises from two principal head streams in Mongolia.

Jerusalem – Jerusalem appears first in Genesis 14:18. Its original name was *Salem* meaning "possession" or "foundation of peace." The Hebrew word is *shalom;* also meaning *peace.*

joust – Jousting is a combat between two knights on horseback with lances.

Julotta – Julotta is an early Christmas morning worship service. (pronounced yoo'-lah-tah.)

juniper – A juniper is any evergreen shrub or tree of the genus Juniperus with prickly leaves and dark purple berry-like cones.

K

Kalevala – Kalevala is a significant epic poem from Finnish folklore in the nineteenth century. It consists of 22,795 verses; (the Finnish *la/lä* meaning "place").

kantele – The kantele is a ten-stringed Finnish instrument.

ketch – The ketch is a two-masted sailing boat with a mizzenmast. The mizzenmast is the mast next to the ship's mainmast.

Kidron Brook – The Kidron Brook is located at the base of the Kidron Valley between Jerusalem and the Mount of Olives. The Kidron Brook was crossed by David and Christ. (Second Samuel 15:23; John 18:1.)

kilometer (km) – Kilometer is a metric unit of measurement equal to 1,000 meters or 0.62 miles.

knead – to work the dough by presssing and folding

knäckebröd – rye crisp bread

Korv – Korv, or potato sausage, is made with beef, pork, potatoes, onions, and spices.

L

Ladoga Lake – Ladoga Lake is located in northwestern Russia; adjacent to Finland.

lance – A Lance is a long weapon with a wooden shaft and a pointed steel head used by charging horseman.

larch tree – The larch tree is a deciduous coniferous tree of the genus Larix, with bright foliage and producing tough wood.

lash – Lash is a sudden whipping movement.

last will and testament – One's last will and testament are directions in legal form for the disposition of one's property before or after death.

lathe – A lathe is a machine for shaping wood or metal by means of a rotating drive which turns the piece being shaped.

Latin – The Latinic language of ancient Rome and its empire.

legacy – A legacy is a gift left in a will; something handed down by a predecessor.

Leviticus 19:32 – "You shall rise up before the gray-headed and honor the aged, and you shall revere your God; I am the LORD."

lily of the valley – The lily of the valley is any liliaceous plant of the genus Convallaria, with white bell-shaped flowers.

linden – The linden is any ornamental tree of the genus Tilia, with heart-shaped leaves with fragrant yellow flowers.

lingonberry – The lingonberry (Vaccinium vitis-idaea) is a low creeping evergreen shrub with pinkish flowers.

lingon bushes – Lingon bushes are mountain cranberry, red whortleberry, or crowberry.

linnet – The linnet is a finch (*acanthis cannabina)* with brown and gray plumage.

Lofoten – The Lofoten islands are an archipelago lying within the Arctic Circle in Northern Norway.

loppan – the flea

Lucia – In Sweden, the longest night of the year, December 13, Swedish people celebrate with the crowning of Lucia who is dressed in a white gown with a crown of candles. Pepparkakor (gingerbread biscuit/cookies), Lussekatter ("Lucia cats"; and/or saffron buns are eaten on Lucia Day.

lutfisk – Lutfisk is boiled ling which is a long, slender, marine fish, (Molva molva), of Northern Europe.

Luther, Martin – 1483–1546; Martin Luther was a German monk, professor, theologian, and the Reformation founder.

M

magpie (pica pica) – The magpie is a crow with a long pointed tail and black and white plumage.

mallard – The mallard is a wild duck or drake *Anas platryhynchos* of the northern hemisphere.

mark – In 1860, Finland adopted the Finnish mark as their unit of money.

Matthew 6:2 NASB – "So when you give to the poor, do not sound a trumpet before you, as the hypocrites do in the synagogues and in the streets, so that they may be honored by men. Truly I say to you, they have their reward in full."

Matthew 7:7 NASB – "Ask and it will be given to you; seek, and you will find; knock, and it will be opened to you."

maxim – A maxim is a general truth or rule of conduct expressed in a sentence.

Melanchthon, Filip – Filip Melanchthon coined the term *psychology* or *psychologia* in 1550. He was a well-known reformer.

midsummer – Midsummer is the summer solstice which is an ancient pagan celebration held on June 24 in Sweden.

migrate – to change an area of habitation with the seasons

Mikael's Sunday – Finland is one of many countries in Europe that celebrates name days called *Nimipäivä* in Finnish. In Sweden name days are called, *namsdag*. The Swedish calendar has one to three names for every day of the year.

miller – The miller is the proprietor or tenant of a mill; a person who owns or works at a mill.

mogul – A mogul is an important or influential person. Historically, the Great Mogul were any of the emperors of Delhi in the sixteenth to nineteenth centuries.

mole – A mole is a small burrowing insect-eating mammal of the family *Talpidae; Talpa europaea.*

mongrel – A mongrel is a dog with no definable type or breed.

Mormässa – Mormässa, or Mother's Service, is celebrated on

September 8th. In times past, a worship service was held for Jesus' mother, the Virgin Mary.

mountain ash – Mountain Ash, or *Sorbus aucuparia,* have delicate pinnate leaves and scarlet berries.

N

negligent – careless

Nordenskjöld – Nordenskjöld is a large glacier flowing north to the head of Cumberland East Bay. It was named after the leader of the Swedish South Polar Expedition of 1901–1903, Otto Nordenskjöld.

Nystad – Nystad means *New Town.* In Sweden, *Nystad* is located on the Gulf of Bothnia. Nystad was founded in 1616 during the reign of Gustavus Adolphus.

näcken – Näcken is the evil spirit of the water.

O

osier – An osier consists of various willows, especially *Salix Viminalis,* with long flexible shoots used in basket weaving or other work.

P

Pagliacci – Pagliacci is an Italian opera in two acts written and composed by Ruggiero Leoncavallo.

palt bread – Palt bread is baked with blood and rye flour.

panhandle – To panhandle is to beg for money in the street.

parishioner – A parishioner is one who is a member of a church.

Pasha – Pasha is the title of a Turkish officer of high rank.

passerine – Passerines are known as perching birds which are the largest of the bird order. They have three toes pointing forward, and a hind toe pointing backward.

pea pod – Pea seeds grow in a pod which is a long seed vessel of a leguminous plant, e.g., a pea.

peduncle – A peduncle is the stalk of a flower, fruit, or cluster: especially a main stalk bearing a solitary flower or subordinate stalks. They are small, white, and red.

peninsula – A peninsula is a piece of land almost surrounded by water or projecting far into a sea or lake.

pepparkakor – Pepparkakor is a thin chocolate mint, ginger, or orange Swedish cookie dating to the 1300's.

pericarp – Pericarp is the part of a fruit formed from the wall of the ripened ovary.

piaffevPiaffe is a horse trotting in place with high leg action.

pier – A pier is a structure of iron or wood raised on piles leading out to sea or lake used for walking and a landing place.

pinnacle – A pinnacle is a natural peak, or a small ornamental turret usually ending in a pyramid or cone.

piracy – Piracy is the practice or an act of robbery of ships at sea.

plume – A plume is a large feather used as an ornament.

plunder – To plunder is to rob forcibly of goods.

polka-mazurka – Polka-mazurka is a lively Polish dance in triple time.

Princess Lindagull – Princess Lindagull is a tale written by Zacharius Topelius.

Q

quadrille – A quadrille is a square dance with five parts.

R

ragamuffin – A ragamuffin is a person in ragged, dirty clothes; especially a child.

Rastekais – The people of Scandinavia believed the trolls were a type of mischievous imp who made their way to a mountain called *Rastekais* at Christmas.

rattan – Rattan is a piece of rattan stem or palm of the genus *Calamus* used as a walking stick.

Rauma (Finnish spelling) or Raumo (Swedish spelling) – Rauma is a town in Finland on the west coast and fifty kilometers south of Pori. Raumo is known for shipbuilding, paper, and pulp mills.

reeds – Reeds are any of a various water or marsh plants with a firm stem.

resilience – recovering from shock

resin – Resin is an adhesive flammable substance insoluble in water, secreted by some plants.

Romans – The Romans are people from the ancient or modern territory of Rome.

rosettes – Rosettes are a crispy bow-shaped treat baked in oil filled with hors d'oeuvres and other tasty foods.

runic – Runic is the early Germanic alphabet used by Scandinavians and Anglo-Saxons from about the third century.

rusks – Rusks are a slice of bread re-baked usually as a light biscuit.

S

saber – The saber is a cavalry sword with a curved blade.

sacristy – The sacristy is a room in a church where the vestments and sacred vessels are kept for the service.

St. Birgitta or St. Britta (1303–1373) – St. Birgitta is known as St. Bridget of Sweden and of Vadstena. She was a mystic and saint who believed herself to have visions. These are recorded in *Revelationes Coelestes*. She is remembered on October 7.

Sami – The Sami's, Sàpmi, or Sàmeednam live in the Arctic Circle region encompassing Norway, Sweden, Finland, and Russia, with a total population of about 70,000.

Sampo Lappelill ('Sampo the Little Lap/Sami Boy') – Sampo Lappelill is a fairy tale written by Zacharius Topelius.

sanctuaryvThe/A sanctuary is a place of refuge.

Scandinavia – Scandinavia includes Denmark, Norway, Sweden, Finland and Iceland.

scarabeus – In Egypt, the scarab was a symbol of resurrection or rebirth.

schooner – The schooner is a fore-and-aft rigged ship with two or more masts; the foremast being smaller.

sea dog – These aquatic, herbivorous mammals inhabit rivers, estuaries, coastal marine waters, swamps, and marine wetlands.

shoal – The shoal is an area of shallow water.

shroud – A shroud is a sheetlike garment.

silver birch – The silver birch is a common European birch, *Betula pendula*, with silver-colored bark.

Sirius (Latin) – Sirius is from Orion and is the brightest star in the sky meaning *searing* or *scorching*. It is commonly referred to as the "Dog Star."

siskin – Siskin is a dark-streaked, yellowish-green songbird, *Carduelis spinus*.

smörgås – A smörgås is an open-faced sandwich.

snuffer – A snuffer is a small hollow cone with a handle used to extinguish a candle or trim its wick.

solder – Solder is a fusible alloy used to join less feasible metals or wires.

song thrush – The song thrush, or *Turdus philomelos,* is from Europe and West Asia.

sound – The sound is a narrow passage of water like an arm of the sea.

Spetsbergen – Spetsbergen is the largest island in the group of islands, *Svalbard.*

sprat – The sprat is a small European herring-like fish, *Sprattus.*

spruce – The spruce is any coniferous tree of the genus *Picea* with dense foliage growing in conical shape.

starlings – The starling is the migratory bird, *Sturnus vulgaris,* with blackish-brown speckled iridescent plumage.

stuga – A stuga is a cottage or small house.

swallow – The swallow is any of various migratory swift-flying insect-eating birds of the family *Hirundinidae.*

T

talon – A talon is a claw, especially a bird of prey.

tenacious – A tenacious person is persistent.

Thor – Thor is the Norse god of thunder who is a son of Odin and Jord.

thrush – The thrush is any small or medium-sized songbird of the family *Turdidae*.

thrush nightingale – Thrush Nightingale is a reddish-brown bird of the genus *Luscinia;* the male sings melodiously.

trefoil – Trefoil is any leguminous plant of the genus *Trifolium,* with leaves of three leaflets and flowers of various colors, especially clover.

trientalis europåa – Trientalis is a Latin adjective meaning a plant that is one third of a foot, or four inches.

trough – A trough is a long narrow open receptacle for water, animal feed, etc.

Tyrann, Kristian (Tyrant) – A massacre occurred in Stockholm under the leadership of Kristian Tyrann II of Denmark between November 7 and 10, 1520.

V

Valdemar IV (1317–1375) – Valdemar IV was the king of Denmark from 1340–1375.

valet – A valet is a person's attendant who assists with one's coat, suit, and other belongings.

Vasa, King Gustav – King Gustav Vasa was the King of Sweden from 1523–1560 who was a liberator of Sweden and a tyrannic ruler.

villain – A villain is a person who is guilty or capable of wickedness.

W

wagtail – The wagtail is a small bird of the genus *Motacilla*, with a long tail in frequent motion.

warp – In weaving the threads are stretched vertically on a loom.

warship – A warship is an armored ship used in war.

waxwing – The waxwing is any bird of the genus *Bombycilla*, with small tips like red sealing wax.

willow – The willow is a tree or shrub of the genus *Salix*, growing usually near water in temperate climates with small flowers borne on catkins, and pliant branches.

willow grouse *(lagopus)* – The willow grouse is similar to the Ptarmigan. It has a laughing call, its plumage is white in the winter, and red/brown in the summer.

willow warbler – The willow warbler or the *Phylloscopus trochilus, are* small birds with grey-green backs and a yellow-tinged chest.

Wipplustig – Wipplustig is a fairy tale written by Zacharius Topelius.

Wittalatorpare – *Wittala* is the name of a village; while *torpare* means *crofter,* or a person who rents a small piece of land.

woof – The threads are stretched horizontally (from side-to-side) on a loom.

wren – The wren is a brown, small, short-winged songbird of the family *Troglodytidae,* having an erect tail.

Z

Zephyrinus – pope from ca. 199–217

zither – a musical instrument consisting of a flat wooden sound box with numerous strings stretched across it; played with the fingers and a plectrum. The autoharp is from the same family as the zither.

Å

Åbo – Åbo is a castle in Sweden dating from the 1280's; a town on the east coast in Gävleborgs Län in Sweden; or it means a farm tenant with permanence.

Ö

öde – Öde is a solitary, wasted, uninhabited, devastated piece of land.

Öregrund – Öregrund is located in Uppland Sweden by the Baltic Sea.

References

Bonniers Lexicon, © 1965 ed. s.v. "piaffe." © 1965

Carpenter, Humphrey; Prichard, Mari. Oxford Companion to Children's Literature, The. s.v. "Topelius, Zachris or Sakari." Oxford University Press. Oxford. Ed. © 1995.

Concise Dictionary of Plants, A. Cultivated in the United States and Canada. Staff of the L. H. Bailey Horatorium, Cornell University. MacMillan Publishing. ©1976.

Encyclopedia Britannica, 15th ed.

English-Swedish/Swedish-English Dictionary, University of Minnesota Press. Bokförlaget Prisma © 1993.

Ericson, Britta. Lässvårigheter och emotionell störning. Reading Difficulty and Emotional Disturbance. Uppsala Studies in Education 12. Almqvist & Wiksell International, Stockholm, Sweden, © 1980.

Goldstein, Arnold P. *Prepare Curriculum Teaching Prosocial Competencies, The.* Research Press, © 1999.

Greek New Testament Fourth Revised Edition. © Page 58. United Bible Society 1983.

Hill's Vest Pocket Swedish-English English-Swedish Dictionary. Jan Förlag, Stockholm, © 1961.

Hägg, Göran. Den svenska litteratur-historien. Nørhaven Paperback A/S, Danmark 2004, © 1996.

Illustrated Oxford Dictionary. Oxford University Press. Oxford England, © 1998.

Johnson, David W., Johnson, Frank P. *Joining Together Group Theory and Group Skills*. Allyn and Bacon, © 1997.

Johnson, Edna; Sickels, Evelyn R.; Sayers, Francis Clark. Anthology of Children's Literature. "Finland," Pages 544–549; Houghton Mifflin Press. Boston, MA. ©1970.

Journal of Moral Education. The Contribution of History and Literature to Moral Education. Vol. 5, No. 2, pp. 127–138. Pemberton Publishing Company, © 1976.

Key to Zachris Topelius. A. s.v. "Selma Lagerlöf: 'Kuddnäs'— out of a chapter in her book, *Zachris Topelius*." Miktor Press Helsingfors © 1998.

Lickona, Thomas. "What Is Good Character?" Bantom Books, New York, NY and London, England © 1992.

MacArthur Study Bible, The. New American Standard Bible. Thomas Nelson Inc. © 2006.

McKay's Modern English-Swedish and Swedish-English Dictionary. Ruben Nöjd; Astrid Tornberg; and Margareta Ångström. David McKay Company, Inc. New York, NY.

Nordisk Familjbok. Encyclopedi Konversationslexicon. Förslagshuset Norden AB Malmö © 1959.

Nordisk   Familjbok.   Encyclopedi   Konversationslexicon.
Förslagshuset Norden AB Malmö © 1960.

Norstedts Engelska-Svensk Svensk-Engelsk Ordbok, England ©
2001.

Norstedts Stora Svensk Engelska Ordbok, © 2000.

Rydåker, Ewa. Lucia Morning in Sweden. Civilen AB, Halmstad,
Sweden, © 2003.

Scott, Franklin D. Sweden—the Nation's History. So. Illinois
Press. Carbondale and Edwardsville ©1998.

Shafer, Marjorie Haney Ph.D. The Bible and Its Influence. ©
2006. BLP Publishing.

Stone, Jon R. *Latin for the Illiterati.* Routledge, New York ©
1996.

World Book Encyclopedia. © 2006 Ed.

The Key to
Zacharias Topelius
Selma Lagerlöf
"Kuddnäs"

—out of a chapter in her book, *Zacharias Topelius*

Zacharias Topelius came into the world on Felix' Day, January 14, 1818 in Kuddnäs Finland. (The Swedish calendar has name days.) He was baptized and given his doctor father's name, Zacharias Topelius. He died on March 12, 1898. He was a Swedish speaking Finnish author, journalist, historian, and the rector of the University of Helsinki. Selma Lagerlöf, a Swedish novelist, short story writer, autobiographer, poet, biographer, and a dramatist, notes in her book, *Zacharias Topelius,* that from the beginning he was loved and adored.

Zacharias' home, the Kuddnäs country house, was a wonderful place for children to be raised. There were two gable rooms on the upper floor; however, the children played freely in the six rooms on the main level. There they could be noisy and carry on as they wanted playing Hide-and-Seek, have a wedding with the dolls, and play theater.

Outside there was a courtyard where one could run around. In the winter they dug into the snow and built a snow house. There was a garden with strawberries and prickly berries. There were the high Heavenly Mountains where one went tobogganing and the Lappo River which surpassed all the other playing places.

This little boy from Kuddnäs pretended to be an imaginary

fairy tale prince who was taught how to build brick fences in gardens. Zacharius began to believe everything in the world was there for him, and that he could build exactly as he chose. His mother did not think he should show interest in such things.

One day Zacharius' father missed an item from his writing table. At the same time mother noticed she had lost a silver thimble, and sister Sophie could not find her amber heart. Zealously they searched and the family wondered how a thief had come sneaking into the house. Finally, it was little Zacharias who asked what they were looking for, and the family finally discovered what happened. They dug in the high snow in the garden where he had made a hiding place for treasures.

It had not occurred to Zacharius that taking something was wrong. One day he played *Robber.* A robber must both lie down with others' goods and keep them hidden. He eventually retrieved them due to Father's scolding.

One cold winter day Zacharius went outside and played like he was in an open sea catching herring and baking the fish in paper. "Do you have to do that? A boy catching herring will never be a successful man," Father exhorted Zacharius.

Zacharius' father had a liking for maxims and he used them for consolation, encouragement, and stimulation. Father wanted to make an impression on his son so that the rules of proper conduct would be a lasting spiritual legacy.

One day there was a tobogganing competition in Himmelsbacken. Joshua was on his toboggan named *Flinken;* while Zacharius was on his splendid, highest, beloved toboggan named *Moppe* which was faster than the other toboggans. Zacharius got on the toboggan and made a dangerous bend along a steep chasm. Moppe passed his competitor with Flinken and Joshua tumbling down the ravine. The Flinken toboggan tipped over, Joshua broke his arm and sprained his foot. He was a good friend and he did not blame Zacharias. He noted how fast the Moppe toboggan was because it was able to catch up with the Flinken toboggan.

"Now the Flinken toboggan lies with broken runners. Where will Joshua get a new toboggan?" Father asked.

Zacharius began to understand what Father meant. Moppe was his pride, love, and joy; being superior to all the other boys' toboggans. Three days later Joshua was given another toboggan and laid down on it with his broken arm.

With tears in his eyes, Father was so happy. He no longer needed to be concerned for his son's future. He saw that Zacharias would be a honorable man with his quick imagination and high intelligence. He would continue with the good family name because he had the ability to overcome himself.

Zacharius' father taught his son to be an outstanding student by working hard for his education. Early in his life, Zacharias began to understand that inside him was a starving, unrelenting spirit waiting to be satisfied. His senses were awakened through observing and consistently writing in his diary. He took care in collecting not only insects and birds eggs; but scenes, events, ideas, thoughts, the contents in books, and whatever gave life with the Word.

—Selma Lagerlöf
1858–1940
Eminent Swedish author

On January 13, 2007, the translator was in the Amsterdam airport enroute to Kenya. She met a couple from Finland who said Topelius' sagas continue to be read among school children in Finland.